CALIFORNIA PIONEER SERIES

261

FIC
SCHULTE Schulte, Elaine L.
Golden dreams

CALIFORNIA PIONEER SERIES

Golden Dreams

ELAINE SCHULTE

LIFEJOURNEY
BOOKS

DAVID C. COOK PUBLISHING CO.

LifeJourney Books is an imprint of David C. Cook Publishing Co.
David C. Cook Publishing Co., Elgin, Illinois 60120
David C. Cook Publishing Co., Weston, Ontario

GOLDEN DREAMS
© 1989 by Elaine Shulte

(Another version of this book was previously published under the title
Dreams of Gold.)

Edited by LoraBeth Norton
Cover design by Dawn Lauck
Illustration by Kathy Kulin

First Printing, 1989
Printed in the United States of America
93 92 91 90 5 4 3 2

Schulte, Elaine L.
        Golden Dreams
        (California pioneer series; bk. 2)
        I. Title. II. Series: Schulte, Elaine L. California pioneer series; bk. 2
PS3569.C5395G65   1989   813'.54   89-23955
ISBN 1-55513-987-6

*In memory of our
sisters and brothers
who brought His love
by clipper ship*

Prologue

B enjamin Talbot stood behind the counter of the Wainwright-Talbot Shipping and Chandlery warehouse, eyeing his visitor. Many a scoundrel had arrived in San Francisco since word of the gold discovery was out, but this man, this Jonathan Wilmington, gave every appearance of being a trustworthy gentleman: sober-eyed, intelligent, and likely in his mid-fifties, too. It struck Benjamin that there was something of great import about his caller.

Wilmington said, "I would appreciate it if your firm would deliver this letter to my solicitor and my daughter Rose in Georgetown." He produced an envelope from the breast pocket of his black broadcloth frock coat. "It is urgent. My last letter was lost with a ship rounding Cape Horn."

"Unfortunately a great many ships are lost there," Benjamin replied. "Our firm has lost its share. In any case, we have a clipper ship arriving soon with my son Joshua aboard as supercargo. I shall ask him to deliver the letter himself when he returns to the eastern seaboard."

His visitor drew a relieved breath. "I thank you most heartily. I have remained here far longer than expected, and . . . of late, I have a terrible foreboding about my daughter."

As I do about my son, Benjamin thought. *As I do about my Joshua.*

1

R ose Ann Wilmington stood in the shade of a maple tree and gazed down from the green hillsides of Georgetown. A warm breeze ruffled tendrils of raven hair around her white bonnet and stirred the bell skirt of her pink gauze frock. Absorbed in the bustling seaport scene on the distant Potomac River, she desperately wished that her father were one of the passengers arriving now by sail.

At length she opened the journal she often carried as a companion for jotting down thoughts and bits of poetry. After dating a fresh page May 18, 1848, she wrote, *Best not to dwell upon the dire possibilities of Father rounding Cape Horn, nor the risks of his travel in the California Territory. Far better to listen to the leaves rustling secrets overhead . . . to delight in the dapplings of shade and sunshine . . . to make melody in my heart—*

"Rose!" The voice, so like William's, jolted her. Her eyes closed for an instant before she turned, knowing that it would be her late fiancé's twin brother, Willard.

"Wait a moment, won't you?" he called out, hurrying down the path from the distant road.

The chimes of Georgetown College pealed over the river bluff where the school stood like a stone fortress against the

3

blue sky. She sat still, feeling as though she were a captive to time while the resonant bell tolled the hour of two.

Willard arrived, breathless. His smile began like William's—a quick curve that broke into an irresistible wide grin that she could not help returning. He looked like William, too: firm, clean-shaven chin and a broad forehead framed by curling locks of brown hair; his body was well-built, compact. On the other hand, he was overly stylish in his forest green vest and frock coat and outlandishly checkered trousers.

"Dear Rose . . . I hoped to find you here."

She stood up, brushing the back of her skirt. "Good afternoon, Willard."

"You remain a most formal young lady considering how long we have known each other," he replied with amusement.

"I suppose I am." She regretted the constraint she had always felt around him. Was it a faulty memory that made the two brothers seem so dissimilar in character, now that William had been dead for nearly three years?

She added into the silence, "It took me aback to see you here during working hours." He had never before followed her after their midday dinner, though he'd joined her occasionally in the parlor in the evening during the past month—since she had temporarily moved into his family's house. He would be late in returning to his father's shipping office near the docks.

"I thought we might just walk . . . and talk."

His meaningful tone and veiled green eyes disconcerted her, but she forced a pleasant, "If you like, Willard."

"I see you were writing in your journal."

She closed the book. "Yes. Yes, I was."

"You don't mind if I join you, I hope?"

"What would you say if I did?" she returned lightly.

He furrowed his brow. "You do say peculiar things for a young lady, Rose."

She was tempted to mention that at twenty-one years of age, she was no longer such a young lady. Instead she smiled. "How would other young ladies reply?"

To her amazement, color flooded up Willard's neck and into his cheeks. Since when had his interest in women become a sensitive subject? William would have chuckled at her question because he was honest and straightforward . . . and because there had been no other young ladies in his life. As for Willard, there were rumors—none of them good. But to be fair, it was merely gossip. There were always people envious of wealthy families like the Stanfords, and such people were often eager to spread scurrilous talk.

Willard leaned back against the maple tree. "How can a man think of other ladies when you're so beautiful? You're the most lovely young woman in all of Georgetown, Rose . . . and even in Washington City."

"How kind of you," she replied, attempting a pleasant tone and looking out at white puffs of clouds in the sky. A honey bee buzzed by in the warm breeze, lighting on a wild iris, and a bird twittered from a clump of azalea bushes.

"You don't believe me, do you?"

Rose shrugged lightly. She had often been told that she was pretty with her dark hair, brown eyes, and light complexion—though she did not think so, particularly because of the circles of high color in her cheeks. She smiled at a recollection.

"What do you find so amusing?" Willard asked.

"Miss Sheffield, the headmistress of my school in New York, once told me to scrub the rouge from my cheeks—but I wasn't wearing any!"

His lips curved up at the corners, and suddenly he felt her cheek with his fingertips.

She drew away from his touch and from the smell of wine on his breath. "Willard . . . please!"

He laughed softly. "I had never suspected rouge because you are not the type. But I did wonder whether your cheeks might be rough. I find they are not."

"I see." To avoid his further scrutiny, Rose glanced toward the silvery-blue Potomac, then allowed her eyes to wander to Washington City four miles distant. The bright spring greenery and the breeze on her face soothed her annoyance.

"I suppose you come out here every day to watch for your father's arrival," Willard remarked.

"Yes. He is already two months late."

"How can you bear to look at the canal?" He sounded more curious than malevolent. "I realize, of course, that your father was not the only man to invest heavily in its construction. A good many investors envisioned it as another Erie Canal, not foreseeing how the railroad would damage the scheme."

"I try not to think of it," she admitted. She glanced at the abominable Chesapeake and Ohio Canal, where mules trudged on either side of the water pulling barges of coal, lumber, stones, and grain to the port. "If Father hadn't invested in it, he most likely would not have sailed to the California Territory on a new venture, though it is beyond me what prospects he'll find in such a foreign place."

Realizing that Willard had pried more from her than she wished to reveal, she lighty mocked him in the same tone he'd used upon her just minutes ago. "What a peculiar and personal topic for a young gentleman to raise!"

He chuckled and reached for her elbow with a show of solicitude. "I do hope you don't find me too much of a gentleman, my dear. I should detest being considered a dullard. As you have undoubtedly observed, William and I might have been identical twins outwardly, but we differed in other aspects." His grip on her elbow tightened, and he fixed her with a piercing gaze.

She was tempted to wrench herself loose and tell him that his late brother had done everything in his power to remain a gentleman . . . and had never been a dullard!

"Come, Rose, let me accompany you on your stroll," Willard urged. "You are too often alone. You're too beautiful to go about unaccompanied on these secluded paths."

She pulled away slightly, and he relaxed his hold on her elbow. He was a flatterer, that was all, she decided. Perhaps he knew of no other way to befriend women. In any case, she dared not treat his attention as an affront since she now resided in his parents' house. If Father didn't arrive soon, she must lease another place. She had already placed their possessions in storage last month, when their leased Georgetown house had been sold and she'd been forced to move in with Willard's family.

They strolled along the path together, Rose calming herself occasionally by admiring clumps of violets and trillium. After a while, Willard cleared his throat. "My dear Rose," he began, "I've known you for many years and have felt so attached to you . . . as a sister, of course . . . when you were betrothed to William." He hesitated, looking around past the bushes and trees to make sure of their privacy. "What I am trying to say is that I—"

Rose felt a stab of panic. To her amazement Willard swept her around to face him, his fingers digging into the flesh of her shoulders. She pushed away, her efforts impeded by the journal and pencil case in her hands. "Willard, please!"

"There's no need to look at me as though I'm a

blackguard," he protested. "My attentions are entirely honorable. I meant to demonstrate that I'm attracted to you, Rose. I fervently hope you will become my bride."

His bride! She faltered. She was not surprised to find him attracted to her—his frequent glances had made that obvious while William was still alive—but a proposal was entirely unexpected. She caught a deep, steadying breath. "Thank you for your proposal, Willard. I do thank you . . . but I—"

His face neared hers again, the reek of wine on his breath.

She pressed away from him. "But I do not think that you . . . like me as I'd want a husband to, Willard. Real love should include caring and trust, empathy, a sharing of faith—"

He must have realized her discomfiture, for his tone grew persuasive. "If you marry me, Rose, you will lack for nothing. We can take a honeymoon trip to London or Paris or Rome . . . anywhere you please. My parents will pay for anything."

"Your parents wish us to marry?" When had that come about? Prior to her betrothal to William, the Stanfords had wanted both sons to marry shipping heiresses—and Willard had been courting one from Baltimore recently.

"My mother and father are fond of you. They would like you to be a member of the family."

Rose recalled how his parents had insisted she stay with them. "After all," his mother had reasoned, "you were William's betrothed. He would be pleased to know you were living with us now." But moving in with them had only been intended as a temporary measure until Father returned.

Willard asked, "You will accept my proposal, won't you, my lovely Rose?"

She recoiled at his oily tone. Didn't he see that she could never marry him? For one thing, his appearance would be a constant reminder of her love for William; for another, she could not endure him! "I am stunned . . . and overcome by your proposal, Willard," she managed. "I would like to consider it for a time if I may."

He nodded, bestowing an indulgent smile upon her. "I know it is short notice, but I hope you will let us know by tomorrow night. Mother and Father would be pleased to announce it at my birthnight ball. We could be married almost immediately." He attempted to draw her to him again. "I know a true gentleman should give a young lady several months to decide—"

Rose heard horses clop along the nearby road. "Please, Willard, the riders—"

He glanced toward the horsemen who peered through the trees at them. "Come," he said huskily, "let me accompany you home."

It occurred to her that his mother might be napping, and the servants would be in the kitchen or back in their quarters now. Rose knew of only one way to evade him and said, "I was planning to visit the burial ground to pay my respects—"

"The burial ground?" He stared at her as if he thought the idea of it unbelievably morbid.

"Yes, I often stop there during my walks."

Frowning, he unhanded her and backed away to make his departure. "Very well, Rose, if you like. We should like to make the felicitous announcement of our engagement with a champagne toast tomorrow at midnight."

No response came to mind, and she returned his nod uncertainly before starting toward the burial ground, a place she had long noticed that he avoided whenever possible.

Lord, he is surely not the husband You mean for me! she thought and hurried on. Not Willard! Of late she had begun to pray that He might send someone she could love and trust as much as she had William, but surely it wasn't Willard!

Glancing back, she was relieved to see him heading down the road toward the docks. If nothing else, he had forced her to face her dilemna. She could not remain at the Stanford house much longer, but where could she go? Most of her friends were married and scattered across the eastern seaboard. If she had attended school here in Georgetown instead of New York, perhaps there might be someone to whom she could flee.

At the Georgetown Burial Ground, Rose passed the glorious stone angel that overlooked the Wilmington family plot and her mother's ten-year-old grave. The words on her mother's tombstone had long been engraved on Rose's heart: The Lord is my Shepherd; I shall not want.

A sense of peace filled her as she strolled in the dappled sunshine among maples, hickories, and oaks to William's grave. She saw nothing morbid here, only that it was a resting place for the body after one's soul went on. She felt free here, almost unfettered from her own body, closer to God.

At William's grave site she sat down in the grass, enjoying the breeze and occasional twitterings of birds. *William Paul Stanford,* was chiseled on the tombstone. *January 3, 1823 — June 15, 1845. God takes the loved ones from our homes but never from our hearts.* Above the words was a broken column, signifying early death.

Her grief had slowly diminished during the three years of visiting his grave. The first month it had been so unbearable that her father had accompanied her here, hushing her as she cried out, "How could God have taken him now . . . just before our wedding? How could He when we loved each other so much? Doesn't God care about me?"

Her father had tried to soothe her. "Of course God cares about you."

After a moment he'd added, "Your mother always said that those who are left behind have more work to do for Him on earth. But she . . . she was the real Christian. After her, I don't know what my work could possibly be—" Her father's voice had cracked, and for the first time Rose had truly seen the depth of his sorrow.

"Oh, Father! I never realized you hurt so terribly, too!"

He had simply nodded, tears rolling down his cheeks.

Day by day another month had passed, then another and another, until Rose had felt peace. When she sat here in the grass by William's grave, she envisioned a golden scene . . . a dream in which she, William, and her mother were with the Lord in the brilliant light of eternity. As each year passed, the anguish had lessened, her golden vision imparting a sense of serenity.

But now—who might have thought that Willard would intrude this way upon her quiet life? What would William have said about it? She knew immediately and closed her eyes to pray. "Heavenly Father, I do ask Thee to show me Thy way in this. In the name of Thy beloved Son, the Lord, Jesus Christ. Amen."

She opened her journal. I must depend upon God, she wrote, for there is no way to escape on my own. She had committed her life to the Lord five years before when she and William had attended a special church service; yet she still had so much to learn. William had called Christianity a lifelong walk, a spiritual pilgrimage into eternity.

When the clock at the college rang out three o'clock, she added in her journal, How my life has changed in just this last hour! Now there is not only Father's delay, but a proposal from Willard to deal with, too.

Rose let herself quietly in the front door of the Stanfords' red brick Federalist house, only to find Willard's mother descending the graceful stairway.

"Rose, I did hope to see you!" she said, her green eyes sparkling. Light spilled through the Palladian window over the landing, shining upon her graying chestnut hair, which was perfect as always, swept up by her personal maid into a French twist. "Let's sit in the music room. It's so pleasant in the afternoon. I asked Maddy to bring in tea when you arrived . . . just for the two of us. I daresay we won't have a chance to talk for a while with another dinner party this evening. Some of Willard's school friends will arrive early for tomorrow night's ball, and a sea captain acquaintaince is in port, and a merchant from Boston."

Rose followed Mrs. Stanford with consternation. Usually four or five ladies were in attendance at teatime, an occasion of great social consequence in Georgetown that involved an arduous amount of traveling and leaving of cartes de visite.

Mrs. Stanford spoke lightly of the lovely May weather, her dark blue afternoon gown rustling as she swept past the English antiques in the formal green parlor and into the music room with its pianoforte and harp imported from London. They seated themselves on the formal side chairs at the Baltimore tea table. "Ah, here comes Maddy now."

Rose smiled at the dear face of the middle-aged Negro housekeeper whom she had known since birth and had brought along to the Standfords'. Maddy wore her best black dress, a white apron tied around her bulky middle and a starched white turban on her head.

"Beg your pardon." Maddy nodded so politely that Rose could not help thinking how very different life in the Stanford mansion must be for her. Life had not been quite as elegant as this at home, but not this stiff and formal either, and Maddy had run the household as she pleased. Now she carried the small Forbes silver tea service and thin slices of fruitcake on a gold-rimmed bone china plate that matched the cups and saucers.

Mrs. Stanford inquired with genuine interest, "Maddy, are the other servants treating you well here?"

"Yes'm, thank you, Miz Stanford."

Rose realized there was no other proper answer for her housekeeper to make. Maddy had not let on, but very likely she was uncomfortable with the other servants since she had been a free black for years and the Stanfords' staff were slaves. Rose felt a renewed responsibility for her welfare.

"That be all, Miz Stanford?"

"Yes, thank you."

Maddy's eyes caught Rose's for an instant, brimming with concern, then she departed as quickly as her heft allowed.

"Well," Mrs. Stanford said, handing Rose a cup of tea, "I trust you had a pleasant stroll this afternoon."

Rose nodded. "Yes, thank you."

Mrs. Stanford smiled, taking up her own cup of tea, and they continued in idle conversation. At length she said, "I hope Willard had an opportunity to speak with you."

Rose sipped her tea and swallowed hard. "Yes, he did."

Mrs. Stanford offered her a slice of fruitcake, but Rose politely declined, uncomfortable about the direction of their conversation. Finally the older woman said, "Both his father and I have discussed Willard's wishes, and we hope you will accept his proposal . . . if you haven't already."

"I—I don't know—"

"It can't be easy for you . . . we know how much you loved William. But you can't grieve forever, dear, although—although sometimes I feel that I myself might."

She bit down on her lip and took a moment to compose herself. "It would be like marrying William in a sense—"

"But they are so different!" Rose protested.

His mother blinked at Rose's vehemence. "Yes, they are different. Willard does need to settle down, and you would have such a wonderfully settling influence upon him. Eventually you and Willard would inherit this house. It's said to be one of the finest in Georgetown. Someday Mr. Stanford and I hope to return to his family's plantation, Oaklawn."

Rose set down her teacup, unsure of how to proceed. Seeing the love on the woman's face, she thought, *If only it were William we were considering, we might be the happiest mother and daughter-in-law who had ever lived!* At length she said, "Willard told me I might have some time to consider."

"Time?" A note of panic accompanied the word.

"He said he must know before the midnight toast at tomorrow night's ball."

Mrs. Stanford looked somewhat relieved. "I see."

Upstairs in her spacious bedroom, Rose felt a warm breeze waft through the open window, rich with the aromas of recently cut grass and boxwood hedges from the garden. She slipped out of her shoes and pink frock, and lay down on the canopied four-poster bed in her chemise and petticoats, trying to put Willard and her predicament out of mind.

Her eyes wandered from the bed's pineapple-carved posts to the elaborate plaster cornices along the ceiling, then around the room. The creamy walls glowed with afternoon light, and the depths of the mahogany furniture gleamed deep red like port wine; the wooden floor around the Persian rug glistened as if it were glass. It was a lovely room in a magnificent house. She ran a finger over the voile summer bedspread that matched the window curtains and the bed canopy. Some young women might be tempted to overlook Willard's flaws and marry him for the house and the prospect of a pampered existence with endless teas, dinners, plays, musicales, and balls.

A knock sounded at the door.

"It's me, Maddy."

Rose sat up on the bed. "Come in; the door's unlocked."

Maddy stepped in and quickly closed the door, her black eyes brimming with concern again. "I doan like sayin' it, honey," she said in a hushed tone, "but keep the door locked."

"I'm sure it's perfectly safe—"

"I jest got a minute, Miz Rose Anne. That Mistuh Willard is gonna ask to marry you 'cause . . . 'cause he has to."

Rose felt her eyes widen. "What do you mean?"

Maddy placed a warning finger at her lips. "Hush, now. I know how you loved Mistuh William, but Mistuh Willard . . . he's bad, full of trouble. Folks say he's a bad seed!"

"Oh, now, Maddy!"

"Now you listen. The high-toned Baltimore gal he was courting got wind of his doings. It be one thing when he was messing around in the Federal City, but another when he takes up with white trash along the canal right here in town! That high-toned Baltimore gal want no part of such doings! She told him there ain't gonna be no wedding!"

"I don't understand—"

Maddy rolled her eyes toward the ceiling. "You doan know nothing much about such doings, Miz Rose Anne. Yo' mama never told you much before she went on to glory, and yo' daddy doan know how to explain. What I got to tell you is Mistuh Willard's got one of de white trash gals by the grog houses in a family way."

At Rose's stunned silence, Maddy continued, "It's that

Megan McCabe . . . and she be telling the whole town even with the Stanfords paying her to hush."

"Oh, Maddy!" The girls at school had hinted at such things, but she'd never quite believed it, nor understood. She did recall that her own mother had underlined a Bible verse warning against fornication. And she recalled Willard's husky voice and the lascivious look in his eyes that afternoon. "But then no proper woman will ever marry him! He won't be received in polite company!"

Maddy shook her head. "You doan understand. Plenty of women would still marry him, jest for his money and the house. But the Stanfords want you 'cause of yo' good name!"

"For my good name?"

Maddy gave a nod. "Now, what I wanna warn you about, honey, is that it be bad enough he's so wild, but he am not in the least bit repentant!"

This was why he had proposed to her . . . and why his family wanted a quick marriage! They wanted to use her to divert attention from the scandal, to smooth it over in Georgetown! Her parents were descendants of prominent eastern seaboard families—the Wilmingtons of New York and her mother's family, the Smithsons of Virginia—and they had been well received in Georgetown even though their fortunes had dwindled. She felt a surge of anger at Willard, although she could not really blame his parents for their hopes for him.

"He doan even care about that gal!" Maddy added. "I expect he ain't never gonna change!"

"Well, you don't have to worry, Maddy." Rose vowed, "I will never marry Willard!"

Maddy wiped beads of perspiration from her upper lip. "I be glad to hear that, Miz Rose Anne, but doan never say never!"

"In any event, Father will be back soon, and we'll be on our own again."

A hopeful smile wreathed Maddy's face. "I hopes so. Oh, I hopes so!" She started for the armoire. "Land, I forgot! That handsome man from Boston came to our house with them pictures three years ago . . . well, he's coming heah tonight for dinner. The cousin of yo' friend, Miz Abby."

"You mean Joshua Talbot?"

Maddy nodded. She opened the mahogany armoire and pulled a out a deep-rose colored silk gown. "You wear that, and he'll be coming back again, Miz Rose Anne. Last time you was wearing black, and I do believe it scares the men away. Reminds them of their own end coming."

"Oh, Maddy!" Rose protested. "You were just fretting about Willard's morals and now you want me to tempt a man!"

The old housekeeper raised her chin. "Be a line between being a lady and being trash, and you know the difference!" She turned huffily. "Now doan you forgit to lock the door."

Closing it behind her, Maddy must have stood in the hallway until she heard the lock click in place. "You sleep for an hour, Miz Rose Anne," she said through the door before the heavy creakings of her footsteps receded.

When Rose lay down again, she attempted to put the entire matter about Willard out of mind; it was too sordid to even contemplate, she told herself. Instead, her thoughts drifted to her meeting with Joshua Talbot. It had been the autumn of 1845, and she had been walking home along a path above the river. Yes, it had been nearly three years ago now.

As befitted an 1845 Sabbath, the autumn scene around the docks had dwindled to a somnolent pace; the canal

17

mules rested from pulling the barges, and in the distant Federal City, people jested that even the politicians were silent. Leaves trembled and fluttered from the trees in the chill wind, their brilliant colors faded, and Rose felt like a brown leaf herself. All the brightness, the color had faded from living. Even in church her prayers had seemed to avail little.

Starting home from the burial ground, she hugged her black cloak about her and not for the first time prayed, *Help me, Lord, help me! William would not want me mourning him so!*

She strolled on through the rustling leaves toward the red-brick Federalist row-house her father had leased until they could build a larger place in Georgetown Heights. As she approached the house, she glimpsed Maddy inviting two well-dressed men in through the front door. Probably business associates who had come to visit her father. Waiting until they stepped inside, she made her way to the rear of the house. A gust of wind swirled the leaves at the kitchen door as she quietly let herself in.

Maddy hurried into the kitchen. "Miz Rose Anne," she whispered urgently, "there's callers in the parlor for you! Gempmum callers! I saw you coming so I asked them in."

"They want to see me?"

Maddy nodded, looking inordinately pleased. "They's down in the harbor from a Boston ship, and they's bringing you a present. Wainwright and Talbot, their names is."

"Wainwright and Talbot?" Rose asked, shedding her cloak. "Is that all they said?"

Maddy rolled her eyes at her forgetfulness. "Here's the cards, chil'. But that's all you getting from me 'cause that's all I knows. Now lemme take your cloak."

Rose read the cards. Joshua Talbot. Daniel Wainwright. Both were with Wainwright-Talbot Shipping and Chandlery as supercargoes, which meant they were the officers in charge of the cargo and represented the owners in all transactions. Important men, thought by some to be as important as the sea captain himself.

Puzzled, she slipped the cards into the pocket of her black broadcloth dress, then removed her black bonnet. "I've seen Wainwright ships in the harbor, but Talbot—I wonder if it's one of Abby's cousins? Abby, my friend from Miss Sheffield's School in New York."

"I doan know," Maddy replied, turning Rose by the shoulders with practiced ease. "Here, honey, lemme fix yo' hair." Her brown fingers brushed and patted the chignon to rights. "You looks like a porc'lin doll with circles of color on yo' cheeks. When you done mourning, won't be a man here in Georgetown or even in the Federal City can resist you. Why, you could marry a man to be sen'tor or even pres'dent.

"Now, Maddy, you know I don't care about other men."

"I knows. Sometimes I jest want to raise yo' spirits. You got to go on with life. It be killing me to see you in black dresses for a year—nine more months—and you only eighteen years old!"

Rose blinked away the tears that so often blurred her vision lately and forced a smile. Sometimes she thought she would mourn William forever, but it was best not to mention that to Maddy. "If the men stay awhile, we'll have tea."

"Jest take me a minute to fetch it."

"Thank you, Maddy."

Maddy nodded. "Now doan you be having one of yo' going-away spells. It scares a soul fierce."

"I shall be fine, I promise."

She ignored Maddy's worried look and started for the hallway. Stepping into the parlor, she saw the two men rise from the blue damask settee. They were both handsome and wore stylish dark broadcloth suits and vests and white linen shirts with high stocks around their necks. A package wrapped in a roseate fabric lay between them on the settee.

The taller man appeared rather taken aback at her black dress. He himself wore a brown vested frock coat that accentuated the engaging brown of his eyes; his wavy hair and mustache were an attractive auburn. "I'm Joshua Talbot, a cousin of your friend Abby. And this is Daniel Wainwright."

"What a pleasure to meet both of you," Rose said, moving forward to offer her hand. She was surprised to find Joshua kissing her fingertips, a gesture becoming more and more rare among northerners. When his eyes returned to hers, she added with a smile, "I must say that you don't look like Abby!"

"I should hope not for Abby's sake," Joshua said with a laugh, "particularly not with my mustache!"

Rose smiled. "I meant that she is blonde with blue eyes and you have . . . such different coloring—"

"Red hair?" Joshua suggested.

"Dark auburn, I'd call it." His hair was luxuriant and wavy and his mustache was magnificent—well-suited to his strongly masculine bearing and stance. There was a sense of daring about him, a dashing air . . . and, she suspected, often a stubbornness in the set of his square chin.

She turned to Daniel Wainwright, who was blue-eyed and darkly bearded—the man whom Abby loved! "Abby wrote about what a help you were to her. I believe I saw you at school in New York when you and your uncle came to get her."

Daniel's color heightened at the edge of his beard, and his blue eyes sparkled. "It was a pleasure to help in any way. And I believe I recall you, too, from your school."

"Shall we sit down?" she suggested and settled in a blue

velvet parlor chair. "I understand that you're visiting Georgetown from a Boston ship."

"Yes," Joshua replied, handing the package to her. "Abby has asked us to deliver her wedding gift and best wishes to you and your husband."

A wedding gift? Rose's heart constricted. She must have turned white, for the next thing she knew, Joshua Talbot was hurrying toward her with a most concerned expression.

"Are you all right, Mrs. Stanford?" he asked.

Mrs. Stanford! "But . . . didn't Maddy explain?" Rose inquired, stricken. Maddy must have been so distracted with her romantic scheming that she hadn't informed them of William's death!

Daniel started toward the hallway. "I'll find you a glass of water."

Rose wanted to protest, but the words did not reach her throat. This was the first time that she had to explain; everyone in Georgetown knew about the horse throwing William and his death just hours later.

Unaccountably, her mind flew to the week before the wedding when a minor reception plan had gone awry. William had said, "Don't worry about things so. Be joyful, my dear Rose. The Lord wants us to be joyful, and you have the most beautiful smile on earth to do that bidding." She recalled the wonder-struck smile of William's last breath.

"Miz Rose Anne!" Maddy exclaimed. "Miz Rose Anne, honey, here's a drink of water!"

Rose came to herself, wondering if she had said anything peculiar. Maddy said she sometimes did.

As if from a great distance she heard Maddy explain about William's death, her frightened words tumbling over each other, ending with "I didn't think to tell them, Miz Rose Anne. I jest didn't think! I hopes you be forgiving."

Rose sipped the cool water. "It's all right, Maddy. It's only that I'd been thinking about—"

"I knows what you thinking about," Maddy interrupted with a sorrow-stricken look.

"Perhaps it's best if we leave," Joshua Talbot offered.

"No, not at all," Rose insisted. "I do hope I didn't faint. If there's one thing I can't abide, it's women who are forever fainting!"

Joshua gave her a small smile. "It seemed more as if you'd retreated into the past for a moment, which is more than understandable. Are you sure you wouldn't prefer that we leave?"

"Of course not," she insisted, her strength returning. Her eyes went to the roseate wrappings of the gift, which was now on the tea table. "How like Abby to wrap my gift in my favorite color. But I fear I'll have to send it back to her in Missouri."

Joshua said, "I am at your service in any event. However, I know she'd be pleased if you'd look at her gift."

"Yes, then I think I shall."

He handed the package to her and sat down tentatively on the settee as did Daniel, while Maddy hovered in the background with the glass of water.

Rose unfolded the cloth from the narrow wooden box. Sliding the box open, her heart leapt with pleasure at the sight of the watercolored paintings. "How wonderful . . . and how like Abby to want to share her adventure."

The first watercolor sketch was *Crossing the Alleghenies*, the crossing by portage railroad between Philadelphia and Pittsburgh about which Abby had written; she had indeed captured the precipitousness of the journey. The second picture was *Frontier Baptism*, the delightful sight Abby had witnessed on the Ohio River. Rose, fascinated, next admired

Mississippi Madness with its river jam of barges, rafts, pirogues, canoes, and steamships. And last, *Summer Tranquillity*, a river scene that captured a summer afternoon in Independence, Missouri.

Rose said, "How I envy her—and both of you—your travels and adventures."

"Perhaps you will travel someday, too," Joshua suggested.

She shook her head. "It seems rather unlikely." She looked again at the pictures she held. "Abby's pictures are the loveliest, most thoughtful of all of our—our wedding gifts."

"I am sure she would want you to keep them for your own enjoyment," Joshua said.

"Yes, probably she would," Rose responded, admiring the watercolor pictures again. "When I think how hopeless Abby's life seemed with her parents' deaths and the estate being bankrupt— I prayed and prayed for her."

Daniel nodded. "Prayer brings about miracles. She is learning to take one day at a time."

"Yes. It's something that I must do now, too."

Joshua stood up uneasily. "We should be on our way."

"Of course not," Rose objected, "not until you tell me all about Abby. And you must have some tea. It's chilly outside. Maddy, would you please bring in the tea things?"

"Yes'm, Miss Rose Anne, if you feel all right now."

"I'm perfectly fine, I promise."

By the time they had finished tea and the men were making their departure, Rose had nearly forgotten her unfortunate lapse into the past. "Thank you for delivering Abby's pictures," she said as the men stood in the doorway.

"Our pleasure," Joshua said. His brown eyes, full of sympathy, lingered on her. "I hope you will recover soon."

"Thank you."

Once the door was closed, she wondered what she had

said during her unfortunate lapse into the past. Still, what did it matter, for she would probably never see them again.

Maddy bustled in from the hallway. "My, what handsome men those two was!"

"Now, Maddy. In any case, Daniel Wainwright, the bearded one, belongs to Abby."

Maddy replied with great earnestness, "Well, that Joshua be mighty handsome with his red hair and mustache—the kind of man who could be pres'dent, I expect."

"Oh, Maddy!"

After that curious afternoon, Rose had decided it was all very well for Maddy to let her imagination run rampant, but her own thoughts had returned to William.

It seemed impossible that her meeting with Joshua Talbot and Daniel Wainwright had taken place nearly three years ago, Rose thought as she slipped out of the canopied bed. Daniel had married Abby during their covered-wagon trip west. And now Joshua would be here at the Stanfords' house for dinner.

She sat down at the table to add to her journal entry of May 18, 1848. After recounting the particulars of her tea with Mrs. Stanford and Maddy's disheartening revelations about Willard, Rose wrote, *Time to dress for tonight's dinner. Tomorrow morning and afternoon there is an outing to Washington City and, in the evening, Willard's birthnight ball.*

She hesitated, then added, *I wonder whether Joshua Talbot will remember our first encounter, since I recall it so vividly.*

2

Descending the graceful Georgian staircase in her crepe-de-chine gown, Rose reflected on how much more she might enjoy this evening's dinner if Willard had not proposed. She continued down the stairs to the entry, stepping on its fine Persian carpet and past the Chippendale furniture.

"There you are, Rose!" Willard exclaimed. He had been sitting near the entry in the green parlor while conversing with guests, and he immediately came to her. His quick irresistible grin reminded her again of William's, and his evening attire might have been William's, too—black suit, white silk vest, and white cravat.

"Good evening, Willard."

He proffered his arm, and she saw no alternative to accepting it. He smelled most disagreeably of French musk, wine, and Macassar hair oil, and his green eyes appraised her carefully. "How very enchanting you look, Rose. I must say that I prefer you in this sort of sophisticated gown rather than your usual frocks."

"Thank you," she managed to say in an even tone. She stepped into the parlor to avoid further discussion of the matter.

The other guests quieted, the men rising to their feet, and Mrs. Stanford smiled hopefully. Willard made the introductions: two of his school friends from Baltimore and their fiancées, both Georgetown belles; Charles Wilkey, her father's soliticitor, with whom she was acquainted; Captain Caleb Svenson and Lars Johnson, a ship's officer; and last, Joshua Talbot, who Rose thought looked even more attractive than she remembered, his luxuriant dark auburn mustache and hair shining, his black broadcloth suit well-tailored. While greeting the others, she had been quite aware of his eyes resting intently upon her.

Joshua Talbot said to Willard, "I had the honor of meeting Miss Wilmington nearly three years ago." He turned to her, his brown eyes aglow with warmth. "I am pleased to see you looking so well now."

So he did remember. "Thank you. I am pleased to see you again, Mr. Talbot."

Willard cast a curious glance at her, and she quickly sat down on the green damask settee beside him.

The others returned to their conversations, but Mrs. Stanford said to Rose, "You are looking especially beautiful tonight. I've often thought that the color of your gown and your name suit you well. Perhaps you should always wear rose . . . as a distinction. Some women in society make their mark by just such an image, you know."

Rose felt her cheeks redden as she acknowledged the well-intentioned compliment, for making a mark in society by the color of her clothing, or any other such superficiality, held absolutely no appeal for her.

She accepted a glass of fruit punch from a servant and turned to Joshua Talbot. "I hope you've brought news of Abby and Daniel from the California Territory."

"Yes, indeed. They have recently had a child."

"A baby! I can scarcely believe—a boy or a girl?"

"A young Daniel."

"How pleased they must be!"

Joshua Talbot chuckled. "Euphoric is a more apt description. It never ceases to amaze me to find perfectly happy bachelors suddenly in the throes of love, then marriage, and . . . finally waxing eloquent over a squalling babe."

The others laughed, and Captain Svenson warned, "Someday you may find out!"

Willard asked Rose, "How did you happen to become acquainted with Mr. Talbot?"

"He's the cousin of my best friend, Abby, from Miss Sheffield's School for Young Ladies."

"Ah, a New York aquaintance." Willard sounded impressed.

Joshua explained, "Abby married my adopted brother, Daniel Wainwright."

"Also of Wainwright Shipping and Chandlery?" Willard inquired of their guest.

Joshua Talbot nodded, a hint of resentment at the questioning becoming evident in the set of his square chin. "As a matter of fact, you have a goodly representation of the firm here this evening—Captain Svenson, Lars, and myself. We sailed into Georgetown on the *Bostonia* two days ago."

Mrs. Stanford looked at Rose carefully. "I'm afraid I still don't entirely understand your connection with Mr. Talbot."

Rose replied, "Abby, his cousin, is the friend who sent William and me the beautiful watercolors she painted on her trip West." She began to feel as though she were undergoing an inquisition while Willard and his mother probed further about Abby's emigration to California by covered wagon two years ago.

Finally Joshua put in, "Abby likes it there very much, foreign though it is."

Willard said to Rose, "You probably find your friend Abby adventurous, but I much prefer a woman who stays in her own parlor. Or at least in her own community."

So one would guess! Rose felt like retorting, but subdued her irritation. Looking at Joshua Talbot, she found his brown eyes sympathetic.

Fortunately the conversation drifted to the Stanfords' plans for the next day. A chartered steamboat would take twenty of the younger crowd to Washington City for the day, while the house was readied for Willard's birthnight ball. Apparently Joshua Talbot and a young Georgetown belle had been invited, too. As Rose looked at him again, she found him glancing circumspectly from her to Willard as if trying to assess their relationship.

After dinner was announced by the butler, Willard proferred his arm again, and Rose saw that she must accept his escort. As they made their way to the dining room, he squeezed her fingers painfully with his other hand. She whispered, "You are hurting me, Willard!"

He relaxed his grip. "I beg your pardon."

Across the room, she saw Joshua Talbot frown, and she quickly looked away from him.

The spacious dining room was beautiful, as always, and featured great bouquets of red roses, two marble fireplaces, and magnificent mahogany sideboards. The Brabant lace tablecoth, a gift from the Duke of Brabant, held Chelsea porcelain in a Chinese design, and a French chandelier sparkled over the Charles II silver and Waterford goblets. Mrs. Stafford graciously indicated where her guests should sit, and Rose found herself seated between Willard and Charles Wilkey.

"I am glad to see a trustworthy gentleman on your other side," Willard commented about her father's gray-haired solicitor.

"One never knows," John Wilkey returned with humor.

Willard smiled sententiously.

Willard's silver-haired father settled himself at the head of the table, erect and radiating urbanity. When everyone quieted he said, "Since we have no clergyman in attendance, perhaps you will say grace, Captain Svenson. We know that sea captains and you, in particular, are often called upon for prayers."

Caleb Svenson smiled, his blond hair shining in the late evening light that filtered through the windows. "Shall we pray?" he began and bowed his head. "Dear heavenly Father, creator of heaven and earth, the stars and the sea, all things great and small . . . we come before Thee with praise and thanksgiving for this day and its many blessings . . . and now especially for this food. We pray that Thou wouldst bless this house and all of its denizens and friends, and show each of us the way Thou wouldst have us go. In the name of Thy beloved Son, the Lord, Jesus Christ, we pray. Amen."

A buzz of conversation began around the table, and Willard raised a brow in disdain. "Denizens of this house indeed! As in denizens of the deep?"

Rose felt a twinge of anger at his critical spirit. "I thought it was a very nice touch from a sea captain."

Willard frowned, turning his attention to the food being quietly offered by the servants.

Rose noted that Maddy had been pressed into assisting and saw her housekeeper's eyes stop upon her and her gown with pride. She and Maddy had sewn the dress themselves and apparently it compared well with the other gowns worn in the room, whether ordered from Paris or New York, or sewn by the finest Georgetown seamstress. While making it, Rose had discovered that she liked to sew herself.

The sumptuous meal began with a first course of buttered sole, then rounds of beef and Virginia ham accompanied by greens, buttered spring potatoes, sweet peas, beans, biscuits with honey and jellies, and endless condiments. The talk at the table, as always, drifted to politics in nearby Washington City. After a time, Rose realized that her father's solicitor was hoping for a chance to converse privately with her. She waited for Willard's attention to shift to his Baltimore school friends, then turned to Mr. Wilkey.

He quickly murmured, "This afternoon Joshua Talbot delivered letters to me from your father."

"From my father!" she repeated. She cast a glance at their fellow diners and was grateful that no one seemed to have heard her. She whispered, "Did he see him?"

Mr. Wilkey shook his head, then spoke rapidly. "It would be wise not to speak of it now. There is a letter for you that I thought you might prefer to read alone. I took the liberty of giving it to Maddy when I arrived. I know she's trustworthy."

"Is he—he all right?"

"Apparently."

At her breath of relief he added, "If there is anything I can ever do to assist you, please count upon me. You know that I was a friend of your mother's for many years. . . ."

Rose recalled that he had courted her mother in Virginia and had remained her friend until death. "Yes, Maddy told me."

"In any case—" His eyes went to Willard, who was turning to them, and the solicitor suddenly said, "I am very well, thank you," as though she had inquired about his health. "How very kind of you to take a sincere interest in my welfare."

Willard said coolly, "Just so she doesn't take too great an interest in you, Mr. Wilkey."

Indignation rose to Rose's throat, but the solicitor nodded pleasantly. "You have no concern there, Mr. Stanford. Even the elderly ladies bring me no more than chicken soup."

Willard chortled. "What a great shame for you!"

The solicitor smiled amiably and turned to his food. "An excellent repast."

"Yes," Willard agreed and peered at Rose suspiciously.

She turned away and took up a bit of beef on her fork. She must not allow Willard to aggravate her so, not when she had far greater concerns with which to deal. A letter from her father! At length she looked across the table and discovered Joshua taking in the entire drama. Rose was certain that he understood; he had, after all, been the one who had delivered the letters to Mr. Wilkey.

The dinner conversation had turned to Manifest Destiny, which had long been the great hue and cry in newspapers and everywhere one went. Those who espoused it claimed that Americans must overspread the continent, carrying democracy and civilization to the Far West. The Polk Administration, in particular, was anxious that more and more settlers emigrate into the California and Oregon territories on the Pacific Coast.

Willard's father said, "There is talk again about gold being found in California. If so, it will soon be sufficiently populated, but I understand that the find north of Los Angeles was insignificant."

"Only enough to cling to some wild onions!" Willard said derisively. "It's too far away—a vast, arid land. It's too foreign a place for most of us, even if Rose's father is there." Before anyone could do more than glance at her, he turned to Captain Svenson. "What is it now, a three-month voyage at best?"

The captain nodded. "Four to six months around the Horn in most ships. The newer clippers make passage in a hundred days."

Rose wished that her father were sailing home on one of the new clipper ships, but they carried few passengers. She could scarcely wait to read his letter. Perhaps he was on his way home!

Someone put in, "I imagine going across Mexico is not safe just now after the Mexican War, but can't one cross by the isthmus at Panama?

Captain Svenson shook his head. "Not easily. It has been nearly abandoned since the days of Spanish rule. And the isthmus is a dreadful place, full of fevers and pestilence."

The diners quieted momentarily, and Joshua Talbot said into the silence, "I have just returned from the California Territory, and I leave for there again this month." His words might well have dropped a cannonball onto the red roses of the centerpiece.

"Are you returning to search for gold?" one of Willard's school friends asked. "There's been talk of gold in California since the sixteenth century."

"I propose to develop the Bay of San Francisco as a major shipping port, and perhaps to sell goods inland at Sutter's Fort," Joshua replied.

Willard sat back in his chair. "Of course, you have the Wainwright ships and firm to support you, Talbot. In your position, all you can lose is your time."

"Perhaps," Joshua Talbot replied, unperturbed.

The servants cleared the table and brought dessert, and everyone turned with delight to the sponge cake and chilled strawberries covered with chocolate.

Maybe Willard was right—California was far too distant to pique much excitement, Rose reflected. Yet Joshua Talbot was going there soon. Abby Talbot Wainwright lived there now, and her own father had been there, too—perhaps was there still. Her mind went again to his letter. She fervently hoped that Maddy would bring it upstairs tonight.

Beside her, Willard murmured, "How well do you know Talbot?"

"As I said, I have met him once before." She added as kindly as she could, "You really have no right to inquire."

"Perhaps not yet, my dear Rose," he replied softly, "but I am under the impression that your reputation is without blemish."

She raised her chin and quickly turned away, fighting her resentment. Her hand trembled at her situation as she lifted her demitasse and finally sipped it. She would not give him the satisfaction of a reply. As it was, he had already imbibed heavily in wine.

He reached under the tablecloth to clasp her left wrist. When she looked up at him, his eyes glittered. "You do have a temper under all of that innocence, don't you, dear Rose?"

She set down her demitasse and slowly brought her right hand under the table, resting her sharp fingernails between the bones of his hand. She pressed them into his flesh until he loosed his grip on her wrist and backed away.

He chuckled. "A warning?"

"If that is how you wish to interpret it."

He laughed heartily. "We shall see."

The diners stood up from the table, and Rose was relieved that dinner was over. The sooner she could get to her room the better, not only to avoid Willard, but to read her father's letter! In the parlor she could scarcely endure the requisite conversation with the ladies while the men adjourned to the library for their brandy and cigars. The evening finally ended with reminders for those going to Washington City the next morning to be ready at eleven o'clock. The moment the guests departed, she excused herself and rushed upstairs to her room.

"There be a letter from yo' father!" Maddy said with excitement. "Close the door."

Rose closed her bedroom door quickly and quietly and locked it.

Maddy had been readying clothes for tomorrow's outing, but now she extracted a folded envelope from the ample bodice of her black dress. "Maybe there be word of Moses."

"I'm sure there will be," Rose replied as she took the envelope. Maddy and Moses had worked for her family since Rose's mother was young. The couple had been married for many years, and sang in the African Church, where members had prayed for Moses since his departure on the trip around the Horn.

Maddy sank onto a nearby chair. "Got a feeling we best sit down."

Rose sat down on the edge of her bed and tore open the envelope. She unfolded the pages and read aloud.

Oak Hill, California

Dear Rose,

What must you think not to have heard from me for so long? I wrote to you some months ago, but the ship—and presumably my letter—was lost. I hope you are not upset that I am not returning home yet as promised, but an opportunity of a lifetime has arisen here. Gold has been discovered in the American River east of Sutter's Fort, and I have found a goodly amount southeast of there myself.

"Gold!" Maddy exclaimed, voicing Rose's own amazement. Still, at dinner tonight the men had not thought much of the news. She read on.

As might be anticipated, we are attempting to keep the news to ourselves. I doubt that news of the extent of the discovery will have reached the eastern seaboard by the time this letter arrives, but it will . . . it will! I have filed a claim and hired a crew of Indians; Moses is their overseer and a good one, too.

As you know I hope to restore the family fortune, particularly that of your mother's family, after my foolhardy financial plunge in the Canal. I see no other possibility than this of recouping the losses, and I cannot continue to carry the guilt of my error. I hope that you will understand.

My greatest concern now is over your welfare. If you require funds, ask Mr. Wilkey, my solicitor. There is not a great deal of money in my Georgetown account, but it should be sufficient to cover your expenses for at least a year. I have written to Mr. Wilkey to this effect, though he knows nothing about the gold. (I ask you not to spread the news, for we fear a rush of gold seekers.)

Moses misses Maddy as terribly as I miss you, and he asks that we extend his best wishes to her. I believe he wanted to say "his love." He has become invaluable to me as both a worker and a friend.

I hope to meet your school friend, Abby Talbot Wainwright, when I visit San Francisco, as Yerba Buena is now called. I expect to send this letter through Benjamin Talbot, whom I have yet to meet. I hear good things about the Talbot family wherever I go. The mail service here in the diggings is nearly nonexistent, so it is best if you write to me in care of your friends.

I pray that all goes well with you. I am comforted by the knowledge that you are sensible and can always turn to the Stanford family for assistance. My blessings no matter what you decide to do. I shall attempt to write again soon.

Your loving father,
Jonathan Wilmington

P.S. I have purchased three log cabins and land from settlers who came by covered wagon several years ago. The cabins are far from luxurious but are quite comfortable. You will be pleased to know it is a beautiful place in the foothills, just below the Sierra Nevada Mountains, as the California Mountains are now called.

Maddy rolled her eyes. "Moses be overseeing Indians! What if they lift his scalp?"

"It must be all right. Father has written about it quite calmly. Surely he would not have them there if they were dangerous!"

"What about us leaving the house?" Maddy asked, vexed. "Doan he remember the lease was up?"

"It appears he's forgotten in his excitement over the gold," Rose replied, vexed herself.

"I expect he want to forgit. That's how men is!"

Rose fought her anguish. "If only Willard hadn't taken an interest in me. If only he hadn't proposed, we might have stayed on a bit longer. Right now, there are no suitable houses available for leasing, and we have nowhere to go if I

CHAPTER TWO

refuse him."

"What we do?" Maddy asked.

Rose shook her head. "I don't know!" What a shame that they couldn't accompany Joshua Talbot around the Horn to California, but that was impossible. Women simply did not sail on such ships.

Maddy sat up, straightening her broad shoulders. "We got to pray. Ain't nothing else in the world to do!"

A sound at the door caused Rose to look at it just as the knob began to turn. Her hand flew to her mouth before she recalled that the door was locked. "Who is there, please?" she finally asked, her voice shaky.

"Willard, my dear," he replied.

Her gaze flew to Maddy, who whispered heatedly, "Tell him I be here."

Rose's words sounded as shaky as she felt. "Maddy's here with me."

"I see," he murmured, and the doorknob moved slowly back into place. "I—ah wanted to wish you pleasant dreams."

"Thank you," Rose forced out. "Good night, Willard."

She and Maddy sat in disbelieving silence as they listened to his retreating footsteps. Strange that they hadn't heard him arrive, Rose reflected, but then they had been talking. She whispered, "What if he heard me read the letter?"

Maddy's eyes widened. "Oh, Lord, doan let it be!"

"Bad enough if he only heard us discussing him!"

"I doan think he was listening by the door, Miz Rose Anne. He strike me as a man who jest walk up and walk in where he please!"

"If only he didn't remind me so of William!" Rose said half to herself. The first sight of him always gave her false expectations, made her remember how wonderful William had been, even though her every encounter with Willard led to bitter disappointment. And in rejecting Willard so entirely, she felt as though she were being unkind to William, too.

After Maddy left, Rose quickly locked the door, though it provided little reassurance since she tossed and turned for what seemed hours. She could not marry Willard, but where could she go? All of her school friends were married or scattered about the eastern seaboard, and her only living relatives were distant cousins in London, with whom there was only rare contact. True, she did have the funds in her father's account. Reassessing all of the possibilities and arriving at no solution, she finally remembered to pray for peace and guidance, and then she slept.

The next morning as she dressed for the day's outing, Rose still felt dismal. Before there had at least been hope that her father would return in time to deal with their difficulties. Even her yellow gauze gown with its prettily flounced bell skirt and puffed sleeves did not lift her spirits. Pulling on her yellow and white bonnet, she gazed into the oval mirror on the mahogany stand and pulled an unconvincing smile. She took up her ruffled yellow parasol and left her room. *Help me, Lord, help me to endure this day!*

Perhaps if she had been kinder to Willard last night instead of threatening him with her fingernails . . . perhaps if she changed and were more loving to him, he might change his attitude. Perhaps God really did intend him to be her husband. In any event, her faith required her to forgive him . . . and to love him as a person. She hurried downstairs, pulling on her white gloves.

Willard's school friends with their fiancées, numerous Georgetown gallants and belles, Joshua Talbot with a lovely Georgetown girl named Caroline—all were congregating for the day's outing to Washington City. The parlor resounded with lighthearted merriment, girls' gay voices mingling with the bass notes of their escorts. The men had dressed for the excursion in daytime frock coats and hats, and the bright spring hues of the girls' gowns, bonnets, and parasols added to the gaiety of the occasion. Rose remembered to smile as Willard arrived at her side. Perhaps if she pretended that he were William. . . .

"How beautiful you look this morning, my dear," he said, taking her gloved hand, "like a yellow rosebud ready to burst forth into bloom."

"Thank you," she said, uncertain how to take his compliment. "You look very nice yourself." At least his enthusiasm about the day's junket imparted a happy glow about him. His ensemble this morning—checkered vest with the dark green frock coat and trousers—was not nearly as garish as yesterday afternoon's checkered trousers.

"Well, then, all twenty of us are accounted for," Willard announced. "Shall we hie ourselves out to the carriages?"

He bowed his guests out grandly, and Rose hoped he would be so occupied with the day's festivities that he would have little time for her. While they waited for the others to precede them, she realized she was older than most of the young ladies by several years; they all looked nearer eighteen, like recent graduates of Miss Lydia English's Female Seminary on N Street. Most of them would probably be married within the year to the gallants escorting them on today's excursion; undoubtedly they considered her on the edge of spinsterhood, nearly beyond the pale!

Outside, she opened her parasol, its yellow gauze as bright as the butterflies that fluttured across the grass. Beyond the lawn and oak trees, four carriages waited on the dusty road, the drivers looking as delighted with the gay occasion as Willard's parents, who were seeing them off. The young ladies were helped into the carriages, and as Willard assisted her in and sat down beside her, she realized that he was her escort. Why had she imagined that they might go off free as children to enjoy the day without being paired?

The drivers called out and the carriages started forward, horses' hoofs clopping along the road, wheels creaking as they stirred up dust. The gay procession traveled from the green hills of the Heights down toward the town with its dignified streets of red-brick houses, where people stopped to watch them pass.

Willard grinned. "I'm sure everyone in Georgetown already knows our day's agenda. There are no secrets hereabouts."

If so, everyone also knew about Willard and the girl by the grog shops, Rose reasoned. The old adage about being known by the company one keeps flashed to mind, and she desperately hoped that the others did not think her the same type. She cast a sidelong glance at Willard. If he fretted about the matter, it was not in the least apparent. He smiled easily at her, causing the other two young women in their carriage and their escorts to smile, too.

At the marketplace an elderly black man sat against the building playing his fiddle in the morning sunshine, and a slim, high-stepping young Negress danced and snapped her fingers to his music, shopping basket proudly balanced on her starched white turban. Around her idlers and passersby who had been clapping to the rhythm paused to glance at the parade of fine carriages on their way to the dock.

As they arrived at the Georgetown waterfront Willard said, "You are quiet today, Rose. I trust that you slept well."

Recalling his attempted visit to her room last night, she responded in a cool tone, "Yes, thank you, I did." She did not meet his eyes as he helped her down from the carriage.

Townsfolk and river roustabouts watched the colorfully attired belles and gallants as they made their way to the *Georgia,* the small steamboat chartered by Willard's parents for the short voyage. The *Georgia*—newly painted white and festooned with colorful streamers in honor of Willard's birthday and the forthcoming ball—looked like a birthday cake itself, outshining the hourly steamers that plied the Potomac between Georgetown and Alexandria.

The silence between them made her feel uncomfortable; moreover, she must be forgiving. "I've neglected to wish you a happy birthday, Willard," she said.

"I hope you will convey your greetings with more felicitous news tonight . . . if not now."

Heat poured into her cheeks. "Please . . . give me until tonight. You did say midnight, I believe."

Anxiety glinted in his green eyes for an instant, but was quickly replaced by his usual self-assurance. "Yes, of course." He kept a proprietorial hand at her elbow as people swarmed about them, and she tried again to pretend he was William.

Once aboard the steamboat, the party headed for the deck and the shade under a white awning canopy to enjoy the river view. Rose was surprised to find Joshua Talbot escorting his exuberant partner, Caroline, toward them. "May we join you?" he inquired of Willard.

Willard gestured grandly at the long wooden bench. "Please be my guest."

Something in Rose's spirit lightened as Joshua Talbot sat down beside her. He did not require garishly checkered clothing to capture one's attention; indeed, he looked dashing in his fawn frock coat, vest, and trousers. He appeared to be over thirty years of age and seemed far more mature than Willard at twenty-six.

"Good morning, Miss Wilmington," Joshua Talbot said,

his brown eyes full of interest.

"Good morning." She smiled, hoping to silently convey her appreciation for his delivery of her father's letter.

He nodded and, after a moment, she turned to watch the enthusiastic young crowd settle on the benches around them, chatting and laughing.

The *Georgia* tootled and steamed away from the dock, its wake flaring and sparkling in the silvery-blue river, then smoothing out again. Rose looked out with pleasure at the picturesque riverside scene with its steamers and sailing ships, and the receding view of the steeples and green hills of Georgetown. The air was so soft, the sun so gentle, the day so glorious that her heart lifted with happiness.

Joshua Talbot said to her, "I am pleased to see that you are happier than at our meeting three years ago."

"Thank you, Mr. Talbot."

"Joshua, if you please."

"Yes, then . . . Joshua. And you must call me Rose. I feel in a sense . . . probably because of Abby . . . that we are already friends."

"I am honored to hear it . . . Rose." His deep, melodious voice spoke her name tentatively, then he smiled, his eyes filling with pleasure.

She returned his smile, thinking there was something about him that she liked a great deal—his directness and a sense of honesty, perhaps.

Rose recalled from last night's conversation that he and Caroline had only recently met, but the diminutive Georgetown belle obviously knew a handsome catch when she saw one and she began to point out the sights to Joshua to keep his interest.

While Caroline discussed the sights and Willard expounded upon the day's plans, Rose felt a peculiar awareness pass between her and Joshua, a consciousness so palpable that she felt certain everyone else on the steamship must see it, too.

Later, when they docked amid gaity and laughter at Washington City, she was pleased to see that Joshua remained near her; his eyes often met hers with curiosity and—when Willard appropriated her arm—a hint of discomfort. As they made their way ashore, she tried to ignore Joshua's presence, reminding herself that he was not her escort. Yet he came to her attention constantly—the richness of his deep voice, the brilliance of his smile, the sun glinting on his mustache and wavy auburn hair. With him nearby, the sights of Washington City took on such a glow that even dusty Pennsylvannia Avenue almost attained a sense of grandeur.

They dined at John Coleman's Hotel, the finest in the city, just a short distance from the President's white mansion. Joshua Talbot was seated across from her at the long banquet table, and, caught up in the merriment, Rose laughed and chatted all around, far too aware of his presence and only vaguely aware of their excellent fare as she ate.

Finally she had an opportunity to ask him, "Have you been to Sutter's Fort in the California Territory?"

He shook his head. "No, but I hope to go there on this voyage. Is that where your father is?"

"Southeast of there." She wished she might ask him if he knew about the discovery of gold.

Willard grinned, interrupting them. "You are having a fine time, after all, aren't you, Rose? You looked rather glum this morning. I am gratified to see you coming around. I suppose you see that I am rather nice after all."

She laughed with disbelief at his conceit. "Oh, Willard!"

He chuckled himself. "Well, what is the point of being

modest?" He caught up her hand and looked as if he might plant a kiss on her palm if the waiter had not arrived just in time to save her from that mortification.

After dinner, the entire party promenaded on the path alongside Pennsylvannia Avenue, where carriages rattled like ships in a sea of ruts and left dust in their wakes; even the Lombardy poplars lining the avenue were gray with dust. Rose noticed that Joshua offered his arm in no more than a gentlemanly fashion to Caroline as they strolled along.

"Someday this will be a magnificent city," Willard said to Rose. "We see the refuse now, and pigs running loose, but that will change."

"It has been like this for years," she pointed out.

"Mark my words, it will change. L'Enfant's grandiose plan will succeed. Let Dickens and the other foreigners make fun of us with their 'spacious avenues that begin in nothing and lead nowhere'! I can visualize great avenues with rows of marble edifices, artificial lakes with pebbly shores, swans floating along on the water in the shade of monuments."

Rose glanced at the elegant Greek Revival buildings nearly completed—the Treasury, Post Office, and Patent Office. "Perhaps you are right."

"Of course," Willard said. "Moreover, we shall be a society of ambassadors, members of Congress, justices, everyone of importance. It will be unlike anything in any other city of the world." After a moment he added in a low voice, "I hope that together we shall play an important part in it, Rose."

"I have never heard you quite so eloquent, Willard," she equivocated.

"It is my dream to play an important role in such a society." He smiled at her meaningfully and slipped his arm around her shoulders. She must have looked aghast, for he threw his head back in laughter, then said, "I must be in disfavor again!"

She glanced away toward the white President's mansion, refusing to dignify his remark or his amusement at her expense.

The Marine Band played on the South grounds of the President's mansion, the martial airs floating over the lawns and shrubs and white gravel walks. Rose thought if she were with William this might be one of the happiest days of her life. Instead, she fought against the sense of urgency that warned her to flee as quickly as possible.

They strolled toward the Capitol, and the band played a medley of sprightly folk songs—"Jimmy Crack Corn," "Old Dan Tucker," and "Zip Coon," then the new ballad, "Oh, Susannah." One of Willard's friends merrily sang out the nonsensical words:

"It rained all night the day I left
The weather it was dry
The sun so hot I froze to death
Susannah, don't you cry!"

"Isn't everyone having a fine time?" Willard remarked as he assisted Rose up the great stone staircase of the stately Capitol.

Rose glanced at the happy faces of their group. "Yes, it's a lovely birthday outing."

They made their way around the Capitol rotunda and discussed the historical paintings and the colossal Greenough statue of George Washington—a scandal to all with its Roman toga, bared chest, and arm pointing upward. Later, they toured the National Institution and marveled at the vast collection of natural history artifacts. The small nuggets and flakes of gold made Rose wish desperately that she could be with her father.

In the late afternoon when they walked through Lafayette Square, all of Washington seemed on display—old Dolly Madison wearing rouge and pearly powder, Daniel Webster carrying a leg of mutton up the front steps of his house, foreign ministers, charges d'affaires, even Vice-President George Dallas with his crown of snow-white hair.

Willard greeted all of them and said to her, "You see the excitement we have here already, Rose. Everyone of importance."

Rose replied facetiously, "The immortals."

"Exactly," he agreed. "We do think alike, my dear."

"But I was jesting," she objected with disbelief. "We are . . . to worship God and never earthly power."

"And who put that into your pretty head?" he inquired.

"Why . . . the Bible and our pastor."

Willard frowned as if she were being morbid again, then gave a belated chuckle. "You are droll, Rose. Droll . . . but a tempting rosebud in that sweet yellow dress."

She turned away quickly. Not only had he misunderstood her point about the immortality of those who worshiped power, but he purposely avoided God. Moreover, she did not appreciate his kind of compliments. Perhaps Megan McCabe and the other young women who worked at the grog shops enjoyed them, but she did not! She could not bear him much longer, but where could she and Maddy go?

3

The scent of newly washed earth filled the air as Benjamin Talbot and Jonathan Wilmington rode their horses through the green California countryside. Benjamin's chestnut gelding and Jonathan's bay mare galloped through the spring sunshine over rounded hills and flat-bottomed valleys where clusters of live oaks shaded the grasses to a darker green.

As they rode toward his ranch, Benjamin prayed, *Lord, let this visit lift the weight from my new friend's shoulders.* They had only met twice before in the past few months, since Walter Colton, the clergyman who was now the alcalde in Monterey, had sent Wilmington to see him.

"Whoa, Warrior," Benjamin said, reigning in his chestnut as the outer reaches of his ranch came into view. "The beginnings of our property lines. We have four leagues, a small place by California standards, as you probably know."

Wilmington nodded. "I have five leagues at Oak Hill, but a good deal of it includes mountainsides." He smiled. "I'm still unaccustomed to speaking of leagues instead of acres or miles."

"The new measurements, like new customs, slowly become familiar," Benjamin said as he sat on Warrior's back, looking over the countryside. "Our land stretches from the old road to what's called Winter Creek to far south of here. We call it Rancho Verde . . . green ranch. A misnomer during dry seasons, but appropriate now after two months of winter rains."

He looked with pleasure at his cattle grazing upon the hills. Beyond the stream, corrals fenced in the horses near the whitewashed outbuildings. "The first sight of the ranch never fails to please me," he acknowledged.

"A beautiful sight indeed . . . as beautiful as my land at Oak Hill." Wilmington smiled at a thought. "You have the Biblical 'cattle on a thousand hills.' "

Benjamin grinned at the allusion. "The Spanish family who sold me the ranch and its livestock told me that a thrifty rancher should have two thousand horses, fifteen thousand head of cattle, and twenty thousand sheep before he thinks of killing or selling them."

Wilmington chuckled. "They think in grand terms here."

"Indeed," Benjamin replied. "Almost as grand as the Lord's provisions for us . . . almost as grand as arriving here after almost five months of body-wracking covered wagon travel and being able to buy a Spanish land grant rancho."

"Mexican rule had just ended then?"

"Yes, while we were toiling through the mountains and deserts," Benjamin responded. "When we arrived at Sutter's Fort, we learned California had become an American territory. We were so done in we could scarcely raise a cheer."

"I can imagine," Wilmington said. He patted his bay's neck, then turned back questioningly. "With so few dwellings here, how did you find the ranch?"

"Most of the Spanish royalist families had already fled during Mexican rule, and those left in the Castello family, the owners, wished to return to Spain." He gave a laugh and patted Warrior's neck, too. "Despite my being 'a lowly Yankee trader' in their eyes, the place fell like the proverbial ripe plum into our hands."

"I am not surprised," Wilmington said. "What does surprise me is your management of such a vast rancho, as well as the shipping and trading establishment in town."

Benjamin explained, "My adopted son, Daniel Wainwright, sailed around the world as a supercargo for years and is invaluable for our shipping work here. As for the ranch, my son Jeremy and son-in-law Luke are in charge. They farmed in Independence, though butchering cattle for hides and tallow still strikes them as callous and wasteful."

"As it does me," Wilmington agreed. "Still, a ranch of these proportions takes many men to run it properly."

"We kept the Indians the Castello family had working for them. We pay them, however, and allow them to stay on as before . . . housed, fed, and clothed."

"A far better arrangement than they'd have with most settlers," Wilmington said. "We have Indians working for us in the hills, too. One wonders what will happen to them and to this way of life with so many men coming to the diggings."

"Yes. It was a pastoral paradise when we arrived," Benjamin said. "Everyone thought our warehouse on the bay would be a failure. I felt like Noah building an ark."

Now that his warehouse was a success, even those who had scoffed at him were building—and not all of them were respectable establishments. "If the gold holds out, we may have a metropolis on our hands," he added. "Do you know of Juan Bautista de Anza coming here in 1776?"

"I have read only a little of his travels," Jonathan replied.

"Anza was most impressive," Benjamin said. "Compared to Lewis and Clark, who journeyed from St. Louis over the

Rockies to the Oregon country thirty years later, Anza's exploratory feat here stands equal. If, however, Lewis and Clark had returned to Missouri, raised and equipped a colony, led them over the same trail again, and finally held the land against a foreign power, they might have equaled Anza's success. As an explorer and colony leader, it's impossible to find anyone in Anglo-American annals with whom to compare Anza."

"Interesting. I had never considered it in that light," Wilmington replied.

"There was a great deal more of interest about his explorations," Benjamin said. "The priest with him wrote of the Bay of San Francisco being a marvel of nature, the harbor of harbors. He thought if it could be well settled like Europe, there would be no more beautiful place in the world. He imagined it with a city rising up the hills and below, shipyards and docks . . . and anything that might be wished."

"And that's why you came?"

"In part," Benjamin said, deciding it was no time to go into the details of his calling. "I never forgot his words."

"I believe that Anza's priest was right," Wilmington replied. "The question for us is how to find men to build a city when they only wish to search for gold."

"Yes, the question exactly."

Wilmington stared out into the distance. "How I wish I had a son to help me at Oak Hill. We only had the one child—"

"Perhaps Rose will provide you with a fine son-in-law," Benjamin suggested. "I've acquired a good son and grandchildren in just that manner."

Wilmington brightened. "Yes, that is assuredly my hope. When I think how my prayers have already been answered and my life changed, everything seems possible!"

"There's nothing like a new convert's enthusiasm to rekindle one's own faith," Benjamin said. Smiling, he nudged his horse onward. "We had better ride on."

They cantered to the crest of the next hill, slowing their horses again as the walled whitewashed houses with red-tile roofs came into sight. "Our houses are built of adobe, baked earth," Benjamin said, "just as our log house in Independence was built of logs, the most distinctive surroundings in that heavily wooded place."

"The reason I have a log cabin at Oak Hill," Wilmington replied. "It's a far cry from the fine houses in Georgetown, but I've become rather fond of it."

"We have dedicated the ranch to the Lord," Benjamin told his new friend. "In fact, we have Sunday worship services at the house, and I hope you might stay the night."

"Your invitation to dine with you already is an honor . . . I am so seldom among civilized people nowadays. I don't wish to be a burden."

"You would be a blessing," Benjamin assured him. "Everyone will be as excited by your conversion as I am. I wonder what special work the Lord has for you."

"I often wonder myself," Wilmington said, his brown eyes lively with speculation. "I believe it concerns my land at Oak Hill and the gold. I want to use my life and my riches for Him." His expression grew sober. "If only I could be reassured again about Rose as I was the first time we met and prayed. Perhaps I am out of God's will. Perhaps I should be sailing back to Georgetown."

"Trust Him to let you know," Benjamin said. "He's brought you thus far; He will give you further discernment." He nudged Warrior onward and smiled ironically. "At least that's what I always tell myself, for sometimes I wonder whether I'm precisely in His will as we try to build His church here. We simply must place our trust in Him."

As they cantered their horses down to the house, he prayed, *Lord, give him and his daughter, Rose, Thy guidance and discernment. Lord, help them! And, Lord, I beseech Thee again in behalf of my son, Joshua. . . .*

When Rose arrived upstairs in her bedroom, Maddy was laying out petticoats, silk stockings, and ivory slippers for the evening's ball. "How was yo' day?" Maddy asked, her honeyed voice as solemn as her creased black face.

"It was a lovely day except—"

"Except for Mistuh Willard," Maddy supplied for her.

Rose nodded and sat on the bed to untie her walking slippers.

"Doan seem like you ready for dancing with that long face. All the help heah be saying the big 'nouncement gonna be tonight . . . and yo' wedding soon!"

Rose blinked angrily at threatening tears. "Oh, Maddy, we have to leave Georgetown! I can't conceive of any other solution. Can't you think where we might go?"

"I doan know, chile. I doan know. I been worrying and worrying my haid, but I can't think of any place . . .'cept maybe going to yo' daddy and Moses in Cal'fornia." Her dark eyes flickered with hope, then turned to the floor at seeing Rose's dismay. "I expect it doan be possible."

"I expect not," Rose agreed, "not that it hasn't occurred to me. This year's wagon trains to California are already en route and most won't take women alone. As for going around the Horn, women seem to be most unwelcome on the ships."

"In the Bible, Job say 'man is born to trouble,' but I say woman sho' is born to trouble, too!" Maddy declared. "Heah, let me help you out of yo' dress. What you needs is rest for tonight, and what I needs is more time fo' prayer."

Rose turned for Maddy to unbutton the back of her yellow frock, regretting that she had forgotten to pray since this morning. Why was it that even in the midst of distress, she allowed her attention to drift away from the Lord?

"Wait 'til you see the gown Miz Stanford send up for you to wear, chile."

"She sent up a gown for me!"

Maddy nodded. "Miz Stanford say it be special fo' tonight. They got mighty big expectations for you and Mistuh Willard."

"But I can't wear it, I can't—"

"Hush, Miz Rose Ann. She say it be in 'membrance of her friendship with yo' mama."

Rose's eyes closed in despair.

Maddy returned Rose's yellow dress to the armoire, then brought out an exquisite silk ivory gown with rich ivory lace inserts and bows, a gorgeous confection with a flounced bell skirt and dropped shoulders. "Flowers be sent up later to wear twined along the buzzum and in yo' hair. Pink roses like yo' cheeks, Miz Stanford say."

"Oh, Maddy, I can't wear it. I can't . . . even if it is the loveliest thing I've ever seen." She noted that, except for its low neckline, it might have been a wedding gown.

"You think on it, Miz Rose Ann. Maybe best you pleases them for a while, jest 'til we knows what the Lord want us to do." Maddy headed for the door. "Now, you lay down, chile, and rest! You got time for one hour's nap."

"Yes, I think I shall. I'm exhausted."

"What you going through, I ain't su'prised! And that Mistuh Joshua, he be watching you at dinner last night."

"Now, Maddy, you musn't start imagining again. I'm sure

he wasn't watching me . . . especially."

"There be watching, and there be watching, and I been heah on earth long 'nough to know the difference." Maddy lifted her chin and headed for the door. "Now you sleep!"

Rose heaved a sigh and locked the door determinedly.

She lay down on the bed and, glimpsing her mother's Bible on the bedside table, felt compelled to take it up. Reading God's Word would help her more than an entire day of rest. She propped herself up on the bed pillows and turned through the softly rustling pages to the Book of Psalms, stopping to read, "For in the time of trouble he shall hide me in his pavilion . . . now shall mine head be lifted up above mine enemies round about me: therefore will I offer in his tabernacle sacrifices of joy: I will sing, yea, I will sing praises unto the Lord."

Praise . . . that was what was missing from her relationship with God, Rose thought. She so often called out *Help me, Lord,* yet she so seldom offered praises to Him. William had often spoken of the need to praise God. He said praise showed one's faith even when all seemed to be going amiss.

Rose thanked God in spite of all of her circumstances, then prayed, "I praise Thee, Lord Jesus . . . I praise Thee . . . " until she felt an awesome reverence that filled her with joy and peace before she slept.

"I be glad you at least wear the dress," Maddy said as Rose looked into the mirror. Maddy had brought up the tiny pink roses, pinning them into the lace along the neckline of the ivory gown, and had helped her into the bustle, crinoline, petticoats, and, finally, the glorious gown. Standing back as if to admire her own handiwork, the old housekeeper pronounced, "You be most beautiful . . . most beautiful, Miz Rose Ann."

Rose protested gently, "You see me through the eyes of love." Yet when she looked into the full-length mirror at herself in the ivory silk and lace gown, she knew what Maddy said was true: she knew she had never looked quite like this. The tiny pink roses tucked just over the ringlets loosed from her chignon were lovelier than a diamond tiara; the intertwined roses along the dress's neckline, more enchanting than jeweled necklaces. Her mother's gold ear bobs were her only jewelry, reminding Rose of her father in faraway California.

A medley of lively Beethoven airs floated up from the ballroom, and outside, the street resounded with the restless stamping of horses, the crack of whips and shouts of coachmen, and the voices of arriving guests.

"Time to go," Rose said in trepidation.

"I be praying for you all night long," Maddy promised as she opened the door. "You think on a Bible verse."

One that William had often quoted came to mind: *I can do all things through Christ which strengtheneth me.* Rose claimed it to hold in her heart, to get her through whatever lay ahead this evening. The path would be opened for her.

Making her way slowly down the staircase, she nodded at the arriving guests. The women brightened the entryway with their colorful gowns, sparkling necklaces, and ear bobs; many of the younger ones wore necklines garlanded with clematis and scarlet honeysuckle. Most of the men were resplendent in evening dress—black swallowtails with white cravats; a sprinkling of ambassadors and chargés d'affaires wore elegant court uniforms.

While the men handed over their hats to servants, the women scrutinized Rose's ivory dress and returned her smile knowingly. How many of the guests suspected the true purpose behind Willard's birthnight ball? She repeated silently, *I can do all things through Christ which strengtheneth me.*

Gay Parisian tunes swirled through the house as the butler led the guests toward the ballroom, Rose following them. Ahead of her a group of Georgetown belles and their escorts paused to exchange greetings with friends, blocking the ballroom doorway, and Rose decided to detour through the library.

Opening the door, she stopped. Mr. Stanford was berating someone . . . Willard! Starting to close the door, she heard her name. "Rose is a lady, Willard," his father said, "and we expect you to treat her as one. For once, resist your baser instincts! This family cannot tolerate any more scandal because of you. And, remember, not one more drink until after your betrothal announcement is made tonight! Do you hear?"

"This is ridiculous, treating me like a child!" Willard retorted. "Rose will be more than grateful to have me as a husband. She is nearly a spinster—twenty-one years old—and with little dowry! She only feigns coyness—can't you see that? Open your eyes, Father!"

His father replied, "I'm not so certain."

"Ah, it's only the way women play. Before midnight, I shall take her into my arms and she will be more than delighted to marry me . . . and quickly." He chuckled. "I am, after all, your son . . . given to like escapades."

"I have always been discreet!" Mr. Stanford protested. "As for your certainty about her, women are often surprising."

Rose closed the door softly. Surely the Lord would not make her enter into this marriage! She repeated the verse, *I can do all things through Christ* . . . . Hopefully that did not mean enduring marriage to Willard!

Her eyes turned toward the merry crowd moving down

the hallway to the ballroom. She stared at them blindly before she was aware that Joshua Talbot was among them, splendid in his black swallowtail suit. He nodded at her as he approached, the diminutive Caroline at his side.

Rose removed her hand from the library doorknob, feeling like a culprit caught at eavesdropping.

"One seldom overhears what one wishes," Joshua remarked with irony.

"I—I . . . " She could not go on.

His expression filled with compassion. "I beg your pardon, Rose. I tend to taunt people too easily. Come, come along with us. Your face is quite pale."

She nodded distractedly and clutched his arm. In the ballroom, gaslight flickered from the glittering chandeliers, and the immense room blurred before her eyes. Although the dancing had not yet begun, the room seemed awash with swirling colors and dizzying movement.

Joshua Talbot said, concerned, "Rose, you must not faint. I recall you once telling me that you couldn't abide women who were forever swooning."

His face came slowly into focus: firm square chin, unsmiling lips, straight aristocratic nose, and the handsome dark auburn mustache and hair; then, at her eye level, muscular shoulders filling the fine black evening coat, a handsome white satin cravat tucked into his white vest. She must ask him about California and how he had received her father's letter, she thought. She must talk to him.

He signaled for the nearest waiter circulating with a tray of crystal goblets with wine and cups of pink punch. "Here, drink this, Rose. Rose?"

She sipped the cool, fruity drink.

"Can you hold the cup now?" he asked.

"Yes, of course." Accepting the cup with trembling

fingers, she brought it to her lips and drank half of it down.

She began to feel somewhat revived. "Thank you." She attempted a smile. "It—it must have been the heat."

Joshua raised a dark brow. "In one form or another, I suspect. Are you feeling better now?"

"Much better. You will probably not believe me, but I have only come to the verge of fainting once before in my life—" She recalled the peculiar spell she'd had when he arrived with Abby's watercolors three years ago and added, "It seems to be your misfortune to have been at hand on both occasions."

He gave her an ironic look. "I trust I do not bring on these spells."

"I am sure you do not," she replied with a little smile. She found Caroline staring at her as if she were one of those ridiculous belles who wore her stays too tight.

Joshua remarked, "It's a warm evening. Shall we make our way out to the terrace?" Without awaiting their reply, he escorted Rose and Caroline through the crush of guests toward the wall of open French doors.

The musicians, sitting among the palms on their platform, played a classical air, too slow for dancing. Their foreheads already shone with perspiration, and Rose knew that hers must be shining, too. Finally they were outside on the terrace, and Joshua handed her his neatly folded handkerchief.

She blotted her face dry with the fine lawn fabric. The cooler evening air was beginning to refresh her damp shoulders and arms. At Joshua's troubled look, Rose recalled Maddy's remark about him watching her last night at dinner.

"Thank you for your kindness," she said.

"My pleasure," he replied.

He is a good man, Rose thought. She judged that he

would never do anything that could not bear the light of day. She returned the handkerchief to him, smiling with gratitude.

From behind her, a hand cupped her elbow. "There you are, my dear," Willard said. "My abject apologies that I wasn't standing at the bottom of the stairway to watch your descent. It was my loss."

She cringed, but managed a "Thank you, Willard."

His irresistible smile elicited a small one from her in return. His black evening attire was flawless, his white silk cravat exquisite with its diamond stickpin. If only he were William!

She said, "How thoughtful of your mother to find this lovely dress for me."

His eyes traveled the length of her with unconcealed pleasure. "I helped her to select it."

"But gentlemen never—"

He drew her close, his hand warm upon her bare shoulder, and whispered into her ear, "But husbands may."

She backed away slightly.

"Soon I shall help you choose everything, and we shall turn Georgetown and the Federal City on its ear." He grinned and turned to Joshua Talbot and Caroline. "Thank you for escorting Rose. I was unavoidably detained."

"My pleasure," Joshua said again, a muscle near his jaw twitching with annoyance.

The musicians played the introduction to the opening quadrille, and Willard offered his arm. "Come, my dear, we must lead the dance. This is, after all, our evening."

"Please, Willard—"

He gave her no opportunity to object as he led her firmly through the throng, then chose three other couples to make up their set.

The first quadrille proceeded with elegance, ladies and gentlemen promenading arm to arm in their formal attire, and Rose was gratified to keep her mind occupied with the dance's changing figures she had learned at Miss Sheffield's School—Le Pantalon, L'Ete. . . . She flinched at the half smiles of her changing partners, for their expressions seemed to ask, *Does the poor girl foresee what life with him will be like? Does she know about the scandal?*

Finally the quadrille ended, the spectators applauding, and the musicians began "Just Like Love Is Yonder Rose."

Willard drew her into his arms. "I requested it in your honor," he murmured, then beamed as they began to dance. "The words alone are mantraps . . . like you."

"You find me a mantrap?" she inquired, incredulous.

"One hears that still water runs deep." At her indignant look he added, "You are, shall we say, intriguing to me."

She stated firmly, "I have never intended to be."

Willard chuckled. "What sweet indignation, my dear Rose."

I am not your dear, nor your Rose! she wanted to protest.

To add to her indignation, Willard began to sing in a smoothly confident, albeit off-key voice, "Just like love is yonder rose, heav'nly fragrance round it throws . . . yet its dewy leaves disclose—" She tried to ignore him but he sang the chorus even more loudly as he whirled her around the ballroom.

Joshua Talbot danced by with Caroline, his brown eyes widening in amazement as he heard Willard. Fearing that Joshua might laugh, Rose averted her eyes to Maddy, who was serving punch across the room. If Maddy was praying for her, Rose admonished herself, she must at least keep her temper under control while Willard sang on.

I can do all things through Christ, she repeated in her mind.

With a great effort, she turned her attention to the others around them, thankful at last when Willard stopped singing.

The ballroom had burst into life . . . women dancing in flower-bright dresses, round white shoulders bare, jewels sparkling at their ears and necklines, and lace shawls hanging from their arms . . . gallants of all ages in their black swallowtails or exquisite uniforms with medals shining in the soft light. It was all very beautiful, but Rose wished that the evening were over. If only she had said a very firm and definite no when he had first proposed yesterday afternoon!

As the music ended, there was much changing of partners, and Rose found herself dancing with Willard's school friends. She noted that Caroline cleverly kept Joshua Talbot to herself.

The evening proceeded apace with vivacious waltzes and quadrilles, and Willard puffed up with pride and certitude as he danced with her again. It appeared he harbored no doubts that their betrothal announcement would be made at midnight. Indeed he said several times as they danced, "Soon, my rosebud, soon."

Her eyes darted wildly across the ballroom to Joshua Talbot and, for the first time in hours, discovered his gaze upon her—and Caroline missing from his side. *Please help me!* her heart cried out as they danced past him. It appeared that he was her only path of escape.

He arrived at her side for the next waltz, and she was forced to remind herself to appear calm, to respond in kind to his pleasantries as they left Willard.

She made herself count out the rhythm silently as they began to dance. Joshua was light on his feet, far more graceful than might be expected for such a large, muscular man. He held her carefully, a polite distance spacing their bodies as they moved to the music.

He inquired, "Was that a plea for help you were sending me across the room?"

"Yes—yes, it was." She must do something . . . say something . . . now! She must ask him what had been roiling in the back of her mind since last night, impossible as it seemed! The words burst from her. "Please, may I go with you around the Horn?"

He stopped mid-step, his brown eyes full of astonishment. After an instant, his feet moved to the waltz rhythm again. "You are quite serious, aren't you?"

"Yes, very serious. My father will not return from the California Territory for a year or even longer. You brought the letters to Mr. Wilkey, and I thought—"

"That I might help you escape?"

"Yes. How did you know?"

"The caged look in your eyes, I suppose. Something seemed amiss." He studied her carefully. "Are you certain that you wish to go? California is not like this," he said with a glance around the glittering ballroom. "It is a raw territory, not what one might call a civilized place."

"Nevertheless, I want to go. I am certain of it."

He danced on gracefully, but his brow furrowed. "A great many risks are to be considered in this, Rose. I'm sure you know that sailing around the Horn is fraught with danger. Shipwrecks are common, and few live through them."

"I don't care!" The next words slipped from her lips: "I would rather be dead than marry Willard." She was horrified at her admission, but it was true.

His hand tightened slightly on her waist, forcing her to look up into his face again. "Have you considered how you might escape from the great announcement that is expected tonight?"

"Maddy and I are praying—"

"Praying!" he repeated incredulously.

"Yes."

He paused for an instant, then gave her a slight smile. "Well, I suppose that I could sweep you away from here in a carriage, and we could sail away in the middle of the night for Boston."

Her spirits lifted, though she feared he might receive an improper impression. "Maddy must go, too."

His expression sobered. "Of course."

Rose's hopes grew. Perhaps it was possible after all! As they danced on, she explained, "I can't go in your ship tonight. It would cause even more talk, and it would be unfair to you and the captain since you are friends of the Stanfords."

"Business acquaintances, Rose. There is a difference."

"Still, I will not ask you nor the captain to take me now, and I know that the ship won't sail tomorrow . . . not on the Sabbath."

Joshua's brows lowered. "What is your plan?"

"I only know that Maddy and I must be able to sail around the Horn from Boston with you." She could ask Charles Wilkey for the funds; he had, after all, promised his help just last night. "We can pay our way. I know it sounds unreasonable, but we must go!"

"It is not as unreasonable as it seems. Very likely, there will be another woman, Nichola Wainwright, the owner's niece by marriage, on the ship with her maid."

"Then we can go?" Rose pleaded, scarcely staying in step.

"Yes," he replied, leading her strongly about the floor, "you can go. There is still room on the ship."

"It will all work out yet!"

Joshua said, "I must give you the address in Boston—"

They both saw Willard across the room watching them,

and Joshua began steering her that way, so they would be with him when the music ended. "At church tomorrow morning," Rose whispered, quickly relating the time and location. "After tonight's ball, the family will be too exhausted to attend."

On the dying coda of music, Joshua said ironically, "We shall see how your remaining prayers prevail."

"They will," she replied softly, ignoring his skeptical tone. "They will." She was surprised at her own peace, at her sudden inner assurance.

She turned to Willard, whose complacent smile and eager hands already reached for her.

"If you will excuse us, Joshua," Willard said. With a nod he claimed her and began to escort her toward the French doors. "You look warm, my dear. I thought you might enjoy some fresh air."

Rose cast an assured smile at Maddy as they passed. She was now helping the caterers set the buffet supper—great platters of oysters, lobster, terrapin, wild turkey, partridge, and quail amid colorful displays of fruits and vegetables—on white damask-covered serving tables.

Willard said, "Gautier, of course, is our caterer. My family has always preferred the finest and that, my dear, is why I prefer you."

Now, Rose thought . . . now it will come.

Her eyes closed for an instant. *Help me, Lord,* she prayed before remembering that she should praise Him, thank Him in all circumstances.

They stepped out onto the gaslit terrace, and earth scents assailed her—the evening damp upon the lawns, newly trimmed hedges, the nearby bed of roses. To her vast relief, a great many couples had congregated on the terrace; even some of the single gentlemen had stepped out for fresh air and were discussing politics vociferously.

Willard frowned. "Come, Rose," he said, leading her as far away from the others as possible, "we can sit on this settee."

She sat down, realizing that God was not going to send a miracle. She would have to tell Willard the truth, just as she should have yesterday when he had proposed.

He caught her hands in his and, after a glance at the others around them, said softly, "You know, Rose, why I have brought you here. It will soon be midnight, and my father would like to make our announcement."

She shook her head, unnerved.

Despite the crowd, he tried to gather her into his arms, and she pressed away. "No, Willard . . . no!"

"Yes, Rose," he whispered hoarsely, "you must say yes. I promise you will never regret it! I am far more of a man than your William ever was—"

She wrested herself from his grasp. "Never!"

Suddenly aware of the quiet all around them, they looked at the crowd on the terrace, but the others were not watching them. They gaped at a red-haired young woman who had come around from the side of the house, a buxom beauty who was not only tipsy, but heavy with child.

"Sure 'n there ye be, Willie Stanford," she said to him as she stood at the edge of the terrace. She turned a derisive smile on him and then on everyone else as if she were an actress upon a stage. "I heerd yer big news is to be out at midnight, so I thought I'd be out and about in my fine condition as well."

Eyes leaped from her to Willard.

"Well, my fine Willie, have ye naught to say to yer beloved Megan McCabe? A lot of fine speeches ye have made me. Oh, the sweet promises—"

Mr. Stanford's voice boomed for the butler. "See this young woman out immediately!" He turned upon Megan. "How dare you come here with your ridiculous allegations! How dare you come lying!" His face was livid.

Servants grabbed Megan and tried to take her away, but not before she glanced at Rose. "So yer the fine Rose he will wed! Ye, in your white silk and laces—"

Rose turned and ran wildly toward the French doors, through the throng of shocked guests on the terrace. She saw Mrs. Stanford clutching her chest; she saw Joshua gazing at her with concern; she saw Caroline and other Georgetown belles pale with shock.

Maddy caught up with her on the far end of the ballroom, her eyes rolling with incredulity, her arm grasping Rose around the shoulders as they hurried through the hallway toward the staircase. "That be the last thing I ever expected! That be a scandal, sho'!" She was puffing, but did not even pause for breath. "What would yo' mama say! And what would yo' papa do if he be heah! Land, this be the worst scandal in Georgetown . . . the worst I ever in my life did see!"

"Hush, Maddy, hush!" Rose whispered as they hurried up the stairs. Despite her tumultuous emotions, it occurred to her that there would be no dull entry in her journal tonight. She nearly laughed at such an odd idea springing to mind now.

Once in the bedroom Maddy found it impossible to suppress her indignation as she helped Rose out of the ivory gown, and Rose had to close her mind to her loyal servant's torrent of outrage.

At length Rose stood in her chemise and petticoats, took a last look at the lovely evening dress, and said, "Please wrap it up nicely and give it to Megan McCabe."

"Give this silk gown to that trash!" Maddy exclaimed. "Is yo' head addled? Why you want to give it to her?"

"Because I want her to see that owning a silk and lace gown really makes very little difference in life. And, I suppose, because it rightfully belongs to her. Willard should be forced to marry her."

"Willard marry her? Ain't no chance of that! Ain't no chance of that at all, even if they do seem like a pair of matched bookends."

Megan McCabe and Willard Stanford—matched bookends! Matched . . . yes, they were perfectly matched! A bubble of laughter escaped Rose, then another and another.

"Honey, it sound like you be undone in the head!"

Rose's laughter felt so free and liberating that she cared not in the least whether she sounded demented or not. They were free . . . free! They still had to leave the Stanford house and make arrangements to travel to Boston, but after the strain they'd endured, all of that seemed as nothing.

Finally she gasped for breath. "We are going around the Horn, Maddy . . . both of us! We are really and truly going around Cape Horn to California! Praise God, Maddy . . . oh, praise God . . . we're going to see Father and Moses!" Exhilarated at their escape, even the dangers of rounding Cape Horn seemed insignificant!

4

Sunday morning in his spacious whitewashed parlor, Benjamin Talbot surveyed the twenty or so neighbors who sat on the old Spanish furniture and backless benches with his family and Jonathan Wilmington. *Lord, guide me,* he prayed. *I might be a pastor's son, but I need Thy guidance and assurance in conducting a divine service . . . and I especially need Thy help with the announcement.*

He rose solemnly to his feet. He was stepping into perilous waters, far more perilous than many a minister would attempt. However, he knew that his father, albeit an eminent Boston minister, would have probably done the same under these circumstances.

Finally everyone quieted. "Good morning to you, my family and friends," Benjamin said. "I regret that our friend Seth Thompson is preaching in town this Sabbath morning. He has promised to pray for us and our divine service, and I have given my word that we shall pray for him. We are excited to receive word about the growing number of Christian gatherings in town, and we hope . . ."

His eyes roamed over them and he wondered how they would take it, for most of this crowd had been accustomed to proper white-steepled churches. " . . . and we hope that many of them—and you—will join us at a great camp meeting here by the stream one weekend this autumn. It may be a foreign idea to you, but such revivial meetings have long been a tradition on the frontier."

Their eyes widened with surprise and, as they murmured, his gaze took in his family: Jessica, his dear older sister, who sat at the small pump organ in readiness to play the first hymn . . . his adopted son, Daniel, with his wife, Abby, and their first babe . . . daughter Martha with her husband, Luke, and their four children . . . Jeremy with his wife, Jennie, and their two babes . . . Betsy, his youngest, now thirteen. Likely they would not all favor a rustic camp meeting, but he felt certain it was the Lord's leading, as did Seth Thompson, who was an ordained minister and promised he would help.

When they quieted, he rushed on, "It gives me pleasure to introduce a new friend and believer, Jonathan Wilmington. Jonathan's daughter, Rose, attended school in New York with our Abby. Indeed, they were best friends. The painting of the dark-haired young lady you see behind the organ is Rose. Jonathan, if you would stand for a moment."

He returned Jonathan's smile, then introduced the others, who also stood in turn. "The Thorton family; the Youngs and their guest, Captain Abel Thomas of the bark, Carolina; Mr. Josiah Benton; and Mr. Frederick Stange. Welcome to our divine service. Scripture tells us that we are not to forsake the gathering of the brethren."

Arthur Young stood again, his English accent most evident as he spoke. "I do not believe that a camp meeting is dignified nor appropriate for honoring God. My family shall not attend." With that, he sat down, and the rest of them darted glances at each other and at Benjamin.

Josiah Benton half raised his portly frame and added, "I am accustomed to dignity in a church . . . stained-glass windows, not an outdoor brush arbor and revival preaching! I shall not attend, either."

Benjamin said kindly, "We must each do as we are led by God, and this is where Seth Thompson and I are led. We all know the two great commandments—to love God with all our heart, soul, and might, and to love our neighbors as ourselves. But let us also remember Christ saying, 'Go ye, therefore, and teach all nations, baptizing them in the name of the Father, and of the Son, and of the Holy Spirit, teaching them to observe all things whatsoever I have commanded you. . . .'"

Josiah Benton and Arthur Young did not look appeased. Benjamin quickly suggested, "Let us sing the new children's hymn whose words Jessica, Abby, and Betsy have written out for us, mindful that we are to come to God as openhearted, loving children."

Jessica played the hymn through once as they all rose to their feet, then they were singing,

"Savior, teach me, day by day,
Love's sweet lesson to obey;
Sweeter lesson cannot be,
Loving Him who first loved me."

As they sang, the time suddenly came to him. Mid-September . . . mid-September . . . yes, that was when to have the camp meeting. Suddenly it struck him: Joshua would be here then!

No need to tell Jessica or the children he'd just remembered that, for it was easy to let the tongue slip. They might tell others or, worse yet, they might tell him. Joshua would think they'd planned the camp meeting for his benefit.

Rose awakened as birds twittered outside her bedroom

window. Last night's ball and its inglorious conclusion leapt immediately to mind, and her spirits lifted again. Unpleasant as it had been, she was free—nearly free! The prospect of telling the Stanfords of her departure was disquieting, but no well-brought up Georgetown girl would be expected to marry Willard after Megan McCabe's performance. The telling and retelling about her dramatic appearance at the ball would likely go on for years.

Slipping out of the canopied bed, she did feel sorry for the Stanfords. Willard, however, would probably find a way to evade the furor. Very likely he would someday consider the entire episode amusing—if he remembered it at all.

Rose dressed in her rose silk gown for church, took up her matching bonnet and parasol, and hurried downstairs. The house was more quiet than on most Sunday mornings; none of the family was up to attend worship services.

In the dining room a maid set out covered dishes on one of the mahogany sideboards, scurrying away before Rose could greet her. What must the servants be saying about last night? she wondered, discomfitted. She helped herself to eggs, sausage, corn bread, and butter from the buffet, then sat at the table and poured hot coffee from the silver coffeepot.

The kitchen door opened and Maddy bustled in, her face wreathed in a broad smile. "Morning, Miz Rose Anne." She was dressed in her navy blue church frock and a matching bonnet trimmed with secondhand white silk flowers.

"Good morning, Maddy."

"The servants all buzzin' about the scandal," Maddy divulged in hushed tones. "Mistuh Willard, he gonna be sent off to London, and his parents gonna go up to the plantation at Oakland . . . for a while, anyhow."

Rose asked in a panic, "You didn't tell them about our trip?"

"Land, no . . . even if I did have to bite my lip. I be dying to tell about seeing Moses soon."

"What happened after you left my room last night?"

"Most of them guests they jest go on home and the caterer, he take most of the food back. Mistuh Willard, he got fearful drunk and they had to carry him off to bed."

"I see." She was not surprised.

"I be back from church early," Maddy said on her way out of the room. "I expect we got fast packing ahead of us!"

I hope so, Rose thought, *oh, I do hope so!* She must immediately make arrangements to get to Boston for the first leg of their journey. She hoped Joshua Talbot would have suggestions when they met at church this morning.

Outside, a soft breeze fluttered the green leaves of surrounding oaks, hickories, and maples, and she started along the footpath toward church, wondering how the day would unfold.

As she approached the red-brick church with its pointed white steeple, she saw Joshua in his black suit awaiting her near the door. Beside him in their dark uniforms with brass buttons were Captain Svenson and Lars Johnson, the ship's officer of the *Bostonia*.

"There you are, Rose," Joshua said cordially as he came toward her on the footpath. His brown eyes glowed warmly, and it appeared as if he might offer his arm, then thought better of it. "We were expecting you to come by carriage."

"It's such a fine day for walking, and it didn't seem quite fitting to request the Stanford carriage now."

"Of course. I should have thought to call for you."

"Thank you, but that might have caused complications."

"Yes, possibly." He turned to Captain Svenson and Lars Johnson. "Do you remember these gentlemen from Friday night?"

"Certainly. I am pleased to see both of you again."

They greeted her politely, their blond hair gleaming in the sunshine. The captain said, "Joshua asked that we attend church with you this morning."

Joshua explained in an ironic tone, "They've promised to restrain me in the unlikely event that I receive a missionary call to the heathen."

The men laughed amiably, though their eyes turned serious.

Bewildered, Rose said, "I hope you didn't bring them to discourage my going to California!"

"On the contrary," Joshua replied, "after they heard of last night's contretemps, they felt that you should sail on the *Bostonia* with us. We would be less than gentlemen to direct you to another ship to Boston."

"But wouldn't it cause . . . trade difficulties for your shipping company here in Georgetown?"

Captain Svenson shook his head. "Our owner, Elisha Wainwright, will be pleased that we've rescued a damsel in distress. And our trade in Georgetown is not dependent upon the Stanfords." He hesitated, then added, "Most sailing ships are entirely unsuited for young ladies, Miss Wilmington. We cannot recommend any Boston-bound ship now in the harbor. In any case, we sail at noon tomorrow, and at least on the *Bostonia,* you would know the three of us and we can guarantee your safety."

"I daresay it will make Maddy and me feel more at ease."

"Then consider your passage arranged," the captain said.

Rose's eyes closed in relief and opened with a glow of gratitude. "Thank you. And I thank the Lord for sending such fine gentlemen."

The chimes of Georgetown College pealed across the verdant hillsides and, from inside the church, the organ prelude burst forth. Rose led them into the familiar sanctuary. Settling into a back pew, they quickly took up the hymnals. She found the page and sang out with exultation and a flood of gratitude,

"Holy, holy, holy! Lord God Almighty!
Early in the morning our song shall rise
    to Thee!"

A shiver of joy rushed through her as they sang . . . joy in the Lord . . . joy that God was leading her into a new life.

To her left, Lars Johnson sang along fervently in a melodious baritone. She hoped to hear Joshua's voice on the other side of her, and she cast a sidelong glance at him. He was singing, albeit without much enthusiasm.

Later, during the service, she darted covert looks at him, studying his profile—the fine straight nose, the strong jawline, the sun-burnished auburn hair and mustache. There was a clean masculine smell about him, the browned skin of a man who had recently spent time in the sunshine and fresh air.

He glanced at her and smiled, and she turned away guiltily.

The sermon dealt with man's rebellion against God. According to the preacher, most people's resistance was directed toward authority—particularly toward the supreme authority of God. Stealing another look at Joshua, Rose was dismayed to see him staring out a window with disinterest. Abby had written that he was the family rebel. Did that mean he was not a believer? His late Grandfather Talbot had been an eminent Boston preacher, but that insured nothing.

After the service, Rose and the men stood outside the church and made arrangements for the trip. In Boston, she and Maddy would stay at Elisha Wainwright's house four or five days . . . however long was necessary before the

Californian, a new clipper ship, sailed for California.

"Are you certain I will be welcome in Mr. Wainwright's house?" she asked uneasily.

Captain Svenson replied, "Not only is he one of the most hospitable men in Boston, but he will make you feel as one of the family. He is a most exceptional man."

Joshua added, "He insisted upon sending me to Harvard simply because I was his nephew Daniel's best friend . . . and, of course, because my father took in Daniel when his family was killed by Indians on the frontier. And now our families have become further enterwined through Abby's marriage to Daniel."

As an afterthought he said, "Uncle Elisha's widowed niece by marriage, Nichola, resides there, so you will not be the only woman in the house. She will be sailing around the Horn, too." He glanced at Caleb Svenson, and a concerned look passed between the two of them.

"It sounds fine," Rose said, although she wondered whether their strange interchange concerned Nichola. "I shall never be able to thank you enough."

At noon, she returned to the Stanford house with apprehension. She would have to explain that she and Maddy were leaving tomorrow morning, and they would want to know where she was going . . . and with whom.

Upon her arrival, Maddy met her at the door. "They's gone! They's left for the plantation up north. Miz Stanford give this letter for you."

Trembling, Rose tore open the heavy white envelope.

Sunday morning

Dear Rose,
We must go to Oaklawn for a time and ask

that you forgive our abrupt departure. I think that we shall return to Georgetown in several weeks, and we hope you will remain here in comfort.

Under the circumstances, whatever I say will be inadequate. Only know how heartsick I am over the entire matter. I have grown as fond of you as though you were a daughter and know how you still mourn William. If only he had lived, our lives would be so different now, but one must go on as best as one can. Surely in time the furor over last night will abate.

If there is anything you need, please ask the servants, and do, my dear, feel perfectly at home.

Affectionately,
Garnet Adams Stanford

After rereading the letter Rose said, "How last night's scene must have pained her. I can still see her standing in the ballroom clutching her chest. Now to feel as if they must flee from Georgetown!"

Maddy nodded. "It be a shame Willard didn't take more after his mama . . . like yo' William."

The Stanfords' departure seemed providential; it appeared that the Lord had paved the way for her and Maddy to leave without difficulty tomorrow morning. She must only see to the packing, obtain the funds her father had mentioned from Mr. Wilkey, leave a note for Mrs. Stanford, and . . . go to William's grave at the burial grounds for the last visit.

When Joshua arrived at the door on Monday morning, Rose was waiting, primly proper in her blue traveling dress and white-trimmed blue bonnet. Her handbag held funds and bills of exchange arranged by the kindly solicitor.

After restrained greetings, Joshua gestured toward the trunks and baggage in the entry. "Is that everything?"

"I sincerely hope so," Rose replied.

His gaze went to Maddy who said, "That be all, suh."

He looked into the parlor. "It's very quiet. How have the Stanfords reacted to your leaving?"

"They were gone when we returned from church. They were already on the way to Oaklawn, their plantation north of here."

The lines between his brows deepened. "It does seem as though your prayers are answered."

"Yes, I had only to leave a note for Mrs. Stanford."

The hired black driver and his young assistant carried out the trunks, and Rose walked out to the carriage in the mid-morning sunshine. Turning back, she glanced at the red-brick mansion. Just two mornings ago such a merry crowd had left for the excursion in Washington City for Willard's birthday. She recalled how badly she had wanted to escape Willard then . . . how she had hoped . . . and now it was indeed time to say farewell to this lovely town.

Joshua handed her up into the carriage, then helped Maddy in before seating himself beside Rose.

She arranged the skirt of her blue frock carefully, not wanting to look out the window. As the carriage started forward, she could not help glancing out past Joshua at the fine Federal mansion of which she might have been mistress.

Joshua inquired, "Are you suffering regrets?"

She shook her head. "No. Only sadness that my ten years in Georgetown have ended like this."

"I hope you won't regret leaving this kind of life when you arrive in California. Many Easterners find it an uncivilized place. The customs and the land are different."

"We shall learn and manage," she reassured him as well

as herself. "It's not as though we'll be alone, since Father and Maddy's husband are there."

Only as they passed the burial grounds was her reassurance pierced with regret. Very likely she would never see her mother's grave nor William's again.

In town they drove across a bridge over the Chesapeake and Ohio Canal, her father's financial nemesis—a place she would be glad never to see again. The nearby grog houses reminded her of Megan McCabe, and she asked Maddy, who sat across from them, "Did you arrange for the delivery of the gown?"

"Yes, Miz Rose Anne. It be delivered tomorrow morning."

Rose ignored Maddy's disapproving tone and hoped that Megan would accept the gown as from a fellow sufferer of Willard. In a sense, the gown was a bond between them.

Georgetown's wharf bustled with activity, and Rose was pleased to see that the *Bostonia* was a handsome bark, its three masts and freshly painted black hull gleaming in the sunshine. Captain Svenson and Lars Johnson waited on its deck to welcome them.

"It's a pleasure to have you sailing with us," they said, and were gratified to hear that their departure from the Stanford house had gone so well.

After the captain and Lars excused themselves, Joshua accompanied Rose to the ship's railing, and they stood absorbing the wharfside atmosphere: stevedores rolling heavily laden barrows up the gangways from nearby warehouses, peddlers hawking their wares, small boats darting about between brigs and barks and steamships. The sailors on the Bostonia sang a hearty pulley-haul chantey as they worked the lines, and Joshua explained their preparations for sea as they set the sails, the staysails, and the jib. His enthusiastic explanations pleased her, even if she didn't entirely understand the intricacies of sailing. Underscoring the sounds of the wharf was the steady lapping of the Potomac against sturdy pilings.

When the *Bostonia* left dock and Rose heard the chimes of Georgetown College pealing out the final notes of the noon hour, a knot of anguish rose to her throat. She tried desperately to blink away the wetness of her eyes as the scene unfolded. Sailors still climbed about aloft as the sails filled in the breeze, then the *Bostonia* turned downriver, leaving behind a sparkling wake. Suddenly Rose realized her departure fully and knew in her heart she would never again see this picturesque seaport and its green hillsides. Hot tears burst from her eyes and ran down her cheeks; she bit her lips as she fumbled in her pocket for a handkerchief, then blotted her tears away.

Joshua patted her arm, and a quiet sob escaped her. "It's a sad departure in many respects," he said soothingly. "For Caleb and Lars, it's their last voyage on the *Bostonia* because she's been sold. They'll command the *Californian* and take the best of this crew on it. Strange as it sounds, seamen grow as fond of their ships as land dwellers become of their surroundings."

Listening to him, to the comforting tone of his voice, helped Rose to bring her emotions under control.

"It's best to look forward," Joshua suggested, "always forward." He gently turned her toward the views ahead on the sunlit Potomac River, and she was glad that the brim of her bonnet shielded her face from him.

He began to intone like a tour guide, no doubt to cheer her, "And here we have idyllic Mason's Island on our right . . . and, ahead, the Aqueduct Bridge . . . in the distance, the magnificent, if still rather pastoral, Washington City rises from the marshes."

She saw that far away along the rail Maddy, too, was wiping her eyes.

Sailing past the beautiful Capitol and the white President's mansion, Rose wondered whether Maddy recalled the remark she had made the first time they had met Joshua. "He be mighty handsome with that red hair and mustache, the kind of man who could be president." She couldn't help smiling at the thought.

Joshua looked perplexed. "One moment you're weeping and now—what are you thinking, if I dare ask?"

"Maddy once said you're the kind of a man who could someday be president."

Joshua erupted with such a laugh of astonishment that Rose gave a small laugh herself. "My thanks to her for the compliment. She is probably the only person on earth to whom such a notion could present itself!"

On their right now was Arlington House, the beautiful mansion built beyond the marshes by George Washington Parke Custis. As they sailed on and remarked on the scenery, Rose felt a growing calm and strength, even a sense of camaraderie with Joshua. She felt as if he were not only a good man, but a friend. It was unlikely that she or Maddy would ever return to Washington, but the Lord had surely sent along Joshua to be their guide. It reminded her of the biblical Joshua who had succeeded Moses after the Israelites' wandering in the wilderness. In a sense she, too, in these last three years, had been wandering in a wilderness.

Later, she and Joshua settled on a mahogany bench on the quarterdeck aft, occasionally looking up at the *Bostonia's* sails billowing with the breeze. It was such a lovely day and their conversation so spontaneous that it seemed only a short time before they sailed by the busy seaport of Alexandria. Rose had visited the town several times by steamboat, but did not much care for it, having once glimpsed a slave auction there.

Already the river was widening, its Maryland bank becoming more forested. Captain Svenson stopped by at the rail and suggested, "Since you are the only passengers, I thought you might enjoy taking dinner out here on the deck. It's simple fare, but the river sights make it more enjoyable."

Rose looked at him anxiously. "Please don't go to any trouble on my account."

"Not at all," the captain assured her. "The truth is that I am hoping to join you myself. When my wife, Inger, sails with me, we often eat outside here along the quieter rivers."

"Then I shall be delighted," Rose replied. Probably Maddy would have a fit at her sitting in the sun and freckling her face, but it was so lovely here in the warm breeze with so many sights to see along the river's bank.

Joshua said, "I would enjoy it myself. There will be few opportunities to eat outside when we hit the rougher waters of Chesapeake Bay and the Atlantic."

The steward carried their dinners up to the quarterdeck. Rose and Joshua remained on their mahogany bench, and Caleb Svenson settled near her, bowl of stew in hand; he looked at them and attempted to conceal his amusement over something, but his eyes gave him away.

Puzzled, she decided he must know something of which she was unaware. She turned her attention to their midday repast. It was a simple dinner of beef and vegetable stew with biscuits, but the fresh air whetted their appetites, and the soft sunshine and passing views made the meal most pleasant. After a dessert of bananas and oranges shipped from the tropics, the three of them sat back to watch the scenery, enjoying their coffee. On the left bank, there was Maryland with its wooded land and creeks; on the right bank, the green countryside and occasional farms of Virginia.

Joshua related, "It is said that Captain John Smith's crew found so many fish here along the Potomac in the 1600s that they lay thick with their heads above the water, as if wanting to be netted. Not having nets, the crew tried catching them with a frying pan, but found it useless."

Rose laughed. "You must be jesting."

"Not at all! It appeared in his journal." He grinned. "We have always been together at such solemn occasions that it would be pleasant to be jesting with you, however."

"Or taunting?" she teased, for she suspected that he was not above using light sarcasm to make a point.

His eyes glinted with humor. "The only time I've been sorely tempted to taunt you was when we began to dance together at the ball. I thought perhaps you expected me to sing 'Just Like Love Is Yonder Rose,' too!"

"Why, Joshua Talbot!"

"Something told me it was neither the time nor the place."

"It was not!" Rose returned with a laugh, "unless, of course, you have a magnificent voice."

Perhaps he didn't have a praiseworthy voice, but she liked the sound of the robust laughter that welled up from deep within his chest now.

Captain Svenson stood up from the bench with a grin. "On that note I must excuse myself to tend to my duties."

As he took his leave, they finally sobered, and Rose wondered whether Joshua had work to tend to himself. Quite likely he was only being so kind to her because he thought it was a gentleman's obligation . . . and because she was Abby's best friend. "Do not feel that you must entertain me if you have work."

"I do have accounts to see to—" he began reluctantly,

then his eyes smiled into hers again. "But it is far more pleasant outside than in my cabin. I might bring my work here, if you don't mind."

"Certainly. not. I must write to my father. Do you think we might post it with a departing clipper ship when we arrive at Boston Harbor?"

"Yes . . . and then hope it will beat us to California!"

She said, "I shall have to fetch my writing paper. And I would like to update my journal."

"Fine." He stood and assisted her to her feet, holding her hand a moment too long. Their gazes held uncertainly, then broke. "Excuse me," she said and hurried away across the deck.

When they returned from their cabins, Mount Vernon was coming into view, and they stood at the railing to admire George Washington's beloved home. Beyond it, the river flowed slowly, grandly, with broad vistas and filigreed shores. Here and there between the forests, farmland edged the banks, fields that had been worked since the 1600s. The beauty of the scene made Rose loathe to abandon the railing.

Finally they returned to the bench, and Rose settled down with her writing paper, discomfited yet gratified that Joshua sat at her side again. She reminded herself not to make overmuch of it, for theirs was the only bench now in the shade of the sails. Deciding to write first to her father before turning to her journal, she thought for a moment about how to begin, then felt her eyes drawn to Joshua.

He was looking at her so oddly that it unnerved her, and quite suddenly she was tempted to return his earlier taunt. "Are you going to sing?" she asked.

Instead of laughing, Joshua's color deepened, and to her astonishment, she found herself blushing, too. She looked down at her journal, not quite seeing it. His hand was reaching for hers on the bench between them, and she made no effort to withdraw it. As his hand engulfed hers with warmth and tender strength, a wave of pleasure surged through her. She looked at their hands together, the dark reddish hairs on his shining in the sun. She lifted her gaze to his, her eyes questioning.

He looked around as if to ascertain their privacy. "Rose?" he asked, his tone of voice fraught with meaning.

Her heart pounded against her ribs. "Yes?"

He brought her hand to his lips, the coarse hair of his mustache prickling her fingers as he dropped a gentle kiss on her fingers. His eyes met hers. "I am growing fond of you."

"We scarcely know each other."

He drew a deep breath. "I was very taken with you three years ago when I brought Abby's watercolors to your home."

Her cheeks felt pinker than ever, and she tried to withdraw her hand, but his grip tightened upon it.

He said, "It is likely imprudent, but I wish to tell you something. The few times I visited Georgetown after our first meeting, I strolled past your house in hopes of seeing you."

"You . . . you truly walked past just to see me?"

He nodded, smiling boyishly. "Worse, I asked Caleb Svenson to use his influence to obtain invitations to the Stanfords' dinner and the ball. It is not something I have ever done before. Please understand that, Rose."

She stared at him thunderstruck. "And that is why the captain smiled so knowingly."

He held her hand in both of his now. "I should not have admitted it, but I want you to know the truth."

Joshua's brown eyes held her gaze with such caring that she whispered, "Oh, Joshua—"

He kissed the palm of her hand most fervently.

Shocked, yet half pleased, she pulled her hand from him.

"Please, no—" She must do something to change the direction of matters, she told herself. She grasped at the first subject that came to mind. "I—I overheard bits of your conversation with Caroline the day we went on the outing to Washington City. Tell me . . . tell me what it is like when you sail around the world?"

He blinked with astonishment. "You want to know now what it is like to sail around the world?"

She nodded, realizing how peculiar her question must strike him at this moment. Still, she must not encourage his attentions. "I—I should think it would be very interesting. I should like to know what your ships carry . . . and—" she finished lamely, "everything."

Drawing a deep breath, he sat back and finally smiled. "Your school taught you well in the art of equivocation."

She had to smile herself. "Perhaps," she admitted.

"Very well," he said indulgently, "if you insist upon that topic of conversation." He hesitated. "My last voyage seems a good place to begin."

"Yes—"

His smile widened, but he began in a dry voice. "We left Boston with a cargo of finished merchandise, then sailed around Cape Horn to the Sandwich Islands, where we disposed of a portion of the goods and took on sandalwood and China silks. From there, we sailed to Sitka, and from there to San Francisco, then to San Diego, trading for cattle hides at those last points. Then we returned to Boston."

"Surely that's not all there is to it," she protested. "What is it like in . . . in Sitka?"

"In Sitka?"

"Y-yes . . . I should think that Sitka and the Russians would be most interesting."

He nodded, his brown eyes full of laughter. "Sitka

86

presents many points of interest. Ladies are particularly interested in the furs we take in trade. There is also a government fortress with fine buildings in the shapes of castles and round towers, each mounted with guns as a protection against their hostile Indians."

"And the Russian people?" she prompted, for he was eyeing her hand again.

"The men are from Russia's nobility. Their wives and daughters are exceedingly beautiful and highly accomplished." He added, "They are of medium height, delicate and symmetrical in form and figure, and exceedingly graceful in their walk and carriage. Their complexions are wonderfully transparent and they have rosy cheeks like yours."

It occurred to her that he must have a great deal of experience with women and that she must be careful. "And do the Russian ladies speak English?"

"Most speak French and English in addition to their own language. And they give family parties and balls for our entertainment, all conducted with great elegance and refinement. In return, we usually give several entertainments on board our ship, decorating it handsomely with the flags of all nations, the Russian flag flying at the foremast. At the arrival of the governor and his staff with their ladies and families, we give a salute corresponding to his rank."

"It sounds rather elegant," Rose said.

"Rather like our conversation," he laughed and caught her hand in his again.

Not removing it this time, she looked him full in the eyes. "Then I remind you of the Russian ladies?"

"You are far more beautiful," he assured her.

Is this the man meant for me, Lord? she wondered. *Is this the one?*

At the realization of someone's approach up the quarterdeck stairs, Rose quickly removed her hand again.

Maddy appeared and gave them a look that took in everything. "Miz Rose Anne, I see that I be falling down in my 'sponsibilities. Expect I got to sit heah in the sun with you two so them sailors doan talk."

"Maddy, I am quite old enough to care for myself."

Maddy raised her chin. "I promise yo' mama in her last hour on earth I be taking care of you. I ain't about to go back on that promise now."

"Maddy—"

Joshua said, "I promise you, Maddy, you can entrust Rose to me."

The old housekeeper gazed at him dubiously and set her sewing kit on the next bench. "I doan trust her to no man, but I expect you be better than most. Miz Rose Anne is more beautiful than she know and sometimes I swear she be innocent as a chile. You just calm yo'self, Mistuh Joshua. I gonna rest right heah on this bench and do the sewing." With that, she settled on the nearby bench and took up her work.

Joshua looked at Rose and, despite her embarrassment, she nearly laughed aloud. He caught up her hand and quietly pressed it to his lips.

Maddy cast a fast glance at them, and he replaced Rose's hand on the bench like an errant schoolboy. "Didn't you say I can trust you, Mistuh Joshua?"

He replied with good humor, "I do have to commend you for your timing, Maddy."

Her thick shoulders squared under her black dress, and she raised her chin again. "I see my work cut out for me heah!" Maddy said, undaunted. "I not be moving one inch."

Rose almost laughed at Maddy's unreasonable

interference, but knew from years of experience that it was quite useless to protest.

After a moment Joshua asked, "And would you also like to know now about the ladies of California?"

"I have already heard they are all lovely and bewitching, and that most of the men are tall, handsome, agile, trustworthy, and weigh more than two hundred pounds."

He chuckled. "You have been reading the accounts of Sir George Simpson's journey around the world."

"Guilty," she admitted. She only hoped that her father had not been bewitched by the Spanish beauties.

Finally they turned to their work—Joshua to his account books, Rose to the letter for her father, although she wondered at first how she could possibly concentrate. When she occasionally glanced at Joshua, she'd discover that he had looked up from his work, too, and a warm smile would flicker from the dark depths of his brown eyes—a smile full of promise.

Her thoughts returned to his admission of being "taken by her" three years ago when he visited her with Abby's paintings. But wasn't that precisely the kind of talk that would take in a woman as well? She was no longer a naive schoolgirl, she reminded herself. On the other hand, he was most attractive.

That evening, after supper in the small salon, they walked about the main deck, Maddy keeping an eye on them. Rose and Joshua spoke of nothing and yet everything, their words disappearing in the rush of the river and the crackling of the ship's sails.

At length they gazed out at the old trading ships that carried lumber and produce to market, the green landscapes and the fecund waters that were the province of farmers, oystermen, crabbers, and fishermen. With the sun shimmering on the water in a kaleidoscope of colors, they felt at one with the evening's transcendence.

Sailing toward Boston in the Atlantic

Dear Abby,

Now it is my turn to write the most amazing news to you. We are coming to California! Truly we are! I can scarcely believe that I am having such an adventure, too. Maddy (Mother's housekeeper and Moses' wife) and I and your cousin Joshua are under way, albeit in the wrong direction. We are now sailing for Boston, where we will stay at Elisha Wainwright's house for a few days until the new clipper, the *Californian*, sails. Joshua is certain there is still room on the ship.

I shall tell you my reasons for leaving in detail when we see each other. To put it quite simply now, I had to flee Willard, who is William's twin bother. When Father wrote that he planned to remain in California for some time, my position became so untenable that I desperately wanted to leave Georgetown, and I believe that Joshua came to my rescue in answer to my prayers. You can imagine how grateful I am.

We sailed down the Potomac River, which was quite wonderful, and the Chesapeake Bay, which was magnificent although very choppy. I think that I acquired my sea legs in stages for I have not been sick on the Atlantic yet. Except for being becalmed for two days, the Atlantic has offered much more rough sailing. Unfortunately, Maddy has not fared as well, but has now recovered.

I enclose a letter for my father, as he wrote that he has met your father and hopes to meet you and Daniel. I would appreciate your somehow getting the letter to him. I look forward to seeing you in mid-September if the *Californian* proves to be as fleet as they expect.

Today is Sunday, and Captain Svenson conducted the worship service with beauty and great dignity. One feels so close to God here, and I am grateful to know you are married to Daniel, who Captain Svenson told me has a great and joyous faith. God bless you and Daniel—and your little Daniel!

Your loving friend,
Rose

5

As the *Bostonia* sailed in, Rose was overwhelmed at the vastness of Boston Harbor. A forest of masts stood alongside the wharves, and a procession of steamships, fishing vessels, brigs, barks, and clippers glided across the blue water. Ships arrived and departed constantly, and stevedores swarmed over the docks. Bales of cotton and tobacco, barrels of tallow, and stacks of cattle hides were carried from cargo holds which were reloaded with manufactured goods from northeastern mills and factories. It was impossible to compare this tumultuous scene with the familiar bustle at the Georgetown wharves, Rose saw. Boston's harbor presented a mighty panorama of world commerce.

The mid-afternoon sun beamed down through the salt air as they finally disembarked on the Wainwright Wharf, and she was astonished to find her legs so wobbly that she could scarcely walk.

Amused, Joshua offered his arm. "Allow me to help you."

She accepted it gladly. "Thank you! I'm staggering like a drunken sailor!"

"An unlikely state for you!" he said with a laugh.

She had to smile. Although she had not allowed him to

kiss her hand nor even hold it again aboard ship, they had come to know each other better. She had learned all about his travels and the Talbot family, not to mention shipping and chandlery, and he had learned about her more limited life at Miss Sheffield's School for Young Ladies and in Georgetown. It was clear that after his adventurous life, he found her rather prim.

The dock officials stared at her, and she nearly laughed herself. What a sight she must make, staggering off the *Bostonia* on Joshua Talbot's arm. It was fortunate that she knew no one in Boston.

Followed by Maddy, they made their way through the noisy crowd toward the Wainwright carriage. Men greeted Joshua with utmost respect and eyed her curiously. Judging by their interest, she and Joshua would be the objects of much talk. She was glad she had worn her blue traveling frock and matching bonnet.

Joshua tightened his grip on her elbow as her legs wobbled under her again. "Steady, Rose."

"Truly, I am trying to walk properly."

He smiled. "Then you will make an excellent Bostonian during your visit. Believe me, Boston cares for nothing more greatly than doing all things properly." She gave a slight lurch, and he added with heightened amusement, "Though Boston is going to enjoy your presence far more if you continue to totter so."

"Your own gait is not so superb," she returned.

"It is you who makes me stagger, my lovely Rose."

She gave him an unconvinced glance and said, "You will forget me once I am not the only female about."

His eyes brimmed with warmth. "It is unlikely that any man could ever forget you, Rose."

Maddy harrumphed loudly behind them, and Joshua

stopped to proffer his other arm to her. Her eyes widened in surprise before she said, "Thank you, Mistuh Joshua, but I don't believe that is proper!"

"Not another proper Bostonian!" he laughed.

In the midday sunshine with the salty breeze blowing about them, Rose thought again how she liked the sound of laughter welling up from deep within his chest. Despite her distrust of his romantic overtures, she liked nearly everything else about him—his intelligence and his appearance, which included his reddish mustache and hair, and his brown eyes which matched his suit. She would surely like his city, too.

Their driver, an amiable Irishman in fine livery, settled them into the Wainwright carriage. *How smoothly matters were proceeding,* Rose thought. Captain Svenson had promised to post her letters to her father and Abby by the first California-bound clipper, and the trunks would be transported to the Wainwright house shortly. All that remained to be accomplished was to take themselves and their hand baggage to the house.

The carriage started forward, the horses' hooves clip-clopping on cobblestones. After they had left the Wainwright wharf and warehouses behind, Rose decided that she liked Boston. The air was clear, the brick buildings were bright red and their shutters bright green, the gilded letters over banks and business establishments gleamed, and the knobs and plates on the shop doors shone brilliantly. Boston resembled Georgetown but on a brighter and far more impressive scale.

"It would be easy to lose one's way about here," she remarked.

"I shall make it my business to show you around," Joshua replied, "or, if I am as busy as I fear will be necessary, I shall have someone escort you." He had already explained that he'd leased out his Boston house for a year because of his recent travels and the forthcoming trip to California, and that he, too, would be a guest in Elisha Wainwright's home.

"Maddy and I shall manage," Rose assured him.

Across the seat from them, Maddy nodded in agreement.

The creases between Joshua's brows deepened. "I must warn you that Nichola Wainwright can sometimes be difficult. One simply has to ignore her."

Difficult in what way? Rose wondered uneasily. She recalled the peculiar look that had passed between Joshua and Caleb Svenson when they first mentioned Nichola's name. All she knew of the woman was that she was the widow of Elisha Wainwright's late nephew; they had met and married in Paris, where she'd been part of the fashionable Russian nobility. Her husband, David Wainwright, had died in a duel, and she had lost the child she had then been carrying.

As she looked out the carriage window, Rose recalled the verse that had brought her through before: I can do all things through Christ which strengtheneth me. He had brought her this far; He would not let her down now.

They drove on through the crowded town, then up a hillside with fine red-brick houses. Looking out, Joshua said, "Almost there."

Minutes later, the carriage stopped at a cream-painted regency house with black shuttered windows that reflected the dappled sunshine. Tall first-story windows stood in shallow arches fronted by exquisite wrought iron balconies; the second- and third-story windows, set off by black shutters, were smaller in ascending order. It was clearly the work of a fine architect, Rose decided. "How lovely it is," she observed, "and what a charming departure from all of the red brick we've seen so far."

"Nichola's idea," Joshua said as he climbed down from

the carriage. "She studied art in Paris and is very good at design and decorating . . . and at spending one's money."

Did he approve or disapprove? Rose wondered.

He smiled warmly and said, "Come, Rose."

When she stepped down, her attention was drawn to a second-story window by movement at the open drapery. She caught a fleeting glance of a woman—a filmy black gown and a cloud of golden hair.

Joshua escorted her and Maddy up the walk. It was lined by a short black wrought iron fence topped with pointed fleur-de-lis on each baluster—probably more of Nichola's lovely French artistry.

The front door opened. At the sight of the tall, kindly gray-haired gentleman in a black suit, Rose's nervousness began to disappear. Elisha Wainwright was thin shouldered and slightly stooped, but his smile was like sunshine and sparkled in his blue eyes, too.

"Welcome!" he said cordially to all three of them and caught Joshua in a great embrace.

Rose felt a surge of joy at seeing his love for Joshua, who affectionately called him "Uncle Elisha," even though they were not related by blood. And when Joshua introduced them, explaining only that Rose was a "damsel in distress, who is Abby's best friend," she was made to feel equally welcome.

Elisha Wainwright said, "You must call me Uncle Elisha, Rose. And you must consider this your Boston home."

"Thank you, but I do hope I am not imposing upon you. Joshua insisted that we come with him. Maddy and I could stay in a hotel until the *Californian* sails—"

"I won't hear of it," Elisha Wainwright pronounced. "What else is a large house good for, if we cannot take in such a lovely young lady?" He was also kind to Maddy and asked a staff member to show her upstairs to a room of her own.

He led Rose and Joshua into the elegant regency drawing room for tea, putting her so quickly at ease that she was reminded of Caleb Svenson's words, "Elisha Wainwright is a most exceptional man." He certainly was. Moreover, he assured them that there was still space for her and Maddy on the ship.

As they visited in the drawing room, Rose expected Nichola to join them for tea, but there was no sign of her. Elisha Wainwright said, as if aware of her curiosity, "You will meet my niece, Nichola, later. She is resting, I believe. She has been exhausting herself and Boston's dressmakers with preparations for the voyage to California."

A new wardrobe for the voyage? Rose wondered. *Did one dress for dinner for sailing around the Horn? Perhaps so.*

Elisha turned to Joshua. "Nichola has planned a grand dinner party for Friday evening . . . a welcome home and farewell dinner all in one. Caleb Svenson, his wife, and others from the seafaring community are invited, and some of her own friends, of course. Fourteen or sixteen of us at the table. I hope that is agreeable to you."

Joshua nodded. "Of course, but please, no other plans. I shall have all I can manage to get my work in order before we sail. What do you hear of our first cargo for the *Californian*?"

"Patience, patience! I will not have you overworking as usual, Joshua," Elisha said. "You have nothing more to prove of your competence; everyone is quite convinced that you are the best merchant on the eastern seaboard. There is no need to surpass yourself."

Joshua lifted his hands in protest. "Thank you for the fine compliment, but there remains much to be done. I often feel I have only begun."

"You are going to consume all of your energy while you are young," the older man warned. His eyes went to Rose for an instant, then returned to Joshua. "It would be a great pity for you not to grow to my age. The aches and pains and wrinkles are as nothing compared to the joy of acquiring more of God's wisdom as one grows older."

Joshua said, "I am not ready to sit back yet, Uncle Elisha." He glanced at the French marble clock on the mantelpiece. "In fact, if I may be excused, I should like to leave for the chandlery office now."

When Rose was settled in a beautiful guest room upstairs, Maddy arrived to help unpack. "Mistuh Wainwright doan want me to even help out . . . say I be a guest!"

"What a nice change for you, Maddy! I'm delighted, especially after all of the work you did for the Stanfords. You must be as tired as I am after nine days at sea." She sighed as she helped Maddy shake the wrinkles from the dresses. "Mr. Wainwright strikes me as a fine godly man."

Maddy raised hopeful eyes to her. "Then maybe he let me work after all. I doan take no joy from sitting around long. Too much sitting makes the bones get stuck in place."

Rose stifled a smile, but at Maddy's indignance said, "Perhaps you are right."

"Of course I be right!" Maddy shook out the pink dress that Rose planned to wear at dinner. "Have you seen Miz Nichola yet?"

"No, not yet. Have you?"

"I seen her up in the window when we came, a'wearing a black nightie, her hair all yellow and hanging down around her shoulders . . . not expecting us with Mistuh Joshua, I guess."

"Maddy! I saw the same woman at the window, but we

don't even know who that was."

"That be Miz Nichola. The servants say she be a scandal. One say Miz Nichola be like a black widow spider waiting to tangle you in her web. They say, 'You watch yo' step, Maddy.' "

"We mustn't listen to gossip."

"Yes'um, Miz Rose Anne, that's what I be thinking now that you speak of it."

"Likely it is someone who holds a grudge. I can't imagine anyone in Mr. Wainwright's house who isn't as fine as he—"

"You done already forget the difference between Mistuh William and that awful Mistuh Willard . . . and they be twins!"

"No, Maddy. I haven't entirely forgotten. But it's unfair to jump to conclusions about Nichola."

"You beginning to sound like yo'. mama," Maddy said proudly.

"Thank you, Maddy. Now that is a compliment," Rose said, taking joy at the thought.

At dinner, she was surprised to find that she and Elisha Wainwright were dining alone at the long white damask-covered table. Joshua was working late and Nichola was being entertained by friends.

Elisha Wainwright explained, "Nichola is being feted with bon voyage parties and dinners every evening until you depart. Except Friday evening, of course, when we have the dinner party. Nichola is very sought after in Boston's small but fashionable continental society."

"I look forward to meeting her."

Uncle Elisha chuckled. "It will most likely be in the evening, for like the stars, that is when Nichola shines brightest."

"I see," Rose replied and turned her attention to the

lobster pot pie and fresh greens being brought out by the servants.

After saying grace with great feeling and eloquence, Elisha Wainwright remarked, "You do look like a rose with those lovely pink cheeks . . . a dewy pink rose that is in its first bloom. I should enjoy taking you out to my rose garden tomorrow morning. Many of the roses there are just coming into bloom now, too."

"Thank you for the compliment, though I would prefer not having pink cheeks! I would love to see the garden with you."

"And Boston?" he asked hopefully. "May I show our fine city to you, too? It would be an honor, and I know how occupied Joshua will be at the chandlery office."

"Aren't you occupied with your work?"

"I have worked all of my life and no longer find it quite so exciting," he replied with a chuckle. "In any case, I would never be too busy to show Boston to you."

He spoke so sincerely that Rose could not help but accept. She thought if she could choose an uncle or a grandfather at this moment, she would ask the Lord for Elisha Wainwright. She wondered if Joshua appreciated how much he was blessed.

The next morning Rose and Uncle Elisha ate breakfast in the lovely garden room which overlooked the terrace and the garden's spring greenery. They were finishing their coffee when Joshua strode into the room smiling, though bleary-eyed. His gaze held Rose's for a moment before she turned to his uncle, who was appraising the two of them.

Uncle Elisha said, "You look exhausted already, Joshua. Did you work all night?"

Joshua grinned guiltily and sat down beside her at the

small garden room table. "Not quite. I slept all of two hours."
He held up his hands to ward off rebukes. "One more good
day's work and I'll be able to enjoy our dinner Friday
evening, and to show Boston to Rose on Saturday."

The older man warned with mock solemnity, "You are
nearly too late. The men hereabouts are already lining up to
show Rose around the city. One doesn't leave a beautiful
young lady sitting about idly. Suitors will knock down the
doors."

Joshua's eyes flew to hers, and Elisha laughed. "She has
already accepted my invitation for today, Joshua, but I will
desist if you merely say the word. I am too old to take up
dueling with you or anyone else."

Joshua gave a laugh and turned to Rose. "If Uncle Elisha
is giving you the tour of Boston, I should like to take you
sailing on my skiff Saturday, if you would care to go. Or have
you had enough of sailing lately?"

"Not at all. I would enjoy it very much," Rose responded.

"Good." His eyes held hers again, and she realized they
had a way of widening when he was pleased.

"Well, now, if I may be excused," Elisha Wainwright said,
rising from the table. He told Rose, "If you like, I shall meet
you in the garden when you've finished breakfast, and we
can discuss today's outing."

As the door closed behind him, Joshua said, "I am sorry
to have missed dinner with you last night, but the work must
be done before we depart. It is my responsibility to fill the
ship with cargo."

"I do understand," she replied, undone by the fervent
look in his eyes. She rose to her feet, and they stood smiling
at each other in the garden room, where the sun shone
through the window upon them like a blessing.

Boston proved to be exciting and interesting. As she and Elisha Wainwright rode in the carriage, she was especially delighted to see Joshua's red-brick town house, which he had leased out. If it were not occupied by others now, she thought she might see his rooms and how he lived. The idea had no more than come to mind than she was thoroughly disquieted that she should be so interested in his living quarters.

Boston offered countless more famous places of interest, and Elisha Wainwright took pleasure in showing her about. They visited Faneuil Hall, where the colonists had gathered in anger at the tea tax, and, later, the site of the infamous Boston Tea Party . . . and North Church, where Paul Revere's lantern lit the flame of revolution—"One if by land, and two if by sea!" They viewed *Old Ironsides* tugging at her warps, deck bristling with the cannon that scuttled the British Navy.

After admiring the spring greenery of Boston Common, they visited Harvard University, which was named after the clergyman, John Harvard. Pausing to see the school's "Rules and Precepts" adopted in 1646, they read:

"Every one shall consider the main end of his life and studies to know God and Jesus Christ which is eternal life.

"Seeing the Lord giveth wisdom, every one shall seriously by prayer in secret seek wisdom of Him.

"Every one shall so exercise himself in reading the Scriptures twice a day that they be ready to give an account of their proficiency therein, both in theoretical observations of languages and logic, and in practical and spiritual truths. . . ."

As they left, Uncle Elisha drew a discouraged breath. "In the seventeenth century, over half of Harvard's graduates became ministers. I fear the place is no longer what the Pilgrims had in mind when they founded it."

Rose said, "I suppose not."

"I fear for our children's schools if they, too, continue in the secular direction that Harvard has taken," he added.

"I don't understand—"

"The Pilgrims began the entire educational enterprise in this country," he explained. "Before setting foot on our land, they signed the Mayflower Compact in which they stated they would create schools so that their children might be taught to read the Word of God."

"And you think that children's schools, too, might go in a secular direction?" Rose asked.

The old man shrugged. "It seems unlikely now, but it is possible. I sincerely hope not."

They rode on, their spirits lifting as they admired the impressive architecture of St. Paul's Cathedral, Charles Street Church, King's Chapel, St. Stephen's, and the State House.

Later, dining in a fine hotel, Elisha smiled and nodded at acquaintances, pleased at the flurry of interest in Rose's presence. He laughed. "I hope their seeing us together makes their day as interesting as it does mine!"

Rose laughed with him. Indeed, she felt so comfortable with him that it was all she could do not to divulge her father's finding gold in California. She longed to share the news and her excitement with someone trustworthy, but her father had insisted she not tell.

In mid-afternoon, Uncle Elisha decided they should stop at Joshua's office near the Wainwright Wharf to surprise him. As they were admitted into his office, Rose wondered how they might be received, but the beam of pleasure lighting Joshua's face as he stood up behind his ebony desk reassured her. He requested that tea be served. When Elisha wandered out of the room to see to "a bit of business," he quietly closed the door behind him.

"This is the best business of the entire day," Joshua vowed. "I am working as hard as I can to finish early. Come, let me show you what I am doing."

Interested as she was in his work, Rose remained on the other side of the desk from him.

Joshua missed supper, and Friday fell into the same pattern—a few minutes with him and Uncle Elisha at breakfast in the garden room and a stop at his office after the day's tour to tell him what they had seen. Elisha reminded him, "Don't forget Nichola's dinner party tonight, or you will be boiled in oil, then tarred and feathered!"

"Wouldn't I be!" Joshua replied.

Rose realized that during her two days at the Wainwright house she had yet to encounter Nichola. There were endless teas and soirees to fete the widow's voyage around the Horn and, of course, she herself had been out sight-seeing.

Late Friday afternoon when they returned to the Wainwright house and stepped into the entry, Rose at last saw the stunning widow. Nichola was making an entrance down the stairway, the picture of Russian nobility; her tawny hair was loosely upswept as if about to tumble to her shoulders, her amber eyes danced with delectable secrets. Her sedate lavender frock with high lace collar and long sleeves was scarcely deceptive for she carried herself voluptuously, her wide shoulders back, displaying a magnificent expanse of bosom above a narrow waist. She was perhaps thirty years old, but with such a ripeness about her that age mattered little. Her lips turned up indulgently as Elisha Wainwright made introductions. She said quite evenly, with a half-Russian, half-French accent, "So you are Rose."

Rose felt as if the woman had immediately evaluated everything about her and dismissed it as negligible. She managed, "It is a pleasure to meet you, Mrs. Wainwright."

Nichola's amber eyes glinted with an instant's displeasure, though her smile did not cease. "Nichola, if you please. I should not want it to be thought that I am Uncle Elisha's wife."

Elisha nodded humorlessly at his niece by marriage. "How are the preparations for tonight's dinner proceeding, Nichola?"

"Very well, naturally, but then we have a well-trained staff. I do hope you won't dismiss them while I am gone. I should not care to train new servants when Joshua and I return from California."

Rose quailed at the familiarity with which "Joshua and I" rolled from the woman's lips. She saw that Elisha's eyes had closed for a moment, and she wondered whether he were praying for patience. She started for the stairs herself, wishing for nothing so much as to escape. Much as it shamed her to jump to conclusions, there was something about the woman that she did not care for at all. "I am glad to have met you, Nichola. Now, if you will excuse me, I would like to rest for tonight."

"But, of course," Nichola responded, her foreign accent giving her words a contintental elegance. "I do hope you don't mind, Rose, but with you we had fifteen at the table. I invited a ship's officer, Lars Johnson, as your escort."

"Yes, I met him in Georgetown—"

Nichola added, "He was delighted, of course."

Rose knew instinctively that Joshua would be Nichola's escort. "How thoughtful of you," Rose managed, knowing quite well that she had no claim on Joshua. With that, she turned and hurried up the staircase, not understanding why she should be so furious.

Upstairs in her room, she reached for her mother's Bible

on the nightstand. She opened it to the Letter of Paul to the Ephesians. Thumbing slowly through the pages, she stopped at the end of the fourth chapter. "Let all bitterness, and wrath, and anger . . . be put away from you. . . ." The apostle Paul had been speaking of how to treat fellow Christians, but she suspected that Nichola was not one of them. It seemed impossible to "put away" her irritation. Nevertheless, she must try to, for that was what the Lord would want her to do. After reading on for a while, Rose took out her journal to relate the day's happenings. Odd how her difficulties seemed less dire after she prayed and committed them to paper.

"That woman be a black widow spider all right!" Maddy said as she swept Rose's dark hair into a chignon with side ringlets. "Her maid, Eula, she be jest as bad. They ain't the least bit happy unless they be stirring up trouble."

Rose said, "We can't be bitter or angry, Maddy. If they are as you say, that is probably how they want us to be, too. And it is exactly the opposite of what the Lord wants for us."

"Expect you be right about that," Maddy replied and backed off to observe Rose in the oval mirror.

Rose added a tiny pink rose from the garden to her hair to accentuate the shade in her changeable taffeta gown. She and Maddy had made the dress from a French pattern, and it was lovely with its demure dropped shoulders and puffed sleeves to the elbows. Blue satin bows lay flat from front to back across her shoulders, matching the waist sash in color. As she turned, the hues changed from pink to deep rose to a gray-blue. But the lovely dress did not distract her from what she had just read in the Letter to the Ephesians. She told Maddy, "The apostle Paul told us to be kind to one another, tenderhearted, forgiving one another, even as God for Christ's sake has forgiven us."

Maddy nodded. "Yes, that's what we is to do, but it sho' ain't easy. Still, yo' mama, she did it. She always say that the Lord help her forgive if she make the first move."

Rose had a feeling she'd have to ask for His help with Nichola. *Lord,* she prayed, *help me now!*

Maddy heaved a deep breath. "Fine help I be, mad at that Nichola and her maid, Eula, too. Well, I gonna set myself to praying. The Lord, He ain't done with us yet." She straightened a flounce on Rose's bell skirt and shook her head. "Why do this woman have to show up now when all was moving along so good between you and Mistuh Joshua?"

"Why, Maddy, I didn't think you entirely approved of him," Rose teased.

"Oh, I be approving all right. But at first it jest look like you was jumping outa the frying pan from Mistuh Willard and into a fire with Mistuh Joshua!" She smiled knowingly. "Ain't that I doan approve of the fire, it's jest that the Lord say it be best all around if the fire be banked until after the wedding vows—"

"Maddy, that's improper talk!"

Maddy ignored her. "Now with Eula saying that Mistuh Joshua and Miz Nichola—" Her eyes widened and she bit her lip.

"What did Eula say?"

Maddy squared her broad shoulders. "You said we ain't to gossip." She raised her chin. "Now about the fire between you and Mistuh Joshua—"

"There is no fire, Maddy!"

"I see how you look at each other. Ain't nothing wrong with me saying the truth when the Bible talks clear as day about real living!" With that, she bustled out of the room.

Later, when Rose walked down the staircase, a crowd of guests was arriving, and Lars Johnson in his dark dress uniform was just stepping into the entry. She saw him speak politely with a servant, hand over his hat, then look about much impressed. He was a handsome young man with his blond hair, though not much taller than she, and he had probably acquired his broad shoulders while working his way up to the rank of first mate aboard ships. She recalled sitting next to him in her church in Georgetown that Sunday when he had sung out so beautifully in his melodious baritone.

Lars saw her and smiled, quickly making his way to her side, his deep blue eyes sparkling. "It was kind of you to request me as your escort, Miss Wilmington. I was most pleased when Joshua Talbot delivered the invitation."

"I beg your pardon?" Rose replied.

Lars's blond brows came together. "Nichola Wainwright gave the invitation on your behalf, of course. I am afraid that I haven't explained quite correctly."

Rose stared at him in dismay. Joshua had delivered the invitation? Joshua? How might that have come about?

"Should I not have mentioned it?" Lars inquired, his face beginning to redden.

She felt a surge of sympathy for him and smiled as sweetly as possible. "Of course not. Come, let's go into the drawing room with the others." Apparently Nichola meant to aggravate her, but—Lord willing—she would not succeed again. *Be ye kind to each other, tenderhearted, forgiving one another,* Rose repeated to herself as they walked in.

Near the marble fireplace, Joshua turned from the guests surrounding him and saw her. He smiled broadly, and it appeared that he was starting toward her when he saw Lars, and apparently thought the better of it. He cast a suspicious glance at Nichola who was escorting new guests into the drawing room.

Rose looked from him to the golden-haired widow, who

was as lushly exotic in her orchid-colored gown as the rare orchid she wore in her loosely upswept hair. Her drop-shouldered gown was the most daringly cut in the room, and her voluptuousness captured every man's attention and every wife's annoyance. Nichola glowed with success, nodding as she led new guests into the room. Even Lars could scarcely take his eyes from her as she passed. Rose thought for a resentful moment that Nichola Wainwright swept through the guests like a ship's brazen figurehead.

Lars attempted to draw Rose out in conversation, but everything seemed so amiss that she could scarcely speak. Finally a servant stopped by with a tray of wine and fruit punch. At Lars's inquiry, Rose again found her voice. "The punch, please."

Lars handed a cup of punch to her and took another for himself. His blue eyes probed hers as if he were aware of her distress. "A fine party, yes?" he asked.

She glanced about the room without seeing anyone except Nichola, who had stopped for a word with Joshua. "Yes, a fine party," Rose responded with an effort.

Elisha Wainwright arrived at their side, taking them both under his wing and introducing them to the other guests. Both of them knew Captain Svenson, but only Lars had met the captain's lovely Swedish wife, Inger.

Most of the other guests appeared to be Nichola's intimates. There was a stunningly handsome baron from Austria, who appeared much taken with her, to the displeasure of his overly plump and bejeweled baroness; there were two French counts with their glittering countesses as well as others without titles. All of them exhibited little interest in Rose or Lars and only a modicum of respect for Elisha Wainwright.

Joshua finally broke away from those around him and

hurried across the room. "Good evening, Rose," he said, his brown eyes holding hers before he bent to kiss her fingertips. The timbre of his voice and the feel of his luxuriant mustache touching her fingers made her knees weak and her eyes close for an instant.

He gazed uneasily at her. "You are looking even more beautiful than usual."

"Thank you." How handsome he looked in his black swallowtail. She remembered he had worn it to the ball in Georgetown. "You look very nice, too," she said, but her heart cried out, *Oh, Joshua, why don't you explain your being paired with Nichola? Why don't you put matters right between us?*

His eyes darkened, and it appeared that he wished to rectify matters, but courtesy bade him shake hands with Lars. "I am glad to see that you could come, Lars."

Lars smiled, but his blond brows came together in perplexity again. "It is my pleasure. It is a beautiful house in one of my favorite cities of your country."

As the men exchanged pleasantries, Rose's brain flashed back to what Maddy had started to say—something about Nichola's maid speaking of Joshua. What was it? That Joshua and Nichola were more than friends? Rose looked across the room at Nichola, and her heart sank with the certain knowledge that many men would be tempted. But not Joshua! Please, Lord, not Joshua!

Rose realized that Joshua was looking at her oddly.

"I must speak with you later, Rose," he said quietly. "Please be patient, I'll explain—" His eyes moved to Lars, and after an instant Joshua inclined his head politely at both of them and withdrew.

The butler stepped into the drawing room to announce dinner and, in the flurry of finding partners, Inger Svenson urgently caught Rose's arm. "Please," she whispered, "on the ship to California, keep Nichola away from my Caleb."

Rose drew back in disbelief. Inger Svenson was pretty herself, albeit in her thirties and wearing mourning for her mother who had died nearly a year ago in Sweden.

Inger flushed, her eyes wide with distress.

Lars was proffering his arm and Rose accepted it blindly, allowing herself to be escorted to the dining room. As they neared Nichola and Joshua at the dining room entrance, the woman was smiling rapturously up at him. They stood waiting for the other guests to enter, Joshua returning Nichola's smile.

Walking by them, Rose spoke animatedly to Lars about what she had seen of Boston . . . about North Church and Faneuil Hall and the Common. She thought she must be prattling wildly, for Lars frowned with bewilderment.

While being seated at the table, she noted that Nichola was sitting at the far end with Joshua on her right and, on her left, the Austrian baron and his plump wife. Elisha Wainwright was at the head of the table, and Rose sat on his left, between him and Lars, and across from the Svensons. She was thankful that Joshua and Nichola were not in her line of vision, for she knew she could not bear watching them.

After Elisha said grace, the servants arrived with the fish course and there was a hum of conversation. Rose threw herself into it unthinkingly, and Lars nodded as though intrigued by her words, as though she were carrying on with great aplomb when all that she wanted was to be elsewhere.

Beside her Elisha Wainwright said quietly, "You must eat, Rose. You look white as death." He waved for a servant's attention and bade him open the terrace doors for fresh air. The coolness brought her some relief.

Elisha said, "How I wish I could sail with you on the *Californian.*"

"How I wish you could, too," Rose replied. Especially in view of what she realized now. She swallowed at the knot of grief in her throat.

The talk at their end of the table was all of the *Californian* since Caleb, Lars, and the crew had made a trial run yesterday, and the new clipper ship had performed even better than expected. When they had done with the merits of the *Californian,* the Svensons engaged Lars in conversation about Sweden, where he had recently visited his grandparents.

Rose picked at the fish course, then at the rich French veal entree. She tried to take an interest in what Sweden must be like, and how it felt to be an immigrant like Inger.

Elisha Wainwright turned to discussing the merits of Scandinavian seamen. "They have an affinity for the sea, and they take their work as seriously as we Americans do."

Caleb launched into a tale about an English traveler who, fearing to be impressed as a British seaman, vowed he would never travel on any but an American ship. "He claimed that the crews are the finest, the ships are the best-designed and hardest driven, and the captains the only ones always in uniform—even in bed!"

They all laughed, Rose joining in belatedly.

At long last, coffee and dessert—chocolate cake and bonbons—were served, and dinner concluded.

The guests wandered out to the terrace, and Rose felt compelled to join them since the gathering showed no signs of dispersing. She and Lars trailed the others out onto the terrace.

Everyone stood admiring the opalescent clouds and the full moon that beamed down upon them; smatterings of conversation and bits of laughter filled the soft evening air. Quite suddenly there was a furious burst of German from the baroness, and she turned on her heel and rushed into the house, followed by the sputtering baron. Rose did not understand German but it sounded very much as though his wife were calling him a fool in no uncertain terms. Meanwhile, Nichola held onto Joshua's arm with a show of wide-eyed innocence.

After a moment Joshua spoke abruptly to Nichola and broke away. He looked about the moonlit terrace at the guests and, seeing Rose, started toward her.

Lars said in a soft voice, "It is time for me to go home, for I see how matters stand between you and Joshua."

"Oh, Lars, I am sorry—"

He smiled. "Do not be sorry. You are my Christian sister, and I wish you only happiness." He hesitated. "Well, then, I will pay my respects to Mr. Wainwright on the way out. I thank you for a fine time in your company. Good evening."

With that, he was gone, and Joshua was striding toward her, his expression remorseful. "I must talk with you, Rose. Please let me explain now."

Her voice trembled. "If you insist." She allowed him to guide her through the guests to the distant garden room.

As he closed the door behind them and turned, they stared at each other in the dimly moonlit room for a long moment. "Oh, Rose . . . forgive me."

Contrition etched his face, then yearning, and she backed slightly away so he couldn't take her into his arms.

He added, "I am so sorry, I didn't realize how far Nichola had gone this time . . . asking Lars to escort you . . . even inveigling me into delivering his invitation. I did not know, I promise. I only told her I would play a role to save her from total disgrace."

"Disgrace?"

Joshua shook his head in dismay. "The baroness is suspicious about Nichola and the baron."

"I see."

He quickly said, "They are as addicted to gambling as some are addicted to alcoholic spirits—"

"I do not wish to hear about it," Rose told him. "Why involve yourself?"

"She is Uncle Elisha's daughter-in-law, and I owe him that much. Nevertheless it was a fruitless attempt to fool the baroness, who holds the purse strings. For all of the trouble it caused, I was not even convincing. Forgive me."

"Of course, there is . . . nothing for me to forgive." The words were no more than out, however, than she knew that she did care. He was the first man she had really cared about since William, and apparently Joshua cared about her, too—at least enough to ask her forgiveness.

6

Saturday morning was overcast as Rose and Joshua set out on horseback for the north shore of the bay. Rose wore her blue riding habit and rode a white mare; beside her Joshua, dressed in brown, rode a chestnut stallion.

What a fine picture we must make, Rose thought. She had not felt so happy while out riding in years—not since William's horse had thrown him—no!—she would not dwell on the past. She would enjoy this moment, this hour, this day. She recalled the apostle Paul's words: "Forgetting those things which are behind, and reaching forth unto those things which are before, I press toward the mark for the prize of the high calling of God."

"You look exceptionally happy!" Joshua called out to her as they cantered along.

"I am!" How often people remarked upon her happiness when she was thinking about the Lord, she mused. If only she felt more certain about Joshua's faith. His grandfather had been an eminent Boston clergyman, but she knew quite well that faith was not inherited. Each person had to reach out to God, through Christ, for his own salvation.

She felt Joshua's gaze linger on her a while longer, then there was a fence for their horses to jump and a pasture for racing. They rode on for a long time, then forded a small tidal creek and surprised a pair of deer. Not long after, they arrived at a weather-beaten cottage near the softly lapping seashore and reined in their horses.

"Here we are," he said, dismounting and tying his chestnut stallion to a rustic hitching post.

Rose slid from her sidesaddle and allowed Joshua to take the reins. She patted the mare's neck affectionately and looked around. "And just where are we?" she asked since he had acted mysterious about the outing. She noted a weathered log boat house by the water.

Joshua took their picnic from his saddlebag. "Why, we are here, of course."

She pulled a wry face, and he laughed. "You will have to be a bit more patient."

"It's not a virtue I have yet acquired," she replied lightly. Curious as she felt about this place, she decided not to press, for there was a tentativeness about him this morning, as though he was uncertain at having brought her here. "Wherever we are, it's quite beautiful."

Rose turned to Joshua and saw that the sunshine was burnishing auburn his hair. She found herself wanting to run her fingers through it, to touch his shining mustache . . . and quite suddenly she yearned to be in his arms.

His voice turned husky. "Rose, you must not look at me like that."

"How am I looking at you?" she asked, only half in innocence.

He took her arm, leading her down the path to the boat house. "You were looking as though you wanted kissing."

Heat rushed to her face.

"I am sorry, I should not have said that," he added. "I sometimes forget—"

He stopped, but she knew he meant he sometimes forgot about her late fiancé. "I have wondered about you and Willard," Joshua said. "He looked so sure of himself around you, as though he had most assuredly kissed you."

She swallowed at the remembrance. "Never . . . though he tried to force a kiss upon me the afternoon he proposed."

Joshua looked dismayed, and she found herself telling what had taken place on that Georgetown path just over two weeks ago. She added, "It was most unpleasant."

Joshua scowled. "Had I known, I would have dealt with him!"

His protectiveness stirred something deep within her. "It was the day you came for dinner," she explained. "You really did not know me yet."

"Perhaps. But I wondered about you and him that evening and the next day, when we toured Washington City. Your attitude toward him was most confusing."

She bit down on her lower lip, embarrassed. "It helped me to tolerate him that day in Washington City by . . . pretending he was William. I would rather dismiss all of it from my mind."

A muscle twitched in Joshua's jaw. "And do you pretend that I am William, too?"

"No . . . never! You are far too different."

He let out his breath softly.

"I—I'd prefer not to speak further of this." She would like to ask him about the women in his life, for surely there must be some, but sometimes it was unwise to be too curious. She smiled, recalling a quote from Thomas Moore: *Eve, with all the fruits of Eden blest, save only one . . . rather than leave that one unknown, lost all the rest.*

His brown eyes held hers until finally he caught her hand and bestowed a fervent kiss on it. "Wait here," he said,

"I'll pull out the skiff."

With admiration, she watched his fluid movement as he strode down the path to the boat house. How astonishing that this man cared about her. She wondered what might come of it.

Behind her, the horses stamped, and she reflected upon what they might think about humans, particularly the sight of Joshua kissing her hand. Smiling ironically, she picked up the canvas sack and brushed off the sand. Were its contents as tossed about as she suddenly felt?

When they sailed out from shore on the skiff, the sail filling with the morning breeze, she was thankful that they were separated by a tiller.

"I find," Joshua confessed, "that I enjoy being with you as much in the morning and the afternoon as I do in the evening."

"And is that so unusual?" she teased.

He chuckled. "Are you going to inquire into my past?"

"No," she laughed. "I withdraw the question."

"I shall answer it anyhow, though in a roundabout way." He gazed out over the sea, changing course with the tiller so that they sailed straight out now from the coast. "I have never before brought a woman out on this skiff."

She blinked. "Oh? Did you just recently acquire it?"

"I have had it here for over five years."

"Then I am honored, especially that you've told me, too." Seeing him smile so boyishly with the wind and salt spray in his hair, she was especially delighted. They sailed in silence for a while before she said, "The only thing that could honor me more is if you told me about your childhood. You never mention it." On the voyage from Georgetown to Boston he had only mentioned living with Uncle Elisha during his Harvard days. He'd spoken, too, of his sea experiences, dealing with merchants and sea captains from China to the West Indies.

He studied her for an instant, then looked out at the sea again. "I suppose talking about boats is as likely a place as any to begin. When I grew up in Missouri, I spent many a summer on the water in a homemade raft, albeit dependent upon oars instead of sails. My brother and Daniel and I went fishing, catching crawdads, and dueling with imaginary pirates . . . all of the things that boys in the countryside might undertake."

"Did you want to be a pirate?" she inquired with a laugh.

"Many's the time I was one in my imagination. I was a pirate and a sea captain and a frontiersman. I must have liked something about all of them, for one needs a little of each for chandlery work, not to mention being a Yankee peddler, and a sea lawyer and a diplomat as well."

"I can understand being a bit of a sea captain and frontiersman and Yankee peddler and more . . . but a pirate?"

He grinned. "I dreamed of carrying a beautiful woman like you off to sea."

"Oh, Joshua, you are taunting me."

"Not entirely. You are the only young woman I have ever carried off to sea . . . so you see that my entire dream has now come true."

She laughed, then she asked, "What was it like to grow up in Missouri?"

His eyes shone as he related growing up on the edge of the Indian Territory, telling about the Indians who came into Independence . . . about his father, Benjamin Talbot, whom she would meet in California. "He unknowingly set up the beginnings of a mercantile dynasty for our family," Joshua said. "He joined forces with Uncle Elisha and his shipping company. It has been an excellent merger, but I'd have liked to have made the success myself . . . without family help or favoritism. I sometimes wonder whether I would have been so successful on my own."

The lines between his brows had deepened, and she deemed it best to change the direction of their conversation. "You have never mentioned your mother."

Joshua drew a deep breath. "She died when Betsy was born, when I was nineteen years old."

"I'm sorry. But what a blessing that you had her that long." Rose recalled how young she had been when she lost her own mother. "What was she like?"

"Very kind. You sometimes remind me of her."

"I remind you of your mother!" Rose repeated, unsure of whether that was a compliment.

He grinned. "Not entirely."

She smiled herself.

As they sailed along the coastline, their conversation turned to the past, to stories of Indians and the French explorer, Champlain, who sailed by this place in 1605. Joshua said, "Champlain wrote that they sighted many camp fires, and natives rushed out to observe their ship. He noted that a great deal of land was cleared and planted with Indian corn, and there was no lack of fine trees."

He gazed out at the coastline as though through the explorer's eyes. "Apparently the Indians used dugout canoes. Champlain said they were made of a single piece and very liable to turn over if one had too little skill. There were diaries about the Indians—burning and clearing forest, planting corn and fishing, taking pleasure in sport, bathing, feasting, dancing, and—" He glanced at her.

"And?" she prompted.

His color rose. "And . . . eating, I suppose."

It was not what he had meant to say, she thought. She

looked toward the coast so that her bonnet hid her face, not daring to imagine more than natives feasting and dancing on shore. Sometimes the passion that was wont to grip her astonished her. As they sailed on, they could find no comfortable topic of conversation.

Fortunately, the sea had whetted their appetites. From the sack Rose took buttered biscuits. While they devoured them, she thought that this time sailing on the skiff and the days on the *Bostonia* were some of the happiest hours she had ever spent . . . despite the uncomfortable moments. They had come to know each other in so many ways, and she was certain he had come to care about her, too. She darted a glance at Joshua and found him staring at her thoughtfully.

When they returned two hours later, her blue riding habit and bonnet were wet, as was Joshua's riding attire. She waited on the beach while he locked the skiff back in the old boat house, then went into the log cabin, returning with a worn but clean quilt.

"Who lives there?" Rose asked, for she had thought the cabin to be deserted.

"An old sea captain keeps the place for us. He rides out from the city sometimes to sail in the skiff, much as he did in his youth. We like it here. It is my dream to buy acres of land hereabouts, and to build a great estate someday."

"That is your ambition?"

"Yes," he replied with a peculiar glint in his eye. "Yes, that is some of my ambition." He spread the quilt on the beach, not far from the water. After a quick glance at her, he removed his jacket and hung it across a nearby bush to dry.

It seemed a fine idea, Rose thought. She cast a shy look at him, then decided to remove her wet jacket, too. In any event, she wore a proper blouse with a camisole under it, and everything felt so uncomfortably damp. She pulled off her bonnet, dropping it on the quilt, and smoothed back her hair, which was falling from the chignon she had so quickly arranged that morning.

Joshua hung her jacket on the bush beside his. "No one else will see if you let your hair down to dry," he suggested in a rather odd tone.

She had never let her hair down in front of a man, not even William. "I don't know—"

His voice was low and persuasive. "It will dry in the sunshine. You don't want to catch cold before we leave on the voyage, Rose."

As though in a daze, she removed the pins from her dark hair and let it fall down in damp ringlets to her shoulders. She sat down quickly on the quilt, her eyes wandering up to him. His fine white shirt clung to his broad chest and shoulders, and quickly looking down at herself, she saw that her blouse did, too. What would he think? She was newly aware of how alone they were with an empty cabin nearby and a forest behind them.

Joshua sat down on the quilt beside her, and she saw the half-constrained look in his eyes. She quickly took out the food from their canvas sack and lay it out upon the thickly layered clean paper in which it had been wrapped. There were fried chicken, cranberry muffins, and pieces of chocolate cake.

"Would you like to say grace?" she suggested.

Joshua shook his head, his expression so baffling that she scarcely knew what to make of matters. "I should like to hear you say it," he said.

Rose bowed her head and took a calming breath. "Dear heavenly Father, we come before Thee with praise and thanksgiving for the blessings of this beautiful day. We thank Thee for the sun that warms us, for the sounds of Thy wondrous sea beside us, and for this food that we are about to eat. We praise Thee and thank Thee for all of these and . . . and for so much more . . . in the name of Thy beloved Son, the Lord, Jesus Christ. Amen."

She looked up at Joshua and saw that he was still gazing at her. He said, his voice low and husky, "Come, Rose, let us eat."

Unnerved, she picked up a chicken drumstick. How hungry she was! How hungry and discomposed.

It appeared they were both starved, for it seemed only minutes before they had devoured the chicken and cranberry muffins, and started on the chocolate cake that was left from last night's dinner.

Finally Rose licked the chocolate frosting from her fingers and, knowing she would find his eyes upon her, peered up at Joshua.

His lips had parted and his gaze was so penetrating that she could not turn away. "Rose, you must not look at me so," he said, his voice as resonant as the sea's deep tones.

"But I am only—" She faltered, unable to proclaim her innocence, for she was overwhelmingly aware of the attraction all but shimmering between them.

"You are driving me to distraction," he filled in for her. He caught her hand in his and kissed her palm fervently, then closed her fingers upon it as though to hold his kiss.

He reached out with both hands to touch her hair, tangling his fingers in the curls and ringlets, and she had no wish to stop him. Then he was kissing her hair, trailing kisses across her forehead, her cheeks, her neck. "Ah, Rose . . . Rose!" His arms bound her to him and he kissed her lips fervently.

She could not stop herself from responding, but before long an inner voice told her to resist, to resist at all costs. She pushed away. "Joshua . . . no!" What was she thinking, allowing him to kiss her in this solitary place? What would he think? No decent woman would allow such a thing!

He looked as stricken as she felt. She used the moment to rise to her feet, then she turned and ran to the water's edge, her hair streaming behind her in the salt air. *Lord, help us,* she prayed, *please help us!* After a long time of staring blindly out at the sea, she was able to breathe evenly again.

When she looked back, she was relieved to see Joshua walking some distance away along the shore. She returned to the quilt and found her hairpins and put up her hair quickly, then pulled on her jacket and blue bonnet.

He returned, a guilty expression on his face. "I am a scoundrel, Rose, and I would not blame you if you never saw me again."

"No, Joshua, not such a scoundrel . . . for I was so . . . entirely willing. I suppose I am not a lady to say so, but that is the truth."

He stared at her with disbelief.

"I hope you do not think badly of me," she whispered.

He took her hand. "I could never think badly of you, Rose. Never."

"I think otherwise. If the Lord had not spoken for me to resist, I would have . . . in the end . . . been a great disappointment to myself and to you and, worst of all, to the Lord Himself."

"Perhaps," Joshua said, the passion in his brown eyes not quite diminished. "Come now, we had better return to Uncle Elisha's house."

She stayed well away from him as they walked to the horses, thankful that he had the quilt to fold while she carried the canvas sack. She could bear no more temptation this day. As he helped her onto her white mare, his hand on her elbow alone caused her to tremble. *Lord,* she prayed, *why do I feel this way? Is this the man You have sent for me?*

He did not answer, except through the magnificence of the earth that surrounded them. Surely the One who had made the earth and the heavens would show her the way, for she had dedicated her life to His Son.

On the way home, the sun disappeared and clouds covered the sky once again. They rode along the sea-smoothed sand in the quiet surf for a stretch, and Rose saw a perfect image of her white horse reflected beneath, with the clouds below them. She could easily imagine herself to be passing, like her spirit, through time—a brightly mirrored reflection of her earthly existence in the soft ebb and flow of the water. *Thank You, Lord, for being in my soul,* she prayed as they rode on. The pounding hooves of their horses barely left imprints, but she knew that this day would be forever imprinted in her memory.

The next morning Uncle Elisha awaited her in the drawing room. "It appears that you and I will attend church alone," he said. "Joshua worked nearly the entire night, and Nichola's bon voyage fete must have lasted until dawn."

"I am happy to accompany you," Rose said with perfect honesty. She would be happier if Joshua were going, too; she had not seen him since their return from yesterday's tumultuous outing and ached to see him now. Yesterday, by the time she had bathed, changed clothing, and come downstairs, he had already departed for his office without having even told her he would be gone. She wondered whether he regretted their day.

As they made their way out Elisha Wainwright asked, "Did you have a fine excursion yesterday?"

She tried to hide her turmoil. "Yes, a lovely time."

"I do believe you are the only young woman Joshua has ever taken out on his skiff," he commented.

Rose was glad the old gentleman was occupied with closing the door behind them, for his confirmation of that fact caused her further tumult. If he noticed anything peculiar about her, he did not say. It had been bad enough last night with Maddy scolding her about her sunburned face and hands, which looked browner than red today. Maddy had been insatiably curious about what had transpired between her and Joshua, and Rose feared she had not fooled the old housekeeper very much.

Rose and Uncle Elisha stepped out into another overcast morning. He said, "Joshua's late grandfather was once the pastor of my church. A shame you can't meet him, at least not here on earth. He impressed upon us that true observance of Christianity was consistent with being cheerful. His emphasis on God's love and the Holy Trinity made our church into a joyful place, which it has remained all of these years. I thought for a while that even Joshua might be converted, but it was apparently not yet his time. You must pray with me for his salvation."

"Joshua is not a believer?" she asked as they started to walk to the church.

The older man shook his head. "Joshua is a fine man, but he has yet to accept Christ as his Savior."

Rose scarcely heard what else he said, for her mind raced back to yesterday before their picnic. That was why he had asked her to say grace! Other confirming thoughts rushed to her mind.

Elisha Wainwright said, "I wish Joshua would use his talent for making money to God's glory instead of his own satisfaction. It's not as though he's vain about success. It is more that he must constantly prove himself—not only to me and to others, but to himself. Proving one's excellence over and over is not an easy road to take through life. Indeed, it strikes me as impossible, for most of us have our failures, though I've yet to see anything Joshua cannot do well."

She thought of when she'd sat next to him in church in Georgetown and he had seemed disinterested, singing so mechanically. Elisha Wainwright had confirmed her suspicions, but she fervently wished he had not.

When they arrived in the church and settled in Elisha's pew, Rose prayed for the Lord's guidance for her and Joshua. Surely He would not allow her to care for Joshua so much if there were to be no future for them.

The organ music was magnificent and the anthem inspiring, but Rose felt stabbed to the heart. The sermon dealt not with her problems, but with abolitionism, the freeing of slaves. She agreed most adamantly with the vision of emancipated humanity, but felt herself fettered in chains of despair. Finally she sang with the congregation:

"I sing the almighty power of God,
That made the mountains rise,
That spread the flowing seas abroad,
And built the lofty skies,
I sing the Wisdom that ordained,
The sun to rule the day;
The moon shines full at His command,
And all the stars obey."

God in His wisdom would not want her to be hurt in any way, she reasoned. She must entrust not only Joshua's salvation but her own path into His hands. What a joy it would be when Joshua did accept the Lord! She would rejoice with the angels, for didn't Scripture say that they rejoiced when a soul was saved? As she sang about the greatness of God, she felt a growing and glowing reassurance.

7

On Monday morning Rose was caught up in the bustle of leaving the house with Joshua, Maddy, Nichola, and her maid, Eula. Joshua chuckled at Rose's excitement about the trip, but she was undaunted.

"This might be just an ordinary voyage for you," she said, "but I am embarking upon a great adventure and I intend to enjoy every moment of it!" Moreover, she told herself, she would not accept his unbelief, for hadn't she placed it—as well as the entire trip—into God's hands?

Maddy appeared equally excited, but Nichola was groggy, having stayed out late again. She might shine most at night like the stars, as Uncle Elisha said, but she'd made certain her five trunks were on the second carriage that was to transport Eula and Maddy and much of the baggage to the ship.

Uncle Elisha accompanied them to the wharf, and they all climbed down from the carriages into the salt air and wharfside tumult. Everyone proclaimed the new *Californian* the most beautiful clipper ship ever to sail from Boston; her masts were tall, her figurehead a golden lion in honor of "the great lion of Judah." Even the stevedores loading the cargo into her sleek black hull appeared proud to play a role in her first voyage.

As Rose hurried along the gangway with the others, she felt the envious gazes of those below. She was going around Cape Horn—around the southern tip of South America to California on this magnificent clipper ship. Despite the dangers, it seemed like a glorious adventure that one might only read about, or perhaps report on, at Miss Sheffield's School for Young Ladies.

"Welcome aboard!" Caleb Svenson said as they stepped onto the deck. He was attired in a new nautical blue uniform with brass buttons, and, behind him, Lars Johnson, also in a new uniform, added his sincere welcome. Seamen busied themselves all over the ship in their own peculiar uniforms: duck trousers that hung loose around the feet, checked shirts, black silk neckerchiefs, and low-crowned black tarpaulin hats, worn back on the head.

Rose and the other passengers were quickly shown to their cabins, their trunks being delivered behind them. The central salon, with passenger cabins adjoining it, differed little from that of the *Bostonia:* overhead skylight, a bolted-down mahogany dining table with benches, black stove, and marble-topped sideboard. After a rapid perusal of her tiny cabin and bunk, Rose hurried up again, unwilling to miss the departure excitement.

At length the small group of passengers had boarded and the cargo hatches were lashed down. A fine wind was coming up.

"Almost time to sail," Uncle Elisha observed to Rose as they stood at the railing, his wispy white hair blowing in the breeze. "As always, a time comes for parting."

A bittersweet sensation swept through Rose and she swallowed with difficulty before managing to bid him farewell; most likely she would never see him again here on earth. "Thank you for your kindness and hospitality." She suddenly embraced him, feeling the frailty of his shoulders. "I shall miss you."

When they drew away from each other, his smile was like sunshine, just as it had been the afternoon she had arrived at his front door. "And I shall miss you, Rose . . . and remember you in prayer." He cast a covert glance about before adding in a low voice, "I pray not only for Joshua's salvation, but if it be God's will, that Joshua should marry you."

"That he—" Rose felt her lips part in surprise.

Elisha gave a hearty laugh. "I am not so old that I don't recognize a couple who are falling in love."

Joshua was approaching and, although he could not have heard, heat flooded Rose's cheeks. Simply seeing him stride toward them, his auburn hair and mustache gleaming in the morning sunlight, set her aglow.

He chided his uncle, "What are you whispering to Rose?"

"Our secret," the old gentleman replied, his blue eyes dancing as they met hers. He started for the gangway to disembark, accompanied by Joshua, and sent her a final wave. "Remember our pact, Rose!"

"I shall, Uncle Elisha. I shall!"

The boatswain shouted rapid orders, and in no time every seaman was in motion, the sails loosed, the yards braced, while the seamen sang out, "Blow, Boys, Blow." On the voyage from Georgetown, Joshua had explained the various sea chanteys that put a timing and a will to each job the seaman did. A song was as necessary to sailors as the drum and fife to soldiers. What an extraordinarily brave lot the seamen suddenly seemed.

Unintelligible orders were rapidly given and immediately executed; there was a wild hurrying about by the seamen and an intermingling of strange cries. Then there was the noise of flapping canvas as the men hoisted sails, which filled with a fair breeze. The *Californian* slipped quietly out from the wharf, the seamen singing,

"Come, all you young fellows that follow the sea,
To me way—aye, blow the man down!
Now pray pay attention and listen to me,
Give me some time to blow the man down!"

Rose waved to Elisha Wainwright, who waggled a long arm at them from the wharf. He grew smaller and smaller as the *Californian* pulled away, sails billowing in the wind. At length the ship turned south, leaving behind it a wake that sparkled like a trail of diamonds.

When they'd left Georgetown, Joshua had urged, "Look forward, always forward," but now Rose watched the great Boston Harbor with its forest of masts and smoke-belching steamboats recede. It seemed that they had only arrived and now they were already departing. She sensed again that she was gliding through time, much as she had Saturday at seeing the ethereal reflection of herself and her white mare in the surf.

"Here you are, Rose," Joshua said, startling her. "Look who has joined us."

She turned and saw Inger Svenson. "What a fine surprise!"

Inger looked a bit embarrassed. "Caleb, he tells me I must come. Yesterday after church." She held her hands out in dismay at her faded black mourning frock that she had worn for nearly the requisite year in memory of her mother's death. "There vas no time to even make ready my clothes. Caleb tells me only that I must come!"

"What do the clothes matter?" Rose responded. She recalled Friday evening when Inger had been so concerned about her husband's proximity to Nichola during the three-month journey. Perhaps they'd had words about it after the baroness and baron made their inglorious departure, Rose thought, then reminded herself it was not her concern. "I'm so happy to have you aboard."

"Thank you," Inger said, tucking a wisp of flyaway blond hair into her black bonnet. She looked at Rose with sincere blue eyes. "I vould like to have you for my friend."

Rose clasped the woman's hands. "And I would like to be yours." Now that Elisha Wainwright was no longer with her, it seemed the Lord had sent her a new friend. In addition, Joshua appeared moved by their declaration of friendship.

"Caleb gives me charge of feeding the chickens," Inger said with a laugh before hurrying off. "I better do it now or maybe he throws me overboard!"

"Chickens?" Rose asked of Joshua.

He gave a laugh at her incredulous tone. "We have chickens, pigs, and even a cow aboard. There is only so much food a ship can carry on such a long voyage before spoilage sets in, so we carry our meat and milk on the hoof, so to speak. Be sure you don't make pets of them or they won't taste as good when their day of reckoning comes."

Rose swallowed with difficulty at the grim thought.

"If you could see how you look," he said with a chuckle, then his hands moved to cover hers on the railing. "I can scarcely believe we have this long time together."

"Nor I," she admitted, and they stood smiling at each other. She could enjoy simply looking at him all day in the salty breeze, but other passengers were passing by them and taking notice, and she removed her hand from his.

They turned to the railing and watched the *Californian* overtake a slow-moving brig at full sail and, before long, a Boston bark. "I remember when we sailed here from Georgetown and a clipper seemed to fly past," she said. "Now we sail past the others with such ease."

As they stood together at the railing, it felt as though they sailed out of Boston Bay on a silvery beam, faster even than the wind. After a time the sea turned gray and choppy, imparting an air of excitement. There was something about being out on the sea in the salt air and the wind that she especially loved, and she knew it had to do with her wonder over this majestic place God had created.

At midday everyone gathered in the salon for dinner. As introductions were made, Rose realized that she already knew many of them: the captain and Inger, Joshua, Lars, and Nichola. The other passengers were a closemouthed young couple, Mr. and Mrs. Barnes from Philadelphia; Mr. Holmes and Mr. Hupple, middle-aged speculators in cattle hides, who would make their way south from San Francisco to the pueblo of Los Angeles; Mr. Zanot, a balding and portly merchant from Salem; and the oldest man, Mr. Willford, who was long, lean, stoop-shouldered, and scowling of expression. Captain Svenson, a staunch abolitionist, had tried to talk Maddy and Eula into dining with them, but they had begged off with consternation and were eating in a nearby cabin provided for them.

They took their seats, Rose between Inger Svenson and Joshua. Across the table, Nichola looked stunning in a well-fitted amber dress that matched her eyes.

Caleb Svenson said, "We have no clergy or seminarians aboard to say grace. Is there anyone here who would care to?

Rose wished with all of her heart that Joshua would offer. He could say grace if he chose. While he attended Harvard, he must have heard his grandfather preach in Boston.

No one volunteered and Caleb led them in giving thanks and asking for a safe voyage. Rose added silently, fervently . . . *and heavenly Father, I pray for Joshua's salvation. Amen.*

When she opened her eyes, Joshua was smiling most

endearingly at her. "Don't forget the better part of valor," he reminded her.

"I shall." On their voyage from Georgetown to Boston he'd suggested it was the better part of valor the first day on the Atlantic to eat dry biscuits and plain potatoes, nothing else. This morning he'd mentioned it to Nichola, Maddy, and Eula, too.

Rose noted as they were served that Joshua followed his own advice, as did the Svensons and Lars. The others covered their potatoes with gravy and ate heartily of the roast beef and peas with bacon. It did look quite tempting.

A brass railing rimmed the table to prevent dishes from sliding off, and someone had just commented, "No need for the railing yet," when the sea became rougher. Everyone held onto their plates and ate rapidly. Across the table, Nichola turned pale and excused herself for fresh air. The portly Mr. Zanot ran out to the deck before the pudding was served for dessert.

Joshua cast a concerned glance at Rose, and she smiled as though reminding him that she was a good sailor. The conversation at the table continued with strained politeness, and when they had finished, Inger invited Rose and Joshua to come visit the chickens and livestock.

"A fine idea," Caleb said with a smile before leaving.

Rose did not see the humor in visiting the livestock until she and Joshua came around the deck to where the animals were penned. None of the seasick passengers, nor the others, would care to pass the farmlike smell of chickens, twenty pigs, and a cow. How incongruous cackling hens sounded against the wind in the rigging as the *Californian* cut through the sea.

"A pastoral sight," Joshua commented with amusement. Catching her hand, he led her on around to the far side of the carpenter's shop, a wooden building on the main deck.

Maddy had not followed them, nor were there sailors overhead in the rigging at the moment. The sky was, however, darkening quickly to the south as though a squall lay ahead, and the scent of rain filled the air.

Joshua said, "How perceptive of Inger to know we might wish to be away from prying eyes."

Rose recalled their romantic morning on the skiff and their kiss on the beach just two days ago. "I said nothing."

"Don't you think that our . . . caring for each other must be evident?"

She returned his smile. "Perhaps."

"And perhaps Caleb told Inger about his obtaining invitations to the Stanfords' dinner and ball for me," Joshua added.

"Do you regret asking him to use his influence?"

Joshua's brown eyes sparkled and he shook his head. "Not in the least."

He reached for her other hand and, remembering Willard, Rose felt a sudden pang of suspicion. "I do hope, Joshua, that you feel more for me than—" She blushed, unsure of how to continue with the subject of physical attraction.

His color deepened, too. "You can trust me, my dear Rose. I want to be with you . . . to protect you . . . to hear my name from your lips. I never realized that 'Joshua' could sound so wonderful."

She felt her defenses melt. He did care for her. He did.

"Last night I dreamed we were dancing at the ball again, that magnetism binding us together. Did you feel it, too?"

She nodded. "Yes, I felt it."

"I must be honest with you, after what you endured with Willard—"

"Please, I don't wish to hear of him. In any case, you are far different."

"I am glad to hear you think so, for I am . . . very fond of you. Very fond—" His warm eyes probed hers.

To her astonishment she found herself murmuring, "And I am . . . very fond of you."

"Oh, Rose!" He looked as if he wished to kiss her, but instead, he lifted her from her feet in happiness, as though he had won a great prize. She thought he might have twirled her around if the sea were not becoming so rough and, when he did set her down, he held her carefully by the shoulders as though he considered her a treasure.

Great drops of rain began to fall, splatting on the deck ever more rapidly. There were loud, sharp orders from the mate, the trampling of feet, the creaking of blocks. The slide of the hatch was thrown back and there was a loud cry of "All hands, ahoy! Tumble up here and take in sail!"

Joshua laughed as the raindrops assailed their faces, and he bent to her to steal a fast kiss that tasted most deliciously of salt. He drew away just as the sailors climbed up in the rigging. "Come, let's run!"

Holding hands, she and Joshua ran laughing like children, slipping and sliding across the wet deck. *He cared for her; he truly did!* she told herself. Laughing with him, she thought she had not been so happy in years.

They entered the salon, wet and shaking off the rain, and though she tried to act entirely innocent in front of their fellow passengers, she knew a poignant sweetness had entered their relationship.

Rose scrawled the date in her journal:
June 11, 1848
We have been at sea now for nearly a week.

The Atlantic has been much rougher than during the voyage to Boston. Great waves rush at us, dashing and thundering against the ship; sometimes we must hold onto the railing with all of our strength.

This time I was ill, but in two days I regained my "sea legs." Inger brought me dry biscuits and broth, and said that Joshua worried so about me that he did nothing but hover about in the salon near my cabin pretending to work on his cargo accounts. Since then, it has been a joy to be with him daily. How tender he is with me. He is not William, but I am no longer the same person I was three years ago either. I love Joshua, I do!

Today is bright and sunny as befits the Sabbath, and later this morning we shall have our worship services out on the deck, Caleb Svenson conducting them for both crew and passengers. I am hopeful that everyone will recover from seasickness soon.

Most of the passengers were sick far longer than I, even Maddy, who does not like me to take care of her. "Ain't fitting, Miz Rose Anne," she insists. I believe, however, that it is "fitting" that we not only love each other, but care for each other. I felt led in love to tell her that it was a blessing for me to help her after all of her years of caring for me and Mother. To my amazement, tears came to her eyes! Doesn't she know how much I love her? I shall have to make it plainer. She was sitting out on the deck bench yesterday, finally on the mend.

Nichola and Eula said little when I tended to

their needs. They were so weak that they could scarcely lift their heads as I washed their faces and fed them dry bread and broth. I tried to cheer them with news of the *Californian's* good sailing time despite intermittent squalls and high seas. I am sorry to say that they accepted my ministrations begrudgingly, looking as though I must have ulterior motives. I have truly searched my conscience and, if there is any motive at all, it is because I wish that they, too, might have my joy in the Lord.

And, oh, I do pray for Joshua . . . on my knees at night in my cabin no matter how badly the ship is tossing! Lord, I pray again now for his salvation! When I think of the dangers of rounding the Horn, I am reminded all too well of our mortality, of our short time on earth in comparison to eternity.

At ten-thirty the crew members and those passengers who felt well met on the main deck for the worship service. Rose was pleased to see Joshua at her side and Maddy in attendance. Her old housekeeper had always attended the black churches, but looked only slightly uncomfortable here. Nichola and Eula, though on the mend, were still not sufficiently well to attend, nor was Mr. Zanot, who according to the cabin boy was not nearly so portly now.

Caleb Svenson conducted a magnificent worship service, beginning with prayer and favorite hymns. Then Lars Johnson sang "The Lord's Prayer" in a rich baritone and with such faith that Rose had to look away to hide her tears. If only it were Joshua singing so powerfully to God!

The sermon was a paean in praise of God for giving not

only His beloved Son, but the wonders and beauties of earth, sky, and sea. Caleb read selections from the Psalms: "The heavens declare the glory of God; and the firmament showeth his handiwork. . . . Blessed is the man that walketh not in the counsel of the ungodly, nor standeth in the way of sinners, nor sitteth in the seat of the scornful. But his delight is in the law of the Lord. . . . I will praise thee, O Lord, with my whole heart: I will show forth all thy marvelous works. I will be glad and rejoice in thee: I will sing praise to thy name, O thou most High. . . ."

How can Joshua fail to be moved? Rose wondered. Yet, despite all of her prayers and hopes, he frowned and a hardness covered his entire countenance.

The service ended with the singing of "Amazing Grace." Abby had written of Joshua's sister, Rena, who had made the hymn especially memorable for the Talbot family on their covered-wagon trek to California. Now it was Maddy's voice rising so deeply and richly above the others that caused Rose's spine to tingle. She cast a covert glance and Joshua and saw him singing, too, a faraway look in his eyes. Was it possible that Uncle Elisha had been wrong about Joshua's unbelief? Perhaps he had once made a decision and was now returning to his faith. She sang the second verse with renewed hope:

" 'Twas grace that taught my heart to fear,
And grace my fears relieved:
How precious did that grace appear
The hour I first believed!"

She recalled the first hour she had believed. What joy had flooded through her, what blessed assurance, what love from the Lord . . . and what glorious adoration of Him. She marveled still that William had been so thrilled for her and not in the least jealous, for she had been a soul transported and transformed.

After the first week, all of the voyagers recovered from their seasickness. The weather turned temperate, the sky and the sea blue, and most of the passengers spent the days sitting out on the quarterdeck benches. For Rose, the transition to complete idleness was difficult. She almost envied the ship's crew, who were constantly occupied with tarring, oiling, greasing, varnishing, painting, scraping, and scrubbing the *Californian*. If it were not for Joshua's presence, she feared she would suffer from tedium.

Maddy said, "Ain't nothing to do but watch the clouds roll by. I hope we be busier than this in glory!"

Rose laughed. "I am sure we will be." She suggested half in jest, "Perhaps you could take up whittling like Mr. Holmes."

"Maybe so. I got Moses' old knife in the truck. You think Mistuh Holmes would show me how to be a whittling a clock like his?"

"He's whittling a clock?"

"Yes'm, he is. You see for yo'self."

Assured that he was, Rose took up the matter with him. He was willing to teach Maddy or anyone else how to whittle a clock. Mr. Zanot and Mr. Barnes joined Maddy for whittling lessons, while young Mrs. Barnes knitted nearby.

Rose spent her mornings reading James Fenimore Cooper's *The Prairie*, sometimes writing about the voyage in her journal while Joshua went over inventory sheets of the ship's cargo. There were pickaxes, shovels, wheelbarrows, mining pans, firearms and shotgun shot, tents, bolts of canvas, blankets, men's sturdy shoes, vegetable and flower seeds in airtight tins, flour, sugar, coffee, barrels of dried apples, peaches, and pickles, Stewart's Sugar House Syrup, and much more. From San Francisco, the ship would continue to Sitka and then to the Sandwich Islands, so Joshua had a great deal of planning to do, even though another supercargo was scheduled to replace him in California for the next few segments of the voyage.

In the afternoon Joshua often read Shakespeare aloud to her, and she sat contentedly beside him on a mahogany deck bench and embroidered a pink hemline panel for a dress. Even she was amazed at her becoming adept at embroidery while bobbing along on the Atlantic. Some afternoons they talked about anything and everything, and she realized she was coming to know Joshua even better than she had William. Sometimes they simply stood silently at the railing, listening to the screech of the lines, the crackle of the sails, and the sailors shouting above the wind and the ocean. Often she wondered about her father and was tempted to ask if Joshua knew of the gold discovery, but she resisted.

Nichola seldom came out into the sunshine and, according to Maddy and Eula, spent a good portion of each day unpacking and repacking her trunks. She invested an inordinate amount of time on her toilette and emerged from her cabin each evening in a voluptuous decolletage as though she were royalty sailing along the Riveria.

Occasionally she directed arch comments at Joshua and turned inviting glances in his direction. At first it gave Rose pause; finally she decided that the woman knew of no other way to get along with men. In the evening Nichola played backgammon in the salon with Mr. Hupple, who though middle-aged was rather attractive and apparently wealthy from trading cattle hides. One evening he brought out a deck of cards, riffling them with expertise, but Caleb Svenson quickly reminded them of the ship's rule against cards, whether they were used for gambling or not.

"No cards, no drinking of hard spirits," he said again to all of them. "They too often cause hardship and trouble in the end." In their stead he suggested reading books from the substantial library kept in the salon.

Surprisingly, Nichola discussed cattle ranching with the handsome Mr. Hupple while they played backgammon. She evinced a special interest in the pleasant lives led by the Californios who had received their vast land grant ranchos from the rulers of Spain and Mexico. Why Nichola had come on the trip at all was still a mystery to Rose, for the *Californian* would be in San Francisco for only a week before sailing on. The only reasons that came to mind for Nichola's presence were that life had become too tedious for her in Boston and she wished to explore exotic places, or that she wished to put time and distance between herself and the baron and baroness.

Most of the other passengers read, wrote in their journals, and sketched to pass the time. They roused when the mess bell rang or to see the unusual sight of flying fish or a distant ship. On the rare days when they did encounter a brig or a bark sailing in the same direction, everyone raised a cheer when the *Californian* sailed past with ease. There was also much interest in the ship's progress, which Lars explained to them from maps in the chart room. When Rose saw Cape Horn on the maps, she always felt an uneasy flutter in her chest. Others must have felt the same trepidation, for there was always a certain tight-lipped concern when fellow passengers asked, "How much longer until we round the Horn?"

In the evenings there was music out on deck led by Lars, who played the fiddle as well as he sang. Sometimes he appeared to be singing to her, Rose thought, then dismissed it as an impossible notion. They sang "Yankee Doodle," "Oh!

Susannah," "Flow Gently, Sweet Afton," and other popular songs, usually ending with hymns to sleep by.

During the singing Rose and Joshua often slipped away to the far side of the carpenter's shop. Together they would admire the stars and the moonlit sea. Since he had not fully declared himself, she kept him at a decorous distance in the daytime, but she was unable to resist him in the moonlight.

He, however, seemed determined that they control their passions. As he forced himself away from her to the railing one evening he said, "I am determined, Rose, to treat you as a gentleman should, but you do not make it easy for me."

She caught her breath. "You said once that you could . . . never think badly of me. Perhaps you do now."

"No," he replied. "However, Maddy has gathered up her courage to speak to me."

"Maddy?!"

"Yes. She is concerned about your reputation and welfare, remembering as she does her promise to your mother with unswerving loyalty. She has spoken to me about—"

"Yes?"

His lips claimed her for a moment, then he tore himself away. "Come, Rose, let's walk around the deck again. I don't wish to speak of it."

The next morning she asked when Maddy came to the cabin, "What on earth did you say to Joshua about me?"

Maddy squared her broad shoulders. "I told him he best decide how serious about you he be. I not standing by and seeing yo' heart broke again."

"Oh, Maddy, how could you?"

"Because I love you, Miz Rose Anne . . . that's how I could do it. Has that Mistuh Joshua spoke to you 'bout marrying yet?"

"No, he hasn't . . . but if you stop meddling, I think he will soon."

"We see," Maddy replied. "We see. If he be bent on marrying, the captain could marry you right now on this ship."

"Maddy, that is not your affair!" Rose warned her. Unfortunately, she'd considered the idea hopefully several times herself. "Moreover, we are no longer children!"

She turned and started for the deck in a huff. Likely, Joshua required more time to make such a lifelong decision, she assured herself. William and even Willard had wanted to marry her; there had been no other offers of marriage, but surely no man she'd loved had not wanted to!

Thereafter Rose noticed that Joshua kept a tighter rein on his passion, and she was equally determined to do so herself. He would propose soon, she thought. Perhaps he wanted to be married in California with his family in attendance. As for his being a believer, she ceased praying for his salvation, she was so certain of it. Didn't he always attend worship services with her on Sundays!

When they stayed out in the moonlight later than usual, they occasionally encountered Nichola at the railing with the engaging Mr. Hupple. One night Joshua saw them first, and he turned Rose about. "Come, Rose, it is time to turn in," he said. He saw her to her cabin door, bidding her a hasty good evening.

She expected they had come upon Nichola and Mr. Hupple engaged in a kiss and was not too surprised, for it struck her that Nichola would be unable to entertain herself with a book or anything else of intelligence.

There was a special dinner to celebrate the *Californian's* sailing through the equator, as well as high jinks and skylarking among the crew. That evening Rose thought that

Nichola and Mr. Hupple smelled suspiciously of spirits, but when they joined in the evening singing for a change, no one mentioned it.

The tropics, however, were nothing to celebrate, for the cabins were far too hot for sleeping, especially when the winds ceased. Pieces of sail were rigged on the afterdeck, and everyone huddled under them to evade the intense rays of the midday sun; even breakfast was eaten under them. Several becalmed evenings the passengers slept out on the deck, the women carefully separated from the men. As though the stifling heat were not enough to bear, their food supplies had dwindled down to salt meat, dried fish, and hardtack.

When the winds rose again, they made sail for Rio, their first stop to replenish supplies and to make minor ship repairs. Rose and Joshua stood on deck watching the renowned port come into view. First there were the high mountain peaks and foothills on the left and, on the right, the massive fortress of Santa Cruz. As the *Californian* passed close under the fortress guns, the magnificent harbor came into sight: the towns of San Domingo and Preia Grande on either end, the breathtaking expanse of blue water with protruding islands.

"What a stunning city!" Rose exclaimed.

Joshua said, "I am eager to show it to you."

After the *Californian* passed inspection by two groups of Brazilian officials, visitors surged aboard: newspaper reporters seeking news of the outer world, agents for local merchants—most of them offering advice on what shops, hotels, and restaurants to patronize. The passengers, restricted from disembarking the first night, lined the rails all evening, drinking in the sounds and sights of the city. It was strange after being so long at sea to hear Rio's church bells ring out and to see lights outlining the shoreline. In the late hours Rio quieted and darkened for sleep.

The next morning ashore, Rose marveled at the beautiful churches, buildings, and gardens opened to them. Outdoors, the vegetation was luxuriant, particularly the botanical gardens in the suburbs. Rio's residents thrust bouquets of flowers and fruits upon her and romantic encouragements upon Joshua. Despite countless opportunities when they were alone in gardens and churches, he did not propose—though twice she was certain the words were in his eyes and on the tip of his tongue.

Four days later, the *Californian* having replenished her food supply and made repairs, they sailed out of the port of Rio, sails billowing in the wind.

At their midday meal Caleb Svenson said, "Rio is always a pleasant interlude before Cape Horn."

Inger replied, "I vould be much happier if you didn't sound quite so grim! Ach, Svedish men!"

Everyone laughingly agreed, but Rose said nothing. Not long ago she'd been concerned about the dangers of her father rounding the Horn, and soon she would be in the same situation.

Now the days grew shorter, the heat less oppressive as the ship beat its way toward the Cape. Before long, the passengers were again seeking the sun, even digging out their warmest clothing from their sea chests for the frigid weather. The change from summer to winter was so abrupt that to Rose it seemed one day everyone simply appeared on deck in their coats and warm gloves. Now Joshua rarely invited her for moonlit strolls. The sea flung icy waves across the decks, blinding and choking the sailors and the passengers who ventured out. In the salon, they often had no light or heat in the evenings for it was too dangerous to light the stove or the oil lamps in such a wild sea.

One afternoon Caleb called them together in the salon to pray as they approached the Horn. Even those who hung back at Sunday worship services appeared serious in the gray glow under the skylight.

The next day violent storms began to hit, one following another. As the *Californian* struggled against the furious seas, Rose wrote in her journal, the words scarcely legible:

> These gales are not mere gusts or squalls, but fierce Antarctic blasts bearing down upon the ship and the sea all around us for endless hours. Thus blasted, the sea produces huge swells over which the *Californian* mounts with a roll, then plunges as though into a final abyss.

She added,

> Joshua is tender and loving, but he still has not declared himself. In this raging struggle with the elements, with the dizzying descents and lurches, my hopes are plummeting, too.

8

Benjamin Talbot rolled over and over in his bed, tossing and turning, then tossing again.

A wild storm raged around him, the ship dropping to dizzying depths, then riding skyward on a huge swell before another mountainous wave lashed them.

"Rounding the Horn!" a deep voice like Joshua's called out. "Rounding the Horn . . . rounding the Horn. . . ."

An icy wave broke over the deck, and Joshua shouted to him, "You are the one who turned me from God . . . you are the one!"

"Me?" Benjamin asked in protest. "Never me!"

"You did not make it plain . . . you did not make it plain enough. . . ."

"How much plainer can a man make it?" Benjamin asked. "I've read you Scripture since your childhood . . . your mother and I took you to church in Independence. You knew there was never a law, or sect, or opinion that did so much magnify goodness as the Christian faith."

"What else, Father? What else?"

Benjamin hesitated. "You might find fault with me, but your mother was as godly a woman as any who ever trod this earth. . . ."

"Ah, there you have it," Joshua said. "Now you approach the heart of the matter."

"Your mother?" Benjamin asked. "I have told you, there was little fault in her!"

"Now you approach the heart of the matter."

Benjamin shouted, "What is it then?"

"Actions speak louder than words."

"What did I do? What did I do?" Benjamin tried to think. "Ah, yes, you were always resentful of our taking Daniel into our household! You still are resentful of him."

"Somewhat . . . yes, somewhat. . . ."

"But that is not entirely it?" Benjamin asked.

"That is not it."

"What did I do then, Joshua? What did I do?"

"You are the one who caused my mother to die! Murderer! Murderer!"

"Murderer?" Benjamin flung back at him. "She died in childbirth!"

"Murderer . . . murderer!"

"I am not a murderer!"

Joshua suggested nastily, "She was never a strong woman, was she . . . ?"

"I loved her! I loved her!" Benjamin called out. "I love her to this day with all of my heart!"

"Murderer . . . murderer . . . "

"I love her as Christ is my witness!"

The interchange ended abruptly, and Benjamin sat upright in bed in the darkness, his body covered with sweat. The words rang in his brain: *murderer . . . murderer . . . !*

"Lord, help me!" he whispered, and it came to him what he must say. "I rebuke the evil one in Christ's holy name! I rebuke him in Christ's name! I loved Elizabeth; I loved her . . . I still do."

The darkness dissipated, and Benjamin saw the starlit sky outside his window. An owl hooted and a coyote wailed into the night. A dream . . . no, a nightmare, Benjamin thought, or perhaps more than that. He leaned weakly against the headboard of his bed, his body still wet with sweat.

In the hallway, Jessica knocked at his door. "What is it, Benjamin? Are you calling out for help?"

"Only a bad dream," he replied. "I am sorry to have awakened you. I am fine now."

"You're certain?" she asked through the door. "I have never heard you shout like that."

"Certain, thank you. Go to sleep now."

"Good land, here come Betsy and Daniel," Jessica said.

"Tell them I am sorry. Send everyone back to bed."

"Good night, then."

Benjamin heard her tell the others that he'd been dreaming, then their muffled replies as they all returned to their rooms. He remained sitting against the headboard of the bed, uncertain whether he was as fine has he had said. In the depths of his memory he realized he'd dreamed the same dream last night . . . and the night before that . . . and before that.

He touched his brow to test for fever, but his skin was cool. Finally he lay down and recalled that it was about now that the *Californian* would be rounding Cape Horn. *Lord, I pray for Joshua's safety and forgiveness and salvation,* he prayed. At length he added, *Hide me under the shadow of Thy wings.*

Many of the *Californian's* passengers were seasick, and Rose and Inger Svenson tried to tend to them. Mountainous waves lashed the ship, and their travel mates clung weakly to their slanting bunks while trunks, valises, and boxes slid from side to side in the cabins.

Finally Rose took to her bunk, too, clinging to it and wondering whether the *Californian* would survive the next shuddering lunge of the oncoming seas. She almost rued the day she had left Georgetown until she thought of Willard. She rarely saw Joshua, for he had experience as a seaman and had offered his assistance. One night when she gathered sufficient strength to come into the salon for tea, he came in from outside with his mustache coated with ice.

The seas grew fiercer, and heavy shutters were lashed over the salon skylight. Now icy waves broke constantly over the deck and could conceivably break into the salon and cabins. The days became as dark as the nights except for the dim whale-oil lamps, and Rose wore three layers of clothing day and night, and still was cold. She prayed for the ordeal of rounding the Horn to be over. She prayed for the crew . . . for her fellow passengers . . . for her father and Abby and her family in California . . . for Joshua . . . and for what the Lord wanted for the two of them.

Finally it was over. They'd rounded the Horn and weakly congratulated themselves on having survived. The ship sailed north now in the Pacific Ocean, paralleling the long coast of Chile. The sea became smoother. But now that it seemed they would live, Rose thought she preferred to die, for she found the answer to her problem with Joshua spelled out with terrible clarity in her mother's Bible.

Rereading the Second Letter to the Corinthians, sixth chapter, it was as though God spoke to her through a verse that she had never given much heed to before. *Be ye not unequally yoked together with unbelievers; for what fellowship hath righteousness with unrighteousness? And what communion hath light with darkness?*

Her eyes flew over the words. *What part hath he that believeth with an infidel? . . . for ye are the temple of the living*

God; as God hath said, I will dwell in them, and walk in them, and I will be their God, and they shall be my people. Wherefore come out from among them, and be ye separate . . .

Now she felt a great conviction that Joshua was not a believer, that she had been fooling herself and was being disobedient to God by even encouraging him. Despite all of her yearning prayers for Joshua, she was disobedient! She must ask him clearly about his faith when the proper time presented itself.

The *Californian* made good time up the coast of Chile, and the passengers emerged on deck again, glad to hear the crew's hearty chantey fill the salt air as they worked the lines. The sailors resumed their endless rounds of tarring, varnishing, scraping, and painting—and Rose awaited the Lord's leading to bring up Joshua's beliefs.

Days passed, then a week. Joshua attended the Sunday worship service, and she never found quite the appropriate time to inquire. The weather grew temperate again as they headed for Valparaiso, their last port of call for supplies and repairs before the last leg of the journey to San Francisco.

She turned to her mother's Bible again, rereading the chapter and verse in hopes she had taken it out of context. Every time her heart was convicted. *Be ye not unequally yoked together with unbelievers. . . .*

Out on the deck she stared at the blue Pacific Ocean, recalling what she knew of Joshua's spiritual life. First, that Sunday morning at her church in Georgetown where he'd appeared uncomfortable, even jesting that he'd brought Caleb and Lars to restrain him in the event he received a missionary call. He had not attended church in Boston, working late instead, and Uncle Elisha had stated that Joshua was not a believer. She remembered his fine town house in

Boston, his ambition to build a great estate on the north shore.

Her mind turned to their romance. He claimed to have been attracted to her at their first meeting, contriving to be invited nearly three years later to the Stanfords' dinner and ball. He'd shown immediate interest in her during their voyage from Georgetown to Boston, then throughout their time there, even telling her she was the first woman he'd ever invited out on his skiff. And now for over two months on this voyage he had paid ardent court on her . . . without saying he loved her or having proposed marriage. One heard of hesitant suitors who did not propose for years, but Joshua did not seem the type. *Help me to know what to do, Father,* she prayed. *Help me to know what to do!*

Early on the evening before they reached the port of Valparaiso, they stood at the railing and peered toward where the Chilean city should be. "No sign of gulls yet," Joshua commented.

She laughingly inquired, "Do you believe in signs?"

"A strange question from you," he replied.

She had spoken spontaneously, excited at the prospect of seeing Valparaiso, but he looked at her with utmost seriousness. "What are you thinking, Joshua, to frown at me so?"

He turned away toward the sparkling sea. "To be perectly honest, Rose, I have been thinking about us. You have been so patient with me all of this time when most young women would have been pressing about future prospects."

A lump of pain leapt to her throat.

He glanced at her, then quickly away. "I am torn in a thousand directions, Rose. You . . . you are the loveliest young woman I have ever known, but I fear that you would be disappointed in me."

"Disappointed?"

"Yes, disappointed." His tone was one of regret.

She drew a calming breath. "But why should I or anyone else ever be disappointed in you, Joshua? You are a fine man."

"Thank you, I do try to be one, but I do not share your beliefs. I cannot make a commitment as you have to God. I am my own man. I have different ambitions, different goals."

"But you've attended worship service on the ship!" she protested, unnerved that he had taken the lead in this matter.

"I suspect there is many a person who attends worship services and holds other gods foremost. I have attempted to walk both roads because I love you, but one cannot teeter forever on the edge. I must be true to myself."

"To yourself?"

He nodded. "Yes, to myself."

"But, Joshua, the Lord gives one such love and joy and contentment that the worldly goals no long have such significance. He has changed my life so, though I still have much to learn. Perhaps I have been a poor example as a Christian."

"No, Rose, you have been a loving Christian woman, fine in so many ways. The resistance lies within me."

"Is there some other reason? . . . some reason why you might be angry at God?"

Joshua's voice turned heavy with regret. "I am not even certain whether God exists. I have decided to listen to the voice of reason instead."

Tears welled in her eyes. "It's so odd, for I've often seen you in my mind's eye as that Joshua of old who said, 'As for me and my house, we shall serve the Lord.'"

He took her hands into his. "You would have made a fine wife for that other Joshua."

I would make a fine wife for you! she thought, blinking frantically to prevent tears from falling.

"Please don't despise me, Rose. I have led you along through my indecision all of these months."

She swallowed with difficulty. "I shall never despise you, Joshua." She saw that others now watched them, and he was aware of it, too. At the remorse on his face she could only say, "I shall always pray for you."

He looked down. "I am sure that you will." And with that he loosed her hands, turned, and walked away.

Rose whirled to stare blindly out at the sea, tears hot on her cheeks. *How could this have happened, Lord?* she questioned. *How can I be expected to give thanks even in this?* A hard sob shook her body, another sob, and another. Finally she regained control of herself. After her vision cleared, she saw sea gulls flying in the distance, and she knew this wrenching pain would assail her the rest of her life every time she saw a sea gull.

That night Joshua did not join the singing on deck, and Inger came to sit beside her.

Rose held herself rigidly to avoid giving way to tears again. She asked Inger, "You know it is all over between Joshua and me?"

Inger's blue eyes filled with sympathy. "I thought so before on the deck. I vas out with the chickens and I saw him valk avay like his heart vas broken. Caleb and I prayed for Joshua long before ve knew you . . . and then for both of you. It is the religious problem, yes?"

Rose nodded, her heart sore with anguish. "Yes."

"Ve put it in God's hands and go on," Inger said. "Tomorrow ve go to see Valparaiso. You come with Caleb, Lars, and me, and ve try to make you forget."

"I cannot forget! I shall never forget!"

"You go vith us anyvay," Inger insisted, and Rose knew that she must. And she knew that she must give thanks in this, too, even if doing so struck her as senseless.

Valparaiso was set on a spur from the Andes Mountains that reached out to the coast, a lighthouse on its edge. Rows of fine white houses with red-tiled roofs looked down upon the town over a three-hundred-foot precipice, and the American flag fluttered over the consul's quarters. The Americans who lived there were cordial, and the natives friendly. Rose noted that the senoritas were most comely, of superb carriage and elegant movement, darting bewitching glances through the mesh of their thin gauze headdresses.

Inger observed to her husband, "If I knew you vere among such temptations, I vould never have let you sail alone!"

Caleb laughed. "A Swedish beauty has no competition in the entire world!"

Lars made no comment, showing more interest in Rose than in the Chilean beauties, while she hoped that Joshua would not be too entranced with them.

In the three days that the *Californian* took on supplies and had repairs made in Valparaiso, she did not see Joshua ashore until the last moment. She was leaving a hotel dining room with Lars and the Svensons, and suddenly she turned and saw Joshua watching her from a distant table. Heat rose to her cheeks at being seen with Lars, and then she realized that Joshua was with Nichola.

Rose turned away, and Lars took her arm. "Come," he urged, "we must get back to the ship."

"Yes," she replied, but her mind said, *We must get away!*

She attempted to keep her thoughts away from Joshua all the way back to the ship, but there were sea gulls everywhere to remind her of their farewell. Even when they sailed, she either saw gulls in the distance or imagined it . . . or she saw Joshua.

Worst of all was sitting next to him at the table in the salon. The golden glow of love that had bound them together was replaced by painful tension that filled the space between them, pushing out over the salon so they were all caught in it. She sat beside him in an agony of emotions, achingly empty yet unable to eat. He did not seem to be hungry either, and when she discovered him watching her, a hardness flared in his brown eyes.

He hurts as much as I do, she thought, *but he is hardening his heart against me. He is turning the pain into anger. Lord, don't let me do that, too!*

As for Nichola, every evening she played backgammon in the salon now with both Mr. Hupple and Joshua, and she wore more and more daring gowns as though in victorious defiance. Once when she encountered Rose alone near their cabins, Nichola swept her with an ugly look and gibed, "Virtue is not its own reward, is it?"

Taken aback, Rose was speechless. She turned and hurried to her cabin. She never saw Joshua so much as touch the woman, yet she could imagine him holding Nichola in his arms and kissing her.

At first Maddy was disappointed, and then furious. "You mean that Mistuh Joshua say he doan want no part of the Lord?" She raised her chin. "Didn't I tell him right in the face, 'I doan trust no man'! I did think he better than most, Miz Rose Anne. I did think so. Well, I be giving that man a piece of my mind he ain't never going to forget—"

"No, Maddy, please, not one word to him."

"I know it ain't Christian, Miz Rose Anne, but I sho' would like to shake him 'til his teeth rattled around in his head. And heah I was planning the wedding!"

Rose cringed. "We mustn't be angry."

"Oh, land, I wonder what yo' mama be thinking if she can see down from glory? I bet she thinking, 'Maddy, you be lax in yo' duty, seeing after Miz Rose Anne.' "

Rose speculated, "I doubt that the Lord allows those with Him to know what transpires on earth, for much of it would grieve them so."

"Expect you right, Miz Rose Anne. I expect so."

Maddy said nothing to Joshua, but Rose noted that she shot chilling glances at him when they passed on deck. When she gently reprimanded her, Maddy replied in all truthfulness, "Well, I be praying for him, too."

The seas, at least, were now bearable, and the ship made good speed toward San Francisco. Still, it seemed to Rose that the voyage had become agonizingly tedious. Lars, however, spent extra time explaining their progress and position on the map and, during the evening's singing, was most attentive to her.

He was a fine young man, she often thought. Most important, he loved the Lord. If he hoped for more than friendship from her, he did not press the matter, which was a relief to her. After all, he would be sailing back on the *Californian* after a week or so in San Francisco. It seemed safe enough to be friends with him.

She spent the daylight hours reading, escaping into books, and after the evening's music, went directly to bed. The days dragged by, slowly merging into one week, then another. The *Californian* sailed across the equator again, then far west of the Mexican coastline. At last, the coast of California was in sight. The coast and its sea gulls.

She reminded herself that in California she would be with her father; she would not have to see Joshua. Abby would be there with her baby and her husband, Daniel. Once Joshua was left behind, her anguish would diminish, just as her pain at William's death had finally ended. Perhaps the Lord had sent Joshua only to bring her here, to change the direction of her life, nothing else.

At long last, after one hundred days at sea, the *Californian* sailed into the long, narrow Bay of San Francisco. At reaching their destination and returning to American soil—albeit only an American territory—Rose felt a resurgence of hope. A new life lay ahead of her at Oak Hill.

She stood at the ship's railing with Maddy, Inger, and Caleb to view what awaited her. Fog shrouded the hillsides, but the spacious landlocked bay was studded with islands and quite beautiful. As they sailed in, the morning sun broke through the fog, transforming the water from gray to bright blue. Finally they saw the harbor. Sailing nearer, it seemed that something was peculiar about the jam of ships.

"What is it?" Rose asked with the rest of the passengers. "What is so strange here?"

Caleb Svenson peered through his spyglass. "They are abandoned," he replied in shock. "The harbor holds hundreds of abandoned ships!"

9

The air was damp, the wind blew in gusts, and there was nearly a mile of choppy water full of abandoned ships from where the *Californian* dropped anchor to the town of San Francisco. Rose stood at the quarterdeck railing, peering through a spyglass at the hillside town beside the bay. One of the waterfront warehouses had "Wainwright-Talbot Shipping and Chandlery" neatly lettered across the front—a gratifying sight. Nearby were trading posts, and there were numerous shanties with "Saloon" painted across their rough exteriors.

Above them on the hillside she saw weathered frame buildings that advertised "Beds" and a long squat brick structure with a sign that proclaimed "City Hotel." Farther up the hill, shacks and sheds were built of rough boards, packing crates, and flattened tin cans. Clumps of weeds and a few wind-twisted trees separated the ramshackle houses that climbed to the crest of the hill. She attempted to conceal her disappointment as she handed the spyglass to Maddy.

The old housekeeper peered through it and scowled. "It doan look good!"

Inger commented, "Seaports usually don't look so good ven ve sail in. You must not lose courage."

Rose recalled the warehouses and grog shops along the

Georgetown wharf. "I daresay you're right." Yet Georgetown and Boston and Rio and Valparaiso had a certain composed look about them, while everything here looked so dreadfully raw. And so many abandoned ships! Not that she looked so wonderful either after one hundred days at sea! Beneath the excitement of soon seeing her father and Abby, she was weary . . . weary . . . as worn as her faded blue traveling frock.

Small boats had already put out from the beach and approached the *Californian*. "Three dollars a head to carry yer in!" a boatman shouted up to them.

"I got payin' work fer carpenters!" yelled another, mentioning an astonishingly high wage per day. Others called high wages for clerks and cooks and, when the seamen aboard the *Californian* countered with laughing disbelief, the townsmen exclaimed with indignation, "We got a gold rush here inland o' Sutter's Fort! We got rivers lined with gold!"

Gold! Rose's eyes met Maddy's with excitement. It was confirmation of her father's letter!

A townsman yelled, "They're bringin' in five- "n ten-pound nuggets!"

The sailors guffawed. "Then why ain't ye out there gettin' gold yerselves?"

"We got to earn enough fer supplies! An' fer burros to git us out to the diggin's! Ain't nothin' come cheap here!"

Caleb Svenson exclaimed, "Then that is why there are so many abandoned ships. It is actually a gold rush!"

The *Californian's* seamen stared at each other, stunned, and Maddy said to Rose, "It do sound like yo' daddy and Moses come at the right time."

"It certainly does!" She couldn't wait to get out to Oak Hill, but it was southeast of Sutter's Fort and at least a nine-day trip.

Rose suddenly realized that Joshua was making

arrangements with one of the local boatmen to take him, Nichola, and Eula ashore. His baggage was already piled beside theirs on the deck. Rose's heart constricted and she said, "I thought we'd all go in on the ship's boats."

Inger replied over the hubbub, "Nichola must be in a hurry!" At Rose's blank look, she added, "Don't you know? Nichola tells Caleb this morning that she is not sailing on after all. She goes to stay in Monterey with friends."

"In Monterey? But why?"

Inger shook her head. "Ve don't know."

"I wonder if that wasn't her plan from the beginning," Rose said. She watched Nichola's progress down a rope ladder toward the water and was heartsick to see her clinging to Joshua as she stepped into the small hired boat. Rose asked, "Is Joshua going to Monterey with her?"

"Yes, he is taking her."

Rose swallowed with difficulty, unable to take her eyes from Joshua's shining auburn hair as the small boat was rowed toward the hilly town. When she finally turned away she saw that Mr. Hupple, the handsome hides speculator, was not only surprised to see Nichola's departure, but furious.

The *Californian's* boats were finally lowered into the water for the passengers to be ferried ashore. Rose embraced Inger and bid Caleb and Lars farewell before hurriedly climbing down into one of the boats. Sitting beside Maddy, Rose waved at her friends above on deck. Her life had become a succession of farewells lately . . . and now Joshua gone, too.

Heart pounding with excitement, Benjamin Talbot stood on shore beside the horses and buggy, pleased to see the fine lines of the firm's new clipper ship. The *Californian* appeared to be everything Elisha Wainwright had promised. What a shame if it were abandoned like the rest of the ships in the bay, when its sailors heard of the gold rush.

A hired boat was already bringing in passengers across the choppy water. Joshua! It had to be him with that dark auburn hair and mustache blowing in the wind. Although he was still a small figure in the distance, Benjamin welcomed his son with a joyous wave. "Joshua!"

Joshua must have seen him, for he returned the wave, and the women in the boat turned to look at him, too.

Another son here with me, Benjamin thought. As though that weren't heartwarming enough, Jonathan Wilmington would have his daughter, Rose, with him again, and Abby would have her best friend. Their prayers surely had been answered, albeit in an unexpected way. According to Rose's letter to Abby, she had fled because of her late fiancé's brother.

Benjamin squinted at the passengers as the small boat approached on the choppy water. Rose had dark hair in Abby's painting of her; this woman with Joshua had golden hair. Nichola!

Yes, it was most certainly Nichola and her maid. What could possibly bring her to what she'd surely term "an uncivilized place"? And where was Rose?

"Welcome to California!" Benjamin called out to them as the sailors helped them ashore. "I have been watching for the *Californian* these past few days!"

Joshua's brown eyes beamed as they shook hands, then Benjamin pulled him close. He pounded his well-muscled shoulder heartily. "Welcome, son . . . welcome."

"It is good to be on solid land again," Joshua proclaimed. "You remember Nichola Wainwright—"

"Yes, indeed. We met at Elisha Wainwright's house in

Boston. What a surprise to see you here." Benjamin waited for her to offer her hand, but she kept it to herself and smiled disdainfully. Nonetheless he added, "You are most welcome to stay with us at our house—"

"Thank you, but I shall visit friends in Monterey," she replied, her half-French, half-Russian accent coming to the fore.

"I see."

Nichola glanced about, then waved at an approaching black carriage, the only one about. "Voilà!" she said with satisfaction. "They wrote about knowing when the clippers came in."

"Shipping news travels," Benjamin said. "We heard the *Californian* arrived in Valparaiso for supplies two days behind the *Darien,* which is unfortunately now abandoned with the other ships out there."

"I couldn't believe my eyes when I saw them all!" Joshua said. "The boatmen say there's a gold rush on the rivers beyond Sutter's Fort."

"Indeed there is," Benjamin replied. "We'll be inundated with gold seekers if the gold holds out."

"Will it?" Joshua asked eagerly.

Benjamin shrugged. "More gold is always found. There were only a few hundred gold seekers in the diggings in May, but the news spread so wildly, we have five or six thousand men out there now. They're finding treasure in gravel beds, steam channels, sandbars, and potholes hollowed in solid rock. It may be the world's greatest bonanza."

"I should like to see it myself," his son said.

"It's a sight to behold!" Benjamin assured him. "This spring many a local man left his fields half planted and his house half built to rush out to the diggings. My friend, Walter Colton, the navy chaplain and alcalde at Monterey, described it best: 'The blacksmith has dropped his hammer, the carpenter his plane, the mason his trowel, the farmer his sickle, the baker his loaf, and the tapster his bottle. All are off for the mines, some on horses, some on carts, some on crutches.' *

"And it's true?" Joshua marveled.

Benjamin nodded. "Though a good many are now returning."

Nichola had listened with interest, but the black carriage had halted behind them and she started for it. "Joshua—"

Benjamin asked his son, "Where's Rose Wilmington?"

"Aboard ship. They'll land the other passengers soon." He glanced after Nichola. "I must go. I promised to see her well settled in Monterey."

"Everyone will be disappointed, but . . . every brave man is a man of his word."

Joshua grinned as he departed. "You are beginning to sound like Daniel with his quotes. In any case, I shall return in several days."

"In time to drive a supply wagon out to the diggings?"

"By Friday," Joshua promised. "I wouldn't miss it!"

Benjamin felt a flood of relief. He turned and watched as a middle-aged but dashing man, doubtless a Spaniard and one of the remaining Californios, kissed Nichola's hand. After a moment, Nichola introduced Joshua while the driver saw to their baggage.

I hope Joshua is not involved with Nichola, Benjamin thought. He'd met her in Boston when her husband was still alive, and it had not appeared that Nichola had married Elisha Wainwright's nephew for love. To be fair, however, perhaps the young man's motives had not been entirely pure either.

Benjamin glanced out at the *Californian*. The ship's

landing boats were now coming in across the bay. He hoped his meeting with Rose would not be disappointing—that she, at least, would come home with him. In any case, matters were evolving most interestingly. The brush arbor camp meeting would take place on the weekend.

Rose sat uneasily in the boat as the sailors rowed them through the choppy water. Despite her weariness, her spirits lifted to see a familiar face . . . yes, it was Abby's uncle awaiting them on the shore. He would not know her, she reminded herself; then to her amazement, he waved.

"Welcome to California!" he called out as the sailors helped her and Maddy ashore. He looked grayer than the man who had come to pick up Abby at Miss Sheffield's School in New York, but that was over three years ago and before his trip to California by covered wagon.

"It's a pleasure to meet you, Miss Wilmington. I recognize you from a painting Abby has done of you!"

"Rose, please," she suggested. "Abby has painted me?"

"Yes, indeed. She portrayed you very well. She can't wait to see you . . . nor can your father.'"

"And I can't wait to see them! Are they fine then?"

"Yes, in perfect health."

Relieved, Rose added, "How good of you to come for us."

"It's my pleasure," he assured her.

"My letters must have arrived."

"Yes, three days ago. I sent your father's letter on with miners headed in that direction. Whether he received it or not, he will be jubilant. What an answer to prayer!"

Rose was unsure of his meaning, but she was glad to have his assistance, for her legs quivered treacherously on the path of stones which served as a landing.

He turned to Maddy, who followed. "I've seen your

husband, Moses, at the diggings. That man can surely sing!"

"I be glad to hear he be alive and singing!" Maddy replied. "I was scared those Indians scalped him!"

"Not at all. Indeed, he has friends among the Indians."

"They be his friends?!" Maddy repeated.

Benjamin Talbot nodded. "Yes, indeed."

Rose laughed with Maddy in astonishment.

"Life is very different here," Benjamin Talbot said. "You will learn that soon enough."

They stopped on the rutted road, and he helped Rose and Maddy into a two-horse buggy, apologizing for its battered condition. "Fine carriages are few and far between. Not only is our waterfront crude, but all of our town, I am sorry to say. Changing its name from Yerba Buena to San Francisco last year has not changed the character of the place from that of a 'good herb' to 'a saint.' "

Rose glanced up the hill at the ramshackle buildings. It certainly was unlike Georgetown and Boston. She said, "I did not know what to expect. I do hope it's not an imposition for us to stay with you—"

"Not at all," he assured her. "We purchased a Spanish rancho with a spacious house . . . a casa, it is called here. Abby's husband, Daniel, and I tend to our commerce in town, but we prefer to let the family enjoy the countryside. We live in what we laughingly call rustic splendor."

"Then if it's convenient, I am most grateful," Rose said. Looking about, she saw no sign of Joshua. She saw only that the dusty road fronting the warehouses was littered with trash and horse droppings. Uncombed, unwashed loafers stood around the nearby saloons, and the stench of privies and dead fish rotting on the beach hung in the damp air. Most unsettling, the loafers stared at her with greedy eyes. The countryside must be better, she hoped, quickly turning away from the men.

Benjamin Talbot flicked the reins over the horses, and they started off. "One has to understand the men here," he said at her reaction. "There are few women in California. Most of the men will treat you with utmost respect, even the loafers. They miss the presence of women and children. Ofttimes men ask if they might look at my grandchildren simply because they haven't set eyes on a child in so long a time."

"How odd," Rose replied, still glad to be leaving the city. Viewing the rickety shops and houses as they drove along, she was even more grateful.

They passed through a town square surrounded with makeshift saloons and gambling tents where grizzled men wandered in out out, prompting Maddy to say, "It still be morning! Those men be drinking and gambling at this time of day?"

Benjamin Talbot nodded. "It appears to get more uncivilized each time a new contingent of gold seekers arrive. Worst of all, many of them drink and gamble their gold away as fast as they find it."

"Is there that much gold?" Rose asked.

"There appears to be vast quantities of it. Your father purchased an extensive piece of land in a prime gold location before it all began."

"How pleased he must be!"

"He will be even more pleased to see you."

She held tightly to the buggy seat as they bounced through the ruts. "Is he truly well?"

"I doubt that he's felt better in years! I saw him last in July when we took provisions to the diggings. Indeed, I stayed at his cabin while I played argonaut for a week."

"How did you fare?"

He laughed. "First, my horse was stolen. Then I caught cold from standing in the cold stream and had to pay a fortune for a doctor's tablets. I scarcely broke even. It seems I'm better off in a business I know."

"But Father is well?" she asked again.

"In excellent health. Indeed, he is euphoric."

She shook her head with disbelief. She could not imagine her staid entrepreneur father being euphoric or living in the midst of Indians on a goldfield, yet soon she would see for herself. As they bounced along in the buggy through town, she looked around for Joshua and Nichola, but there was no sign of them. Not wishing to inquire directly of their whereabouts, she asked, "Where is Monterey?"

"On a bay to the south. It's a more established place, having been the capital of Upper California. The presidio was established there by Anza, and now that we're an American territory, it's the seat of our military government." He added, "Nichola has friends there. Joshua will return before we leave for Oak Hill."

She let out a quiet breath of relief. If nothing else, Joshua didn't plan to remain there with Nichola. Rose said, "I don't wish to cause you any difficulty. I thought perhaps Maddy and I might go to Oak Hill by stage or hire a driver—"

Benjamin Talbot gave a laugh. "There are no stages here, at least not yet, and I doubt you'd find a wagon or driver. It is no trouble at all for us. We are taking five wagons of provisions to Sutter's Fort and to Oak Hill next week. There is really no other safe way for you to go, and Abby is eager to come with us. Is that acceptable to you?"

"Yes, if you're sure—"

"We're certain. Our problems lie elsewhere. With all of this gold madness, it is difficult to find dependable drivers. I spoke with Joshua when he came ashore, and he agreed to drive one of the wagons. Another facet of the chandlery business for him to explore."

"Then he will be traveling with us."

His father cast a sidelong look at her. "Yes, he is eager to see the goldfields."

"I see." Rose turned away, wondering how much he had guessed.

Benjamin Talbot was saying something about the deserted ships in the harbor, that the sailors on the *Californian* would probably join the other seamen in jumping ship.

She shook her head. "It seems impossible that men would become so crazed over gold."

"You will see proof enough when we arrive at the diggings near Oak Hill. 'Gold fever' is not a meaningless expression. For some men, it is a mania, the passion that drives their lives."

They rode through golden hills and flat-bottomed valleys with clusters of dark green live oaks for a stretch, then the ranch came into sight. "There's our place," he said, "Rancho Verde . . . green ranch, though it surely is not green now."

Indeed, the land was a golden brown except for greenery along a small stream where men were clearing the brush and building a kind of arbor; beyond the stream stood corrals and whitewashed outbuildings. As they rode to the crest of a hill, she saw the three white wall-enclosed houses with red-tiled roofs—the two newer houses for two of the married children and their families.

"We call the old house Casa Contenta . . . house of contentment. That is where you will stay with Abby, Daniel, and their little Daniel. My sister, Jessica, and my youngest daughter, Betsy, and I also reside there."

"It's Spanish architecture," Rose remarked about the

style. "We do not have it in the East."

"Only one of the differences you will find here."

"I like it . . . and the name . . . house of contentment."

He smiled. "It has been one until recently. Unfortunately, since spring it has been almost impossible to find men to care for the cattle. Everyone rushes off to the goldfields, although some have straggled back now that the rivers are low."

"A strange state of affairs," Rose said.

"Indeed!"

Riding through the opened gates, Rose saw her beloved friend Abby hurrying to them from the house. Her golden hair gleamed in the sunshine, and she beamed with joy.

Tears suddenly filled Rose's eyes. "There she is!"

Benjamin laughed. "As excited to see you as you are to see her." He reined in the horses at the hitching post, and Rose clambered down from the buggy and threw herself into Abby's open arms.

Abby held her tightly. "Oh, Rose, how happy I am to have you here! I couldn't believe you were coming!" They moved from each other's embrace, then held each other joyously again.

"And I am so happy to be here, Abby. I thought we would never see each other again!"

Abby shook her head, her blue eyes shining. "I did, too."

Rose stepped back. "It seems much longer than three years since you left school in New York . . . it seems an eternity . . . and to see you looking so wonderful and so happy!"

Inside, she met the other Talbots who had survived the wagon trek to California with Abby and Daniel in 1846. Aunt Jessica, who was Joshua's aunt and a sweet-spirited elderly lady, said, "Abby has so often spoken of you, and Joshua has, too. We are elated that you've come, to put it mildly."

Joshua has mentioned me? Rose marveled. It must have been after bringing Abby's pictures to Georgetown. What might he have said?

Betsy Talbot, Joshua's thirteen-year-old sister, had freckles, clover-green eyes, and long auburn braids. "I have heard so much about you that I was scared I might be disappointed," she said. "But you are just like Abby sketched you."

Rose turned to Abby. "You truly sketched me?"

Abby laughed. "You are not only sketched, but watercolored, framed, and hanging on one of our adobe walls. Come see for yourself!"

They led her into the spacious whitewashed parlor and to where the picture hung behind the small pump organ. Rose was surprised to find herself portrayed in her green silk ball gown, stepping down the stairs into the magnificent marble entry of Miss Sheffield's school. Abby had captured her pink cheeks, widespread brown eyes, and even the sweep of her chignoned raven hair perfectly, but she had added such gracefulness and joy that Rose protested. "Oh, Abby, you've romanticized me. I didn't look that beautiful—"

"You most certainly did," Abby insisted, "and you still do. In fact, I've entitled it *Debut of a Beauty.* You have never realized how beautiful you are."

Rose objected. "You are the one who made such a lovely picture that evening in your sapphire gown. When Daniel looked up at you, I was certain he was smitten at once."

Everyone laughed and Rose asked, "Where is Daniel?"

"He will be here later this afternoon," Benjamin replied. "Then you can gaze upon married bliss."

Abby blushed happily, and Betsy shook her head and

said with hopelessness, "They act like newlyweds."

If only she and Joshua—

Aunt Jessica said to Rose, "You must be exhausted. Let us show you to your room."

The old house was huge, having once held a family of Californios with twelve children. Its center was occupied by a large hall to which the dining room and bedrooms seemed mere afterthoughts. The huge hall's loveliest feature, Rose thought, was the intricate coral and green border Abby had stenciled above the green wash at sideboard height.

Aunt Jessica explained, "Everything in Californio houses is subordinate to the halls, which are meant for dancing. Notice how even the wooden floor springs under our feet."

Rose asked with a laugh, "All the better for dancing?"

Abby shook her head. "Unfortunately the wood has broken down from so much dancing, I expect."

At Rose's incredulous look, Abby added, "The Californios themselves say they'd hardly pause in a dance for an earthquake and would be sure to be dancing again before the quake's vibrations ceased! At their weddings, they sometimes dance three days and nights, keeping the newlyweds on their feet!"

"It's difficult to believe," Rose responded.

"I could scarcely believe it myself," Abby said, "until we were invited to one of their fiestas."

Aunt Jessica put in, "The dance and a dashing horse are the two objects of greatest importance to them, though their fiddle has quieted a bit since our flag went up in '46."

After settling in, Rose met little Daniel, a six-month-old baby who came happily into her arms, crowing his welcome. "How blessed you are to have a sweet little babe, Abby."

"I couldn't be happier," Abby admitted, then added with amusement, "though Californio ladies consider one child only a beginning. They say a woman with only one child is like a hen with one chick; she makes an eternal scratching about nothing!"

Rose laughed, and Abby said, "Many families have sixteen or eighteen children. Why, there's a woman in Monterey who has twenty-three live children now."

"Twenty-three!"

"And another on the way, according to Aunt Jessica."

"One hears that everything and everyone thrives especially well here," Rose said, amused, "but that seems a bit extreme!"

They sat cozily on Rose's bed, and Abby said, "I was sorry to hear about your troubles with Willard, but it is well worth it to me to have you here."

"It seems so long ago now," Rose replied. "I feel as though I am on the other side of the world."

Abby smiled. "Not quite."

Rose bounced little Daniel on her lap. "How I envy you having this beautiful babe and Daniel."

"And how I wish I could change your life for you," Abby replied, her eyes brimming with sympathy. "Is there . . . has there been anyone else, or should I not ask?"

Before she could think, Rose blurted, "Yes . . . Joshua."

Abby stared at her in alarm. "Joshua?"

Rose nodded. "That appears to have come to an end, too."

"Oh, Rose," her friend said. "As Aunt Jessica so often puts in, I am going to bear down in prayer for you. I've been praying for your safety, but I see it is in other quarters that you need help. I can't quite believe it . . . you and Joshua."

"It's over," Rose told her again.

That night when Daniel returned home and welcomed her, he added, "With you here, Rose, surely Abby is now the happiest woman on earth."

Abby winked at Rose. "Not quite yet."

Rose smiled uneasily, almost wishing she had not told her about Joshua. As it was, she found it a bittersweet pleasure to see Abby with Daniel, for they appeared as blissful a couple as the others had warned.

The next day she met Benjamin Talbot's other children—Martha, her husband, Luke, and their children; Jeremy and Jenny and their one-year-old son. They were a closely knit family, the men involved in the Talbot chandlery or in the ranch, the women busy with their young families.

After two days Rose had her land legs again. She and Abby rode out on chestnut mares across the golden hillsides. At the top of a hill they reined in their horses and looked out to the ocean in the distance. "What a magnificent sight!"

Abby replied, "I shall never have enough of this place, nor of my new life."

"You glow with happiness, Abby, and, with little Daniel, you look like . . . well, if it were a painting, I should entitle it *Madonna and Child*.

Abby laughed. "I can't help myself from looking so happy, but a madonna . . . not quite." Her expression sobered. "I am concerned about you though, Rose. At first I thought you were merely tired from the voyage, but I know it is far more than that. It is Joshua—"

A pang of anguish assailed Rose. "He is not interested in . . . entangling alliances."

"He still rebels against God?"

Rose nodded. "He attended worship services at sea so faithfully that I hoped he might turn to the Lord. Indeed, I deluded myself for a while, trying to think he already had. But he told me he has different ambitions—" She patted the mare Chessy's warm neck wistfully, then looked out at the distant ocean. "We were so happy and so in love for a time that I wished it would never end. Then, just before we reached Valparaiso, he concluded on his own that I'd be dissatisfied with him because he is not a believer."

"He put it that plainly?"

Rose sighed. "Yes, he put it very plainly indeed . . . and then . . . and then he spent his time with Nichola."

"Oh, Rose—I shouldn't be prying, but he will be here soon, and this weekend people from all around are going to meet here by the creek for a camp meeting."

"A camp meeting?" Rose asked, having only vaguely heard of such a thing. "What is it?"

"Singing and preaching outdoors all weekend. It will be the first one held here in California, as far as we know. I have never been to one myself, but in other parts of the country where there are no suitable buildings for church services, they sometimes last for weeks."

Rose brightened. "It sounds exciting."

"I hope it will be," Abby said. "In any case, I wanted to know how matters stood between you and Joshua. I'll divulge nothing of it."

Rose nodded sadly. "You've always been trustworthy."

Abby reached out a hand. "Come, let's join hands and pray for Joshua. The Lord told us that where two or more are gathered in His name, He would be in the midst of them."

Rose held her friend's hand as they sat on their horses. It still astonished her that Abby was now a believer, and Rose asked, "Please, would you pray?"

The morning breeze blew through the dried grasses all around them, and Abby spoke with veneration and joy, "Heavenly Father, we know that Thou art everywhere, but we feel so close to Thee now in the sunshine and breeze on this beautiful part of Thy earth. We know that the wind of Thy spirit blows everywhere, and we pray now that Joshua's heart might be turned to Thee, and for Thee to show Rose where Thy wishes in this matter lie. We pray for peace and joy for her now. We pray in the name of Thy beloved Son, our Lord, Jesus Christ. Amen."

"Amen," Rose added fervently.

She opened her eyes, and the sun was blindingly bright. Slowly her eyes adjusted to the light, and it seemed that the earth had never been so beautiful—the vast open sky, the glorious golden hills rolling toward the distant sea.

A great reverence surged through her, invading her body, mind, and spirit—and she found herself praying, *I rededicate my life to Thee, Lord. I see now that I was beginning to place Joshua above Thee, and I do repent of that. No man is as important as Thee. I want only Thee.* Slowly her heart filled with a wondrous peace and joy.

When they rode back over the golden hills to the house, she felt an idle curiosity about what might happen to her and Joshua, but her anguish over him was gone. *Thank Thee, Lord, thank Thee, Lord!* her heart sang to the rhythm of Chessy's quick hoofbeats. If only Joshua's heart could be so joyous.

That night Rose and Abby laughed over their old school escapades. In the midst of their merriment Rose realized she had not laughed so much since the evening in Georgetown when she knew she had escaped Willard. That bout of laughter had been a catharsis; this laughter was in happy fellowship.

The next day Rose joined Abby, Aunt Jessica, and Maddy in the big whitewashed kitchen to cook and bake for the camp meeting. Tables held huge pots of steaming boiled potatoes, carrots to be sliced, dozens of half-made apple pies, and trays of little raisin cakes ready to bake in the big, black stove that had also traveled around the Horn.

Rose sat at the old oak kitchen table peeling hot boiled potatoes for salad. "How many people are you expecting?" she asked, eyeing the vast amount of food.

"Only the Lord knows," Aunt Jessica replied with a smile. "Everyone is talking about it, and people will be glad to have a chance to visit." She deftly trimmed dough from the edge of an apple pie. "Seth Thompson is a good preacher, too, and he has friends all around from the wagon train. In any event, we need plenty to eat. People are bringing basket picnics and old quilts, but there are so many argonauts without families, and we doubt they'll be able to bring much food."

"That's why Uncle Benjamin decided to roast beef," Abby explained. "And why we need to make so much extra food."

"It does sound a bit uncertain," Rose said.

"If we trust the Lord in it, we'll have miracles," Aunt Jessica pronounced firmly. "We had camp meetings when my husband Noah and I lived in Kentucky. I'd been accustomed to Father's proper church in Boston and was a bit wary of going to a camp meeting . . . at least until I saw their effect on the people. They helped to civilize the frontier."

Abby responded, "At the rate life is going with this gold rush, we shall need a great deal of civilizing influence here!"

Aunt Jessica nodded. "Back East, there were times when a whole community was transformed by God's spirit during a tent meeting. Why, they'd stamp out drunkenness and gambling, wife beating and stealing, and even dishonest business deals. As if that weren't rewarding enough, a good many young men dedicated themselves to the ministry at such meetings."

"I am eager to see it myself!" Rose decided.

"I doubt we'll have much commotion unless it's begun by the miners," Aunt Jessica said, "but I remember a dozen different hymns being sung at the same time by the thousands gathered at a meeting. And they loved to shout out their faith!"

"Are you serious?" Rose asked.

Aunt Jessica laughed. "Indeed I am! Of course, most of the ministers and the more sedate church members were dismayed by such a wild display. They thought it was a better revival when there was quietness and dignity."

Abby urged her aunt, "Tell Rose the story about Gabriel blowing his horn at a camp meeting."

"That was in Newton, Maryland, not Kentucky," Aunt Jessica said smiling. "On the Pocomoke River, back at the turn of the century, I believe."

"It's a good story anyhow," Abby said to urge her on.

"Well, there was a strong religious element in Newton," Aunt Jessica began. "The famous traveling preacher, Lorenzo Dow, addressed two thousand people there. Now, I don't know if this is a true story or not, but it's said that on his way to a meeting the Reverend Mr. Dow once overtook a little colored boy named Gabriel, who happened to be carrying an old tin horn. The combination of the boy's name and the horn gave Mr. Dow an idea and, after thinking about it, he took a dollar from his pocket and handed it to the boy. He promised him another dollar after the meeting if he did exactly what he was told.

Aunt Jessica continued, "Then Reverend Dow said, 'You climb up into the big elm tree above the brush arbor and sit quietly while I'm preaching, until I say, 'Blow, Gabriel!' Then you blow like anything!'

"Well, the meeting took place, and Mr. Dow preached on resurrection and the day of judgment. He preached like one inspired. Working up to his climax, he described the angel Gabriel standing with one foot on the sea and the other on land, his long silver trumpet in hand. 'Blow, Gabriel, blow!' shouted Mr. Dow, and was instantly obeyed.

"An unbelievable scene followed. The congregation fell on the ground, crying out for mercy and shouting for salvation. Their horses, hitched nearby, added to the uproar with wild whinnying and stamping. Presently the boy was seen in the tree, and the shamed sinners eyed Mr. Dow threateningly. But he was equal to the occasion. 'If one little boy can strike such terror into your hearts,' he shouted, 'what will you do when the great day truly arrives?' "

Rose laughed and Maddy, still chuckling said, "I heard that story myself. Ain't nothing like making folks think hard in a church meeting."

"Indeed," Aunt Jessica agreed. "Indeed."

Joshua arrived Friday mid-afternoon and was heartily welcomed. He was, Benjamin thought, rather subdued except for his interest in the diggings.

"Are you taking gold dust in trade as they do in Monterey?" Joshua asked.

Benjamin laughed. "I am not only taking it in trade, but sending it off to the Islands in gallon pickle bottles! At first, no one was sure of its value, but after I sent a jar full with the captain of the schooner *Honolulu* for trade on goods, I learned it was worth over double what we'd expected. None of it has brought less than sixteen dollars an ounce!"

"In pickle jars . . . that much!" Joshua marveled.

"At the rate it's coming in, I wish we had glass barrels!"

"No wonder the sailors jump ship."

Benjamin nodded. "Unfortunately they have jumped from the *Californian*, too, though I can't say it wasn't expected."

The whole family came for dinner, excited to be with

Joshua. Benjamin noticed, however, that his son kept slightly distant, never opening himself entirely to his own brothers and sisters or to their children. He did give Rose a peculiar smile across the table, but her composure made it appear they were only friends. Joshua's eyes sought her again and again, and several times she turned from him to Abby to ask about one thing or another.

As they left the dinner table, Joshua said, "You look different, Rose. Rested after the hard voyage, I presume."

"Yes," she replied. "I feel quite rested now."

Benjamin noticed Abby smile at Rose from across the room. Something was in the wind.

Joshua turned to him. "I saw men cleaning up the brush by the stream and constructing what looked like an large arbor when I rode in. Don't tell me we are getting ready for Betsy's wedding!"

"Oh, Joshua—" Betsy protested. "You know I am only thirteen!"

Benjamin laughed, though he thought if it were Jeremy or Daniel jesting, one of Betsy's braids would likely have received a good tug.

"That will come soon enough!" Benjamin said. "Actually, we're celebrating autumn with divine services here this weekend. I hope you will help."

Joshua shot him a suspicious glance. "Help with what?"

"Welcoming the neighbors and whatever else comes to hand. We've decided to do as the Californios did, roasting beef. We expect a large crowd, including miners who have returned from the hills now that the rivers are low."

"Indeed? I'd like to speak to the miners."

Benjamin grinned. "You might speak to me."

"You've been to the mines?" Joshua asked with disbelief.

"I have. I was at Oak Hill for a week when we took

provisions out to the diggings."

Joshua's eyes widened. "And did you find gold?"

"I did. Like most miners, about an ounce a day."

"That's all?" Joshua asked.

Benjamin laughed. "I almost caught pneumonia as well!"

"How does one find gold out there?" Joshua asked.

"The great Hebrew proverbialist says there are three things on earth about which there is no certainty: the way of an eagle in the air, the way of a serpent on a rock, and the way of a ship in the sea. He might haved added—the way of a thread of gold in a vein of California quartz!"

Joshua chuckled, though Benjamin could see that his son disliked the biblical allusion. "There will be far more successful argonauts to question at our camp meeting."

"Perhaps it will be interesting."

Benjamin sincerely hoped the meeting would be of special interest to Joshua. Like all men, he needed a firm foundation. One could see the lack of such a foundation so clearly at the diggings, where gold seekers ran from one rumored strike to another. They were like driftwood floating with the strongest current, like migratory birds that lighted where they could find the best picking or the softest repose.

The next morning Benjamin looked out at the bright sunrise and was grateful for the beautiful day. *Time to get going,* he thought after his prayers. Seth Thompson had promised to come early and to bring another preacher from town, and the meeting was to begin at ten o'clock.

After a fast breakfast, he and Jeremy rode out to the stream to inspect the arbor. "Looks like you and the men made a good job of it," he said to the youngest of his red-haired sons. The arbor, built of fir poles including its rafters, was thickly covered with leafy branches from laurels, live oaks, buckeyes, and madrones. The rustic benches under it could hold about a hundred and forty people, Benjamin calculated.

"It is a pleasure to do work for God's glory," Jeremy said in all earnestness, then looked at the arbor again. "These trees are different from those in Missouri, but they'll give good shelter from the sun. I only pray there is no strong wind to blow off that brush."

"Looks like you made a good job of tying it down."

Jeremy grinned. "I figured the livestock could use it as a shelter for a few years after we're done with it."

"I expect they'll enjoy its shade far longer than we do," Benjamin replied. "Could be we might use it again, though." He eyed the lane the men had cleared through the dried grasses from the road to the stream. "Everything appears to be ready. We will have to trust the Lord for the rest of it. If He isn't in it, our work is wasted, but we surely have bathed the entire effort with prayer."

Seth Thompson and the other preacher, William Palmer, rode in at nine-thirty, just when the neighbors began to arrive with their friends.

"Seth!" Benjamin exclaimed.

He embraced his young brown-haired minister who'd come by wagon train with them from Independence. A moment later, he was shaking hands with William Palmer, a blond-bearded evangelist, who had a calm and intelligent demeanor, and the love and fire of the Lord in his eyes.

Before long, horses and buggies and farm wagons were settled under the trees along the stream. People were arriving from all directions: men mostly in shirtsleeves and wearing broad-rimmed hats, women in long dresses that brushed over the dry grasses, excited children who eyed each other carefully. They all settled on the rustic benches under the arbor.

From the corner of his eye, Benjamin saw Jessica, Rose, Abby, and Betsy give out the small raisin cakes to the children to "hold them over" until the midday meal. And there, finally, came Joshua on his horse.

It begins, Benjamin thought.

As he greeted more and more people, it seemed that a great living tableau had come alive by the stream. The Lord had given him this land, and this was the season to use it to His glory. He knew that Arthur Standford, the Englishman who attended their Sabbath services, and his family were not coming, but to his surprise, here came Josiah Benton and his wife and children.

"Welcome, Josiah," Benjamin said, then greeted Josiah's wife and their children, as well as his stiff-necked sister, Josephina, who looked as if she had been coerced to attend.

Josiah said, "Thought we'd come to see what takes place."

"Glad you're here, my friend," Benjamin said, then sent up a prayer for all of them.

The benches were nearly filled, and he was still greeting families and miners when the singing began. The familiar words to "O Happy Day" joyously filled the morning air, and Benjamin sang out with his guests, "Happy day, happy day, when Jesus washed my sins away. . . ."

After the first two hymns, Seth said, "What a pleasure to find so many of you here. Now, if you would sit closer together to make room for latecomers. . . ."

When they'd settled themselves, he led them in "More Love to Thee." The sweet words seemed to reach to the heavens, and Benjamin thought that God must be pleased.

Seth introduced William Palmer, who stepped forward with confidence. After greeting the congregation, he read from Romans: "He that spareth not his own Son, but delivered him up for us all, how shall he not freely give us all things?"

He smiled at them. "How freely does God love the world!" he declared joyously. "He not only gave us the beauty of the earth and the heavens which we see before us this fine autumn morning, but while we were yet sinners, Christ died for the ungodly. While we were dead in sin, God spared not His own Son, but delivered Him up as the perfect Savior for each of us!"

Benjamin glanced about and saw that even the children listened attentively. Jeremy and Daniel had charge of roasting the beef, and Joshua listened with them by the cook fire. He crossed his arms and raised his chin stubbornly. *Lord, touch his heart,* Benjamin prayed. *Let him not be so hardened!*

After a moment Joshua caught his eye, and Benjamin nodded, then returned his attention to the sermon.

Just before noon, William Palmer came to the sermon's climax. "Hear this, ye who forget God! Ye cannot charge your death upon him! God speaks in Ezekiel, 'Have I any pleasure at all, that the wicked should die?' "

Palmer let that sink in, then added, "Repent, and turn from your transgressions so iniquity shall not be your ruin. Cast away from you all your transgressions. 'As I live,' saith the Lord God, 'I have no pleasure in the death of the wicked. Turn ye, turn ye, from your evil ways, for why will ye die, O house of Israel?' The Lord God asks you to turn to Him through Christ so you might come into His kingdom."

After the call to repentance and salvation was given and the final "Amen" said, Seth Thompson led them all singing,

"My faith looks up to Thee,
Thou lamb of Calvary,
Savior divine!

Now hear me while I pray,
Take all my guilt away . . . "

At midday the people spread their quilts on the ground and visited while they ate. "This morning's the best time I had since I came to Californy," Benjamin heard one of the women say.

"Me, too," another agreed. "Ain't this the way more of life should be!"

The children gobbled their food, then hurried off along the stream to play.

As people visited, a miner said to Seth Thompson, "We need meetin's like this every Sunday. We need a real church built near town for when it rains."

"Aye, it's been on my heart for some time," another man said. "Without churches, it's a lawless society."

Before the meal was over, a dozen or so men committed themselves to help put up a church building close to town.

In the afternoon, Seth Thompson spoke on Christian liberty, quoting from Luther, "Many have thought Christian faith to be an easy thing, and not a few have given it a place among the virtues. This they do because they have had no experience of it, and have never tasted what great virtue there is in faith. It is impossible to understand faith unless a man has tasted the courage and wisdom faith gives when trials oppress him. Faith is a living fountain springing up into life everlasting!"

In the evening, William Palmer delivered a fiery sermon on God's judgment, which was punctuated with the crowd's lively "hallelujahs!" and "amens."

The sermon ended to mighty "amens," and to everyone's amazement a little old lady shouted,

"This day my soul has caught on fire,
Hallelujah!

I feel that heaven is coming nigher,
O glory Hallelujah!"

Others took up the shout, which was apparently familiar to them, and when things finally quieted, William Palmer asked if any had made decisions for Christ. The little old lady was first to run forward, followed by three miners and two children. At the very last moment, who should hurry forward but Josiah Benton's stiff-necked sister, Josephina, to make a first-time confession of faith.

By sunset, the day's meeting was declared a success, and many of the families and the miners pitched tents to spend the night alongside the stream. Some decided at the last moment to stay and sleep in their wagons so they wouldn't miss any of the excitement or fellowship.

Benjamin already had his bedroll so he could sleep out with them. When he settled in near the camp fire he told Seth Thompson, "I have a feeling this will be one of the times of life we will always remember."

"I do as well," Seth replied. "I do as well."

One of the men called out to Benjamin, "Tell us what it was like in town in '46 when you came, Benjamin."

"I am not sure I know where to begin," he replied. "Things were quieter with only two hundred and fifty of us living in the community. The greatest excitement back then was the great battle of San Francisco."

"I ne'er heard o' that," someone said.

"Nor I," Seth Thompson added, then urged him to tell it.

"Well . . . " Benjamin said, collecting his thoughts. "The battle began with Captain King, who arrived from the Sandwich Islands and brought with him a newly patented coffeepot, the like of which no one had ever seen. It held about a gallon and a half of coffee. On the top was a large iron wheel, which fitted tight to the rim; over that was a cover; on the outside was a screw to turn down so tight no steam could escape. Captain King had a Kanaka steward from the Islands with him, who'd learned how to use the coffeepot safely. . . ."

Someone asked, "Be this a true story? "

"It is true all right," Benjamin replied. "In any case, it was their habit to make coffee in the pot every day, but it happened one day that the steward had urgent work to do, and after fixing the coffeepot, he left it in charge of the second cook, with the instructions that if too much steam escaped, to turn the screw tighter. Well, the cook turned it down so tight no steam could escape. The consequence was that the coffeepot exploded, blowing the cook twenty yards from the kitchen and scattering utensils throughout the room.

"Captain Hull's headquarters were on the north side of the hotel then. When he heard the explosion, he ran to the barracks and ordered the long roll to be beat to let everyone know the Spaniards had come to take the city. They called out all the citizens, and he ordered them to fall into line, to be ready to fire at the word of command. He sent out marines to scout out the strength of the Californios, and he made signals for the men on ships to be ready, if needed on shore. Everyone was ready for action when a man came out, saying a coffeepot had exploded in the hotel."

Around the camp fire people began to laugh, but Benjamin said, laughing himself, "That's not the end of it. Captain Hall turned to his troops and thanked them in all seriousness for their ready response to his call, saying if they were needed in the future, he hoped they would show as great a readiness to respond as they did on that day. He then discharged them from further duty."

Benjamin concluded with a wry, "This, I believe, was the

last call to fight the great battle of San Francisco."

Everyone laughed heartily, and someone said, "Tell about the clergyman named Roberts who sailed in last summer on the bark *Whiting*."

"This one is ironic, but not so comical," Benjamin said, sitting back. "I will begin, as is appropriate, at the beginning, which was when the bark *Whiting* stopped in the harbor for a few days en route to the Oregon Territory, and the clergyman, Roberts, came ashore. He informed John Brown, the innkeeper at the Portsmouth House, that if it were convenient and agreeable to the citizens, he would like to hold services on Sunday.

"Well, Brown was pleased and gave him use of the dining room for Sunday morning, and he posted a notice that there would be preaching that day at the hotel. The room was filled, and the Reverend Mr. Roberts preached a good sermon . . . the first Methodist sermon ever preached in the city. The congregation was not very fashionable, but deeply attentive, and well pleased with the sermon. I'd say that many at that meeting had not been in any place of worship for ten or fifteen years. One old sailor put a five-dollar gold piece in his own hat and went around the room and collected over fifty dollars, which he gave to the minister, then invited him to dinner.

"The dining room opens to the billiard room and saloon, and on the other side are card-playing rooms. I doubt another instance could be cited where under the same roof there was preaching, drinking, card playing, and billiards all taking place at once. Those who didn't wish to attend the religious services in the room had too much respect for the minister to make the least noise or disturbance. That much at least can be said for the early San Franciscans. On the other hand, God gave them free will, and they didn't give up their love of hard drink or gambling either. They heard, but chose other gods."

"Didn't know there had been any Protestant clergy in these parts until lately," someone said.

Daniel Wainwright replied, "In '47, we had a Sabbath school organized through the Oregon Methodists with J. H. Merrill as superintendent, and we met Sunday forenoons at the alcalde's office. We've had Walter Colton in Monterey as naval chaplain and now alcalde, and there's Adna A. Hecox preaching at Santa Cruz."

Someone added, "Captain Thomas, the Welsh gentleman has been reading prayers every Sunday in the schoolhouse, and Mrs. Gillespie has organized a Sabbath school, as well."

"We can only trust that God will send us more preachers and devout laymen as they are needed," Benjamin said.

At length, Seth Thompson led them in singing around the camp fire, reminding Benjamin of their covered-wagon days, especially "the hymns to sleep by."

Later, when he lay down on his bedroll and looked up at the stars in the night sky, Benjamin thought how his wife, Elizabeth, and their daughter Rena would have enjoyed the meeting. Perhaps the angels in glory had told them about it, for Scripture said the angels rejoiced at the salvation of even one sinner.

On Sunday, the weather remained fair and even more people came to the camp meeting. "We heard about the wonderful prayin' and singin' and preachin' yesterday," they said. When the benches were filled, they sat on their quilts at the edges of the arbor, moving with the shade as the meeting proceeded.

When the gathering ended that evening and people started home, Seth Thompson and William Palmer assured Benjamin that a good many more souls had been dedicated or rededicated to God.

"Not Joshua?" Benjamin asked, already half resigned to the answer he feared he would receive.

Seth shook his head. "Not Joshua. I am sorry to say, not Joshua."

10

E ager as she was to set out for Oak Hill to see her father, Rose bade Aunt Jessica, Benjamin Talbot, and Betsy a reluctant farewell.

She and Abby rode out on horseback from the ranch on the chestnut mares alongside five mule-drawn covered wagons loaded with supplies that had arrived on the *Californian*. Nearby, in a wagon that Daniel drove, Maddy happily held little Daniel on her lap, and Joshua drove another wagon with good humor. "I am as anxious as anyone to see the goldfields," he'd said.

They had hired five men, all of them going to the diggings. Three drove the remaining wagons, one scouted ahead on horseback, and the last herded extra horses as well as cattle and burros they would sell at Sutter's Fort and Oak Hill. The trip to Sutter's Fort would take five days, and it would take another four to ride on to Oak Hill.

"I can scarcely wait to see Father," Rose said as she rode along on Chessy. "It has been nearly two years."

"I hope he received your letter," Abby replied, "though it never hurts to surprise any man."

Rose laughed. "Are you already such an expert on men?"

Abby dimpled. "Daniel thinks so."

As their horses trotted alongside the wagons, Rose thought again how much she and Abby had shared laughter together over the past few days. They had shared the solemn moments at the brush arbor meeting, but even that had had its humorous moments like Benjamin Talbot's tale of the great battle of San Francisco. Smiling, she turned and noticed Joshua's interest. Well, he could think what he liked.

He called out, "You two are quite a picture!"

"*Riding Out to the Diggings,* I'd entitle it," Rose returned. The memory of wearing this blue riding habit the day they had sailed in his skiff came to mind, but she forced it away, for she should never have allowed him to kiss her like that. She turned to Abby. "You'll have to sketch this outing for posterity."

Abby smiled. "I shall. Nothing is safe from my pencils."

"Nor from my journal," Rose returned. She looked about. "I must remember this atmosphere . . . the scent of dried grasses filling the air . . . the warm autumn breeze."

"Did you record all of your voyage?" Abby asked.

"Regretfully not all of it. But I do try to write about everything of importance. Perhaps someday others will want to know what it was like to sail around the Horn . . . or how this countryside looks now . . . or about this gold rush. God willing, I should like to make my voice heard."

Abby turned pensive, and Rose thought she must capture in words, too, how beautiful her friend looked riding alongside the wagons in her fawn-colored riding habit and bonnet.

Abby said, "It is so good to be with you again, Rose. With you, I can speak seriously about my painting or your writing, or feel utterly frivolous—like a girl again."

"And I feel the same about you," Rose replied.

Abby smiled. "Daniel has remarked upon how different I

seem when I'm with you."

"Different?"

Abby glanced back at Daniel in the nearby covered wagon, and gave a laugh. "He says he has never seen me so giddy."

"Giddy! Is that what they think? Well, then let's give them some real giddiness to talk about!" Their eyes danced with mischief, and they laughed again, then, looking at their fellow travelers' confusion, burst into wild laughter.

Abby gasped for breath. "They think we are daft. And Daniel always proclaiming 'a merry heart doeth good like medicine'!"

Finally the others began to smile at them, then to be caught up in the merriment. Daniel called out, "You two are going to scare off the desperadoes, as Aunt Jessica calls them. We sound like a traveling asylum."

Even the most taciturn driver could not conceal his smile now. And Maddy, chortling with little Daniel at the front of their wagon, finally sobered enough to call out, "That Rose do take up laughing at the strangest times. I sho' glad she ain't the only one! Must be something they learned at that New York school fo' young ladies."

"Scarcely!" Rose returned, then asked Abby, "Can you imagine what Miss Sheffield might say if she saw us now?"

They laughed all the harder.

Later, when Abby went to nurse her little Daniel in the wagon, Rose rode on alone. At length, she felt Joshua watching her and she turned and smiled blithely at him.

His expression was so peculiar she thought he must expect her to start laughing again. Buoyant in spirit, she had to restrain herself.

At midday they stopped for their nooning. They had brought chicken stew, biscuits, and apple pie from the hacienda, and they built a camp fire to reheat the stew and to make coffee. Rose busied herself with setting out food and utensils, feeling Joshua's eyes on her again. When they sat down on the ground with their "eating pans," which they held by wooden handles, he settled as far from her as possible. His firmly set jaw reminded her of how stubborn he had looked at the brush arbor meeting over the weekend.

An hour later they began their afternoon ride. When they stopped to make camp for the evening, they were agreeably tired, but not exhausted. After supper they sat around the camp fire, and Abby and Daniel shared tales from their covered wagon trek across the country which made this nine-day trip to Sutter's Fort and Oak Hill sound like a Sunday outing.

The stars came out, and Daniel led the evening's singing. His low voice filled with amusement at the nonsensical words of "Oh, Susannah!" and "On Top of Old Smoky," then with faith when he led them in "Beautiful Savior."

Rose heartily wished it were Joshua singing out with such love; she pressed the thought aside and sang resolutely to the Lord,

"Fairest Lord Jesus, Ruler of all nature,
O Thou of God and man the son,
Thee will I cherish, Thee will I honor,
Thou, my soul's glory, joy, and crown."

She remembered Lars leading the evenings' songs on the *Californian* and wondered where he was now. The last they'd heard, Captain Svenson was still seeking more sailors to replace those who had jumped ship. No doubt Lars was helping him.

When it came time to sleep, the men decided their hours for night guard duty. Troublemakers were known to be about—army deserters, runaway sailors, and others running from the law in the states, not to mention the riffraff among the gold seekers who had come from other countries. Moreover, the local Indians had never learned the concept of personal property and were known for their prowess at stealing everything from food and clothing to horses—and occasionally women.

Rose crept into her bedroll under the stars. Nearby, Maddy slept in a tent in hopes of avoiding too much night air. To Rose's surprise, Joshua lay his bedroll near hers, albeit at a respectable distance.

He explained, "We do not know these drivers as well as we might, and Daniel must care for his own family."

Joshua, like the hired drivers, carried a pistol and a rifle, which he now placed beside his bedroll.

Discomfitted, it was an instant before Rose could speak. "Thank you, Joshua, but the Lord will take care of Maddy and me. You must not feel responsible."

He gave her a long look in the firelight. "I shall sleep here nonetheless." He got into his bedroll and, saying nothing else, turned away.

Coyotes yowled in the distance as she stared up at the scatterings of stars. *Lord, don't allow me to fall in love with Joshua again*, she prayed. *I ask for his salvation, that is all. His salvation is sufficient.*

She watched a falling star trail through the night sky and then, with a sense of quiet assurance, closed her eyes and quickly fell asleep.

The days took on a pattern. In the morning the camp fire was lit by Joshua, who had the last night watch. Rose, Abby, and Maddy made their hasty toilettes behind a canvas screen and started breakfast—eggs, bacon, and flapjacks. The men tended the livestock and readied the wagons for the day's journey. More than anything else, Rose enjoyed helping to care for little Daniel. Holding him made her yearn for a child of her own.

The late September days remained warm and glorious as they rode through the golden hillsides. Only the food became tiresome. At first there was fresh beef at the noonings and beef stews for suppers, but soon they were down to salt pork. Still, they were glad to have it, and cooked it with onions, carrots, and potatoes, then served it with wild greens which protected against scurvy.

On the fifth mid-morning they approached Sutter's Fort, and Rose marveled at the whitewashed fortress with cannons protruding from its towers. Now the most famous place in California, it was surrounded by hundreds of wagons and tents—and thousands of people, mostly men, and among them, scores of half-naked Indians.

As they rode through the vast encampment, they saw Captain Johann Augustus Sutter himself riding toward them with two aides. "Welcome to New Helvetia!" he called out, pronouncing the words with a Germanic accent. "Wainwright, good to see you again . . . and ze supplies," he said, then assessed the rest of them.

Rose heard a man from a nearby wagon group remark, "They say the old humbug was never a captain and escaped from Switzerland."

Fraud or not, she found Captain Sutter rather charming as he blustered and bowed from his horse to her and Abby. She couldn't help remember, however, what Benjamin Talbot had said about Sutter's reception when he came upon them holding a divine service after they'd toiled down the Sierra Nevada Mountains. "On my land," Sutter had said, "we bow to no other's flag and to no god." He appeared to be in his mid-forties, his dark hair receding from a shiny pate. He wore a short curly beard, and his clothes, like his courtly European manner, were the most impressive around.

Garrulous, he talked with all of his might while the men directed the drivers about unloading the Sutter shipment. He even suggested that little Daniel be seen to by Maddy, whose eyes widened with disbelief at such effrontery.

Finally, still on horseback, he led Rose, Abby, Daniel, and Joshua through the encampment and into the primitive splendor of his whitewashed kingdom, where he pointed out the well, storehouses, his two-story house, and headquarters. The air reeked of animals, liquor, and unwashed humanity, but apparently that mattered little to him. His manner reminded Rose of that of several chargés-d'affaires in Washington City, except that this self-proclaimed ruler fortuitously owned a sixty-mile-long kingdom near the goldfields.

In his headquarters Sutter dispatched a storekeeper to deal with the Wainwright delivery, then turned to Daniel and Joshua. "If you and your good wives will accept my hospitality for the night, I have two rooms at your service."

Rose felt her cheeks turn pinker. Wives!

Joshua's color had risen, too. "I fear that our introduction was unclear. This is Jonathan Wilmington's daughter. We are accompanying her to Oak Hill to be with him. We thank you for your hospitality, but I regret that we must move on."

Sutter said, "I beg your pardon, Miss Wilmington." His eyes swept over her with admiration. "I am certain you will not be unmarried for long. Men will be begging for your hand here, bags of gold in hand. And what do you say to that?"

"I am not particularly interested in gold."

Close to him now, she realized that he reeked of brandy.

"And what does interest you in a man?"

She replied with firmness, "His love for the Lord."

Sutter said, "I see you are like your father."

"Like my father?" Her father would never make such a reply! He was a good man, a man who attended church on most Sundays, but he was reticent about speaking up for the Lord. Perhaps Sutter was befuddled by his brandy.

An aide rushed to Sutter's side with an urgent matter, and he apologized profusely at having to depart. Immediately Joshua excused himself and started for the storehouse, where the shipment for the fort was being delivered.

Daniel said, "Let's ride back to Maddy."

Rose took closer notice of the encampment with its smoky cook fires. Most of the men looked as though they had not changed their rough shirts and trousers in weeks, and there was open drinking of liquor from bottles. Not far away a man angrily cursed at two Indians. Mules and burros brayed, oxen lowed, horses whinnied, all adding their droppings to the befouled panorama.

When they returned to their two wagons, Maddy was holding off a crowd of grizzled miners. She stood indignantly with little Daniel in her arms. "These men doan take no for an answer! They wants to buy the shovels, picks, and food from the wagons now. I told them these goods be ordered for Oak Hill. Then, top of it all, some of them tried to steal!"

A man guffawed. "Ain't but little chance o' that with her standin' guard!"

The miners laughed uproariously.

Daniel, still astride his horse, turned to the crowd. "You'll have to buy your supplies from Sutter. You're camped on his land, and he owns the store here. We're selling the goods on these remaining wagons up at the diggings."

The men grumbled, but backed off and slowly departed.

Daniel thanked Maddy as they all dismounted. "I didn't realize how rough some of these men are now. The kind of men coming in seems to be worsening."

The old housekeeper handed little Daniel to Abby with a sigh of relief. "I sho' was glad to see you all riding down here. I doan think I could of held them off much longer."

Daniel scowled. "We'll leave as soon as Joshua returns. In fact, let's drive on a way now. We can wait for him at the edge of the encampment."

They had already eaten supper when Joshua rode out from the white fortress, and Rose was careful not to look at him. Two hours of daylight remained, and they immediately started off. They moved faster, for he had sold not only supplies and the three wagons to Sutter, but most of the burros and cattle as well. Four of the hired drivers had been paid as promised and each was free to make his own way to the diggings; only one remained to drive the cattle and the burros behind them.

Once they had left Sutter's Fort and the surrounding encampment behind, the air became clearer and the golden foothills pristine. They encountered several covered wagons on the trail; more often they saw miners with burros to carry their belongings, and occasionally a miner with a horse to ride.

As they rode along in the twilight, Rose's thoughts turned again to her father and to their arrival at Oak Hill in four days. Perhaps he had not received her letter. Benjamin Talbot had assured her that Father would be pleased that she'd come, but she wished to be entirely certain.

Looking out at the fields she recalled the Bible verse about the lilies of the field, and that the Lord did not want her to be anxious about anything. She patted the mare's neck. Very well then, she would not be anxious. As for Joshua, he would leave after the supplies were sold, and he would never again cause her a moment's heartache.

The autumn wind was warm as the horses and wagons churned up the dusty trail that bordered a stream in the golden hillsides. The nights were far cooler, but Rose rejoiced to find the scenery becoming more magnificent in the four days since they had left Sutter's Fort. Above them stood foothills forested with oak, cedar, and pine, and occasionally there were glimpses of distant cloud-crowned mountain peaks.

Driving the wagon beside her, Daniel Wainwright pointed to a cleared hillside high above in the distance. "There's Oak Hill."

She had not expected such a majestic setting. "To think Father's there! I am so tempted to gallop up there and leave the rest of you in my dust!"

Joshua surveyed her, his square chin firmly set.

"Only tempted," she promised airily. "I am not going to ride ahead! And, please, no more lectures about Abby and me remaining alongside the wagons."

He allowed himself a wry grin. "I was unaware that we lectured you."

"Only warned . . . and warned again," Rose returned.

They had not encountered desperadoes, as Aunt Jessica called them, but kept constant watch. Moreover, Joshua had slept near her on his bedroll every night . . . more aloof then friendly. His continued nearness, however, had not helped her to forget their former relationship. She would forget him, she had reminded herself time and again for soon—very soon—she would no longer see him.

Riding on, she reminded herself, too, that the actual mining camp of Oak Flats—on this stream below Oak Hill—might not be so beautiful. To avoid more disappointment, she began to brace herself mentally for a raucous scene resembling the encampment around Sutter's

Fort. Yet as they wound through a ravine toward Oak Flats, forested hillsides still towered majestically, overshadowing the widely spaced miners' tents.

At length they rode a rutted trail through the small camp, the miners gawking at her and Abby. One shouted at Joshua, "What ye carryin' fer sale?"

Joshua's replied, "Sluice pans, shovels, pickaxes, frying pans, clothes, boots, foodstuffs, and burros. We'll set up shop this afternoon. If you've got a butcher among you, you might tell him. We have a couple of cattle to sell, too."

As they rode through Oak Flats, Rose turned her attention to the miners. They stood in the stream, swirling water and gravel in metal and wooden pans as well as other containers. One used a bed-warming pan and wore such a grim expression that she doubted anyone even dared to smile at the sight.

Joshua called to one of them, "Still finding gold?"

"Ain't good like at first. Be better come spring when the river's full. Wasn't nothin' but puddles this summer. But it's been rainin' up in the mountains since the first o' September so we at least got a stream again." Like most of the others, he stood to his knees in the water.

It would be a wonder if they didn't contract rheumatism, Rose thought. *How impossible men could be!*

Beyond Oak Flats, the stream made a wide bend and the land rose steeply. Blackberry vines tangled the underbrush near the trail where the two wagons, horses, and livestock ascended the slope to Oak Hill. At last they rode up into the clearing where three log cabins were clustered in the shade of trees. Behind them were log outbuildings and a corral that held burros and two horses. Cattle grazed in the pasture.

Someone shouted, and Rose saw her father run out from the largest cabin, his gray hair shining in the sunshine. She nudged Chessy with her heels and they galloped toward him, Rose knowing from his broad smile that he was as delighted to see her as she was to see him.

Within moments, she was in his arms.

"Oh, Rose, how I've missed you!" He embraced her mightily, then held her out at arm's length. "You look—" The sparkle in his brown eyes dimmed for an instant and words failed him, and she knew that she reminded him of her mother.

"You look so different!" she quickly put in. Instead of staid business attire, he wore a red flannel shirt, rough trousers tucked into knee-high boots, and an air of well-being. His hair had turned entirely gray, yet he appeared taller, his shoulders broader. "All you need is a beard, and you would look like a miner!"

He laughed. "I am a miner!"

She stood gazing at him with happy disbelief. "This life must agree with you. I can't remember you ever looking so healthy and full of . . . joy."

Moses came running from the main cabin. "Welcome, Miz Rose Anne!" he called delightedly. Despite his grizzled gray hair, he looked strong and energetic; he, too, wore a red shirt, rough trousers, and knee-high boots. Moses' grin widened to see Maddy arriving in the lead wagon, and he ran to it to help her down and envelop her in his embrace.

Rose told her father, "You don't seem surprised at our arrival. You must have received my letter."

"It arrived two days ago. Moses and I have been like two housewives at spring-cleaning ever since!"

"You cleaning the cabins?" Rose marveled.

He grinned boyishly. "Even me! What's more, I managed to shoot a deer yesterday. Moses and I have learned to cook. We shall be dining like royalty upon venison."

Amazed, Rose said, "I can't imagine you hunting or cooking! And you even found gold!"

Her father nodded, his brown eyes aglow. "As Providence would have it, we were in the right place before the swarms of gold seekers arrived. The Indians knew where it was. I had only to show them a sample, and they led Moses and me into the mountains and directly to it."

"I don't quite understand. Didn't they want it?"

"They have seen gold nuggets all of their lives, but acorns hold more value for them. Unfortunately now the miners are cutting down the oak trees." He drew a regretful sigh. "For the Indians' sakes, I sometimes wonder if it hadn't been better if we whites had never arrived."

Rose realized that the others were approaching and stepped back to include them. "Father, you know Abby and Daniel, and their baby."

They greeted each other heartily, and her father tickled little Daniel's chin to coax a gleeful chirrup from him.

Rose turned to Joshua. "Father, this is Josuha Talbot."

She puzzled at Joshua's strained expression as he shook hands with her father. Did Joshua suspect that her father might press him to marry her after their ardent courtship? If so, Joshua could forget his apprehensions; she did not intend to mention their courtship to her father, nor to anyone else.

After the men had herded the cattle out to the pasture, everyone inspected the acreage and three log cabins. The main cabin, overlooking the stream far below, boasted a kitchen, a small parlor-dining room, two bedrooms, and an upstairs loft. Rose's father said facetiously, "It's what one might call rustic, particularly the furniture." Everyone laughed. The homemade furniture was fashioned from uneven tree limbs, "finished" by having the bark removed.

Outside, vegetable and herb gardens grew near the

kitchen door. Nearby was a smaller cabin, which Moses had begun putting to rights for Maddy and himself. The third cabin, also small, had fallen into disrepair even before her father had purchased the place from settlers moving on.

The men unloaded the supplies her father had ordered, carrying barrels of flour, sugar, dried apples, peaches, and other foodstuffs into the main cabin, then hauling shovels, pickaxes, and other equipment to the log outbuildings.

At midday they sat down outside at a plank table and benches, their tin "eating pans" in front of them. The warm autumn air imparted a feeling of well-being, and there were venison steaks accompanied by provisions just brought in—onions, carrots, potatoes, and honey for the biscuits.

After grace, Joshua inquired of her father, "What is the best method for finding gold?"

While they ate, they discussed the pros and cons of panning in the streams or pickaxing for gold veins in the hills. Rose was surprised to hear that there were large nuggets being found in riverbeds and even occasionally under rocks.

Joshua said, fork in hand, "I would like to try my hand at it after we sell the remaining supplies. I can return to San Francisco in the second wagon. I'll only stay for a few days, a week or two at the most. This is probably the one opportunity of my lifetime to find gold."

Rose's stomach constricted, and she dared not look at Abby or the men. He planned to stay! Had that been his plan all of this time? Her hand trembled as she stabbed her fork into a bit of carrot on her tin eating pan.

"I'll give you half a day," Daniel said to Joshua. "That's all I needed to convince me that there are far better ways on this earth to make a living. With all due respect to you, Mr. Wilmington—"

Rose's father held up a hand. "I'm not in the least

offended. I'd never have had success without Moses and the Indians. I'm too old to stand knee deep in water all day or to climb through these hills."

Joshua asked, "How did you find it, sir, if I may ask?"

"Indians led us to it in the mountains."

"Do they know where more is?" Joshua asked.

Her father shrugged. "They say not."

Joshua looked out toward the foothills. "I can camp in the wagon."

Rose felt herself grow tense. She had expected—no, nearly hoped!—to see the end of him soon. She needed to avoid him for her own good! But now—now—if he stayed, she resolved to be no more than friends with him. She bit into her honey-spread biscuit without tasting it.

Her father was saying, "Nonsense. It's becoming quite cold at night now. You can use our third cabin if you don't mind cleaning it up a bit."

"Thank you, sir. I accept gladly," Joshua replied.

No! Rose thought.

She darted a glance at him. His broad shoulders and strong arms awakened bittersweet memories, and, as their eyes met, his curious gaze stirred her so deeply she could scarcely endure it.

After dinner he and Daniel returned down to Oak Flats to sell the remaining goods, cattle, and burros, and Abby took little Daniel inside for his nap.

Rose's father showed her the chickens and two milk cows, then they stopped at the corral by the horses. "Is there something I should know about you and Joshua Talbot? It's obvious that you are more than mere acquaintances."

"There is nothing, not anymore."

Jonathan Wilmington's gray brows raised thoughtfully. "He's a handsome man . . . well-educated . . . personable."

She inhaled deeply. "He is a fine man, Father, but he does not know the Lord."

"I see. And are you praying for him?"

Rose stared at him, surprised at his question. "Yes, for months. And the Talbots and Elisha Wainwright have prayed for him for years."

"Then I shall add my prayers, too. I'm sure Joshua wishes to remain here for reasons other than gold." He paused, then asked her, "Would you marry him if he were a believer?"

Despite her prayers and determination not to love him, she was suddenly face-to-face with the truth. "I don't know."

Her father's brown eyes looked steadily into hers. "That sounds like 'possibly' to me, Rose . . . perhaps even 'yes.' "

She bit her lip and looked away.

Jonathan Wilmington remarked, "I was not such an avid believer myself when I married your mother, but now—now—" He laughed heartily. "I see Him every-where. . . . He was always there, of course, but I had no true notion of it. My life has altered so in the past months, Rose, that it would strike one as impossible."

She stared at him. "How did it change?"

"It began with the naval chaplain in Monterey, who sent me to Benjamin Talbot. I told him I'd always attempted to be a good man. To my dismay, he explained that being good is not the same as being godly . . . that Christ—not good works—is the path to God."

"But you often attended church on Sundays in Georgetown. You must have heard that."

He nodded. "Yes, but I'd never truly consecrated my life to God without reservation, and I didn't in Monterey, either."

Rose asked, "What happened then?"

"A few of the miners here invited me to come to their Sunday worship by the stream. None of us sing very well, so on Saturday they came up and asked Moses if he would sing a solo the next morning. Well, Moses was reluctant. He had only sung in the black churches. They insisted that it didn't matter. Finally he agreed to sing, but for the Lord—not us."

"And then—"

"He sang a spiritual, that deep voice of his overflowing with love and faith . . . and suddenly I felt God right there . . . all around me, full of power and love. Before Moses sang 'Amen,' I'd consecrated the rest of my life to God."

Rose embraced her father with tears in her eyes. "I knew there was something different about you when we arrived . . . a sense of joy and well-being."

"Joy—yes, what joy! Now I need only know God's plan. At first Moses and I thought we were to return to Georgetown, because—I've neglected to tell you—we've discovered enough gold here to last a lifetime. Sufficient to cover my losses on the canal and other ventures. Oddly enough, money no longer seems of such great import." He had to laugh. "I never expected to utter those words . . . nor to find my security in God."

"Oh, Father, how wonderful!"

"It is indeed. In any case, when we learned that you and Maddy were arriving, we felt we were meant to remain here. Benjamin Talbot assures me that God will direct us in what we are to do."

"And I am beginning to understand why Maddy and I felt so compelled to leave Georgetown." Her mind returned to the brush arbor service, and she realized that this place also was ideally suited for an outdoor service. "There is a special reason for us to be here," she said. "I wonder what it might be."

Her father answered, "Benjamin Talbot assures me that God will let us know."

11

Two glorious days later, Abby, Daniel, and little Daniel departed for Rancho Verde. Rose waved until their wagon disappeared from sight, consoled by their promise to visit in the spring. It was a great consolation, as well as a reminder of their visit, that her father had bought Chessy for her to ride.

Joshua had cleaned out the spare cabin, and there seemed no alternative to their seeing each other, for Jonathan Wilmington invited him to take meals with them. Rose decided she simply must avoid being alone with him.

His first day out panning, Joshua discovered a three-ounce nugget and joined them for supper in buoyant spirits. She and her father laughed with him as he related how he found the nugget while sliding into the cold stream.

After supper Rose retreated to the kitchen, trembling. She had confined her interest to his story, to his gold-seeking exploits, nothing more.

On his second day out, he pickaxed out a chunk of gold large enough for a signet ring. At the supper table, Rose avoided his eyes, avoided looking at him entirely.

After he had panned for several days in Oak Flats, he rode in on his bay stallion early one afternoon when Rose was out by the corral. At his approach, she turned to hurry away.

"Rose!" He dismounted quickly and caught her arm. "I only wish to speak to you."

She swallowed at the distress in her throat. "You are hurting my arm, Joshua."

"I'm sorry," he said, unhanding her. "I wanted to speak to you alone."

She backed away a step. "Yes, Joshua?"

He said huskily, "What I want, Rose . . . is for us to try again."

Her hands trembled, and he must have noticed for he captured them in his.

"Rose, I am a stubborn, hard fool, but I can't look at you without wanting to change matters between us. I remember the happiness we had sailing from Georgetown, then in Boston, and sailing around the Horn. Never in my entire life was I so happy . . . until I decided to be so forthright. I've been miserable ever since. I can't help myself!"

"No. . . ." She could barely speak, then the strength came. "You were right in what you decided on the ship. If you had not so courageously spoken then, I would have had to. I am at fault for allowing matters to have gone so far!"

"I cannot believe that your faith means so much to you," he said, his tone full of anger.

"I love the Lord more than anything else in this life."

"Do you love me?"

To her amazement she said, "Yes, I love you, Joshua, but I love the Lord more."

He stared at her for an instant, his brown eyes suddenly glinting in a way that made her want to weep. Turning away to his stallion, he vaulted up into the saddle. "Then love your God. And don't expect me for supper. Don't expect me for anything, ever again."

"Joshua, please don't be so angry—"

"What do you expect?" he flung at her. "You say that you love me, but you love an imaginary god more!" He dug his heels into the horse and rode off, his shoulders stiff with hurt and resentment.

She stared after him and began to sob, hard sobs that shook her body so that she had to catch hold of a corral post for support.

At supper, her father and Maddy looked at her eyes and said nothing about Joshua's absence. She appreciated their silence, for his empty place at the table was heartbreaking enough.

On Sunday morning, five miners arrived for a worship service in the parlor. Rose found the men quiet of manner, self-possessed, and devout. They joined heartily in the singing, and during the Scripture readings and short sermon, they listened with fixed attention and a glow of faith.

I thank Thee, Lord, Rose prayed, *I thank Thee for allowing me to see the reverence on their faces, to see spiritual truth shining in them!* These miners worshiped and loved the Lord as much, if not more, than many men in fine attire in the churches of Georgetown. Not that she had doubted it, but it was reassuring to witness the sight with her own eyes.

The next morning there was a new gold find down in Oak Flats—pockets of nuggets trapped in the riverbed. Within days, miners swarmed in from other diggings. The hordes of newcomers chopped down the trees for tent poles and cook fires until most of the remaining oak trees were gone. Oak Flats began to be called "The Flats." Word came up that a gambling tent had arrived, replete with a gambler and two women who themselves dealt cards at the tables. At night there were fights and drunkenness, even a shooting.

Rose and her father began to pray every morning for the boisterous mining camp. As they read the Bible together in their rustic parlor-dining room, they tried to discern God's will. One morning, reading in the Gospel of Matthew, the answer to their prayers seemed near. Jonathan Wilmington read the verse again. "Ye are the light of the world. A city that is set on an hill cannot be hid. Neither do men light a candle, and put it under a bushel, but on a candlestick; and it giveth light unto all that are in the house. . . ."

The phrase seemed illuminated before them, shimmering like gold. "Giveth light unto all that are in the house."

Rose mused aloud, "A house could mean more than this cabin." Suddenly it came to her. "A church is a house of God for an entire community!"

"Yes!" her father replied with excitement. "A church for the whole of Oak Flats and Oak Hill . . . and elsewhere!"

They stared at each other in amazement, then Jonathan Wilmington said, "I know in my spirit that is our answer. We must invite the entire community to our Sunday morning worship meetings. We're to begin a church for the local diggings. That is God's will for us."

"Yes," she said, "I feel certain myself."

"But how do we begin?" her father asked.

"We could meet outdoors as they did at the brush arbor camp meeting at Rancho Verde, though I don't know what we could do when the winter rains begin. Last Sunday we scarcely had room for five visiting miners in the parlor."

She paused, eyeing their chinked log parlor-dining room. "Even if we removed this furniture and made simple benches, there would be space for only a few worshipers."

"We can build a log church next to the spare cabin so it will overlook the river," her father responded. "There's the forest nearby for wood and slate along the river for floors."

"But what shall we do for a pastor?" Rose asked.

"There are men who have attended divinity school among the miners."

"What a curious situation," Rose remarked.

"Curious, perhaps," her father agreed, "but God can make use of that, too, just as I believe He can use an old nominal Christian like me who has finally seen the light of glory."

A knock sounded at the door, and they stared at each other again before Rose stood.

She hurried to the door and, opening it, she could not believe her eyes. "Lars Johnson!" It seemed in that moment he was another part of their answer.

"Yes, it is I," he replied, blinking at her great astonishment. "Am I so much of a surprise?"

"I don't know— You are the last person I expected to see at our door. I—I think you may be part of an answer to prayer."

"I hope so," he said as joy filled his eyes.

"As do I!"

"I did not expect to be here," he said, "but most of our sailors jumped ship. Caleb Svenson sees no chance of sailing until after Christmas. He hopes for a crew when the rains drive the men from the hills."

"Benjamin Talbot told us of your troubles with the sailors, but it just didn't occur to us that you might visit."

Lars shifted his feet uncertainly on the doorstep, looking rather out of place in his blue uniform. "Daniel Talbot told me how to come here. He felt led—"

"He felt led?" Rose echoed.

"Yes, that is what he said."

She was still so astonished that it was a moment before

she invited him in. "Come meet my father. We have just been praying." She scarcely knew how to explain what had happened and said instead, "Come into our elegant parlor."

She laughed, half because of what was happening to them and half because the parlor's most elegant features were the wooden floor and the rustic bent-branch furniture. She and Maddy had made new canvas cushions stuffed with dried grasses for what they jestingly called their "settee" and "parlor chairs." In the midst of it all, it occurred to Rose that if they could learn to make such furniture, they could surely learn to build a church as well.

Rose's father stood to shake hands as she made the introduction. "We were just praying to know God's will," he said.

Lars sat down slowly with them. "That is what Caleb and Inger Svenson did . . . prayed to know God's will, since the ship is still in the harbor. The Lord made it clear to them what to do. Now they are using their unexpected time to help build a church in San Francisco."

"To begin a church there!" Rose echoed. She looked at her father, whose brown eyes were surely as wide as hers.

Jonathan Wilmington said, "That is precisely what we have discerned His will is for us! You are our confirmation. I wonder if other churches are being begun now in California as well—"

"It gives one something to think about," Lars replied, amazed now himself.

"It surely does!" Rose said.

Lars offered, "I could help you until Christmas, but only if you wish to have my assistance."

"Of course," Rose's father said. "You are welcome to stay in our spare cabin. Joshua has moved out. It is next to . . . next to the church site."

"Thank you very much, but—" He looked at Rose hopefully.

"Of course, Lars," she agreed, "we would be pleased to have you stay here with us."

"Then I will," Lars said, "I will help you with the church."

Jonathan Wilmington spoke thoughtfully. "I am beginning to understand why a church should be built here. When the gold dust is gone in The Flats, the miners will realize the gold has been washed down from the mountains. This is the likeliest site for a town when they take their search higher. Someday we may have a town, even a school. With the direction matters are taking in the diggings, we will surely need godly influences."

That morning they began to clear away the brush. The next day was Sunday, and they would be able to share their leading and to show the site to the worshipers. It wasn't until they sat down to eat at midday that Lars asked Rose, "Do you know who is running the gambling tent down in The Flats?"

"No. Is there a reason why I should?"

He nodded unhappily. "Nichola Wainwright and the baron."

"Nichola and the baron!" It was a moment before she could take in the idea of it. "How ever did that come about?"

Lars sat back in his chair. "Nichola waited for him in Monterey. The Talbots think she came early to fool the baron's wife. Whether he got enough of the money, no one knows, but he had enough for his passage on the next clipper ship . . . on which gambling was allowed."

Rose's father said, "And, of course, he won."

Lars nodded. "Yes. From the captain and several passengers. Not enough money to live like rich Californios, but enough to buy a gambling tent and make a beginning."

Rose heaved a sigh of regret. "So many of the miners have no other interests . . . and time on their hands at night. The gold rush appears perfect for Nichola and the baron. But why . . . why did they choose The Flats?"

"There are already gambling tents at Coloma and some of the other diggings." Lars said, then eyed her hesitantly. "I think, too, because Nichola knows Joshua was here."

"She wanted to be near Joshua?" Rose inquired.

Lars shrugged. "Perhaps she hopes to fall back on him if matters do not go well. I think she is a woman who—how do you say it?—hedges her bets."

Rose's mind flashed back to the dinner party in Boston and Nichola pairing herself with Joshua to deceive the baroness. "She has used Joshua before when she had difficulties."

"Yes," Lars said. "And maybe she has them again. The baron brought along a beautiful young woman, Gilda, from his ship, and Nichola does not look well by comparison. The miners say she is furious."

"I can imagine!" Rose replied. Yet instead of being pleased at Nichola's trouble, something in Rose's spirit went out in sympathy. Nichola's husband had been killed . . . her unborn baby lost shortly thereafter. And now, now to be compared to a young woman—"She may need help. I think I should invite her to our worship service tomorrow."

Her father said, "You can't go down to The Flats alone, Rose. If you feel led to see her, let Lars go with you."

Lars replied, "Yes, that is best."

"I suppose it is," Rose agreed.

Later, when she and Lars rode down to The Flats, she was appalled to see the place. Despite its beautiful mountain setting, the mining camp was becoming as befouled as the encampment around Sutter's Fort. Not only had most of the trees been chopped down, but the place looked as unkempt as the unshaved, unwashed miners who gaped at her.

She dismounted in trepidation in front of the grimy white gambling tent. It was still early afternoon and a few miners were already making their way in. "I think it's better if you wait here for me," she told Lars.

The tent flap was open, and she could see in partially. A few men gambled at tables, and, at the far end, a bartender poured drinks. Rose sent up a prayer as she walked in.

What a ridiculous notion it was to come, she thought as the miners turned to stare at her. She was tempted to flee, but her feet felt rooted to the dirt floor. Everyone inside the tent stared at her now . . . the miners . . . the bartender . . . the young raven-haired beauty in a deeply cut jade-green dress . . . and the baron.

"What may we do for you, Miss Wilmington?" the baron asked with a trace of hostile amusement.

"I—I would like to speak to Nichola."

"Escort her to the lady's boudoir," the baron told the bartender.

Rose thanked him and followed the bartender, certain she had not aroused so much curiosity in her entire life. She was led out through the back of the gambling tent to one of three smaller tents.

"Nichola?" the bartender called out. "You got company."

"Who?" Nichola asked from within her tent.

"A Miss Wilmington."

Rose said through the grimy canvas, "It's me, Rose."

Nichola pulled aside the canvas flap. "What do you want?" Her blonde hair hung wildly about the shoulders of a stained purple robe, and her eyes were red as though she lacked sleep.

The bartender hurried away, and Rose stood there alone.

"I—I wished to speak with you," she said. "Perhaps we could . . . go for a walk somewhere."

"I never walk in this camp," Nichola said. "Come inside."

Rose stepped into the small tent, appalled at the disorder, wondering what had become of the woman's maid. There was no place to sit, only a makeshift bed from which Nichola had apparently just risen.

"What is it?" Nichola asked.

Rose had not planned what to say, and her words surprised her. "I merely wished to tell you that if you ever needed help, Nichola, I should be pleased if you would ask me. You know we live up at Oak Hill—"

"Everyone knows you live on Oak Hill!"

"Well . . . yes—"

"I do not require your assistance!" Nichola said vehemently. "I have always managed by myself."

"We never know when we will need help."

Nichola glared at her. "Did Joshua send you?"

"No, of course not!" Shaken by the mention of his name, she rattled on, "We are starting a church for the community, and I wished to invite you—"

"Out!" Nichola snapped, furious. "Get out of here and stay away from me with your church and your God!"

Rose backed out of the tent. "I did not mean to annoy you, Nichola, only to let you know—"

"Out!" Nichola slapped the tent flap shut.

Rose faltered. How terribly she had mishandled this! *Forgive me for not awaiting Thy leading, Lord,* she prayed with remorse. *Please forgive me!*

Looking about, she saw that a path had been worn behind the gambling tent. At least she would not have to walk through the tent again. She rushed around and out to the front where Lars still stood.

One look at her face and he untied the reins from the hitching post, and handed Rose up onto Chessy while the nearby miners stared at her.

They rode away from the gambling tent and past the saloon tent, then alongside the stream where hundreds of miners now panned for gold. Joshua, she noticed, was not to be seen among them.

When they started up the hill, Rose took a deep breath. "I mishandled it badly, Lars."

"Perhaps not," he replied. "We do not always know."

"And I must give thanks even in this!" she said, and forced herself to do so at once.

Sunday dawned so warm and beautiful that Rose could scarcely believe it was nearly the end of October. The six miners who came up to worship happily carried the plank benches to the site where the new church would be built. Excited at the plan, they decided what days and hours they might log the trees for it.

It had rained daily in the Sierras, even snowed on the peaks, and the stream below had widened, adding the sound of rushing water to the worship service. They sat outside in the pleasant sunshine, Rose between her father and Lars. One of the miners, Adam Townsend, had attended seminary and led the service: prayers, reading selections from the Scriptures, and a brief, pertinent sermon.

Together they said The Lord's Prayer and sang "Old Hundredth," followed by Maddy and Moses singing a spiritual. Rose thought she had never heard more fervent prayer or music, nor had she ever been in a more beautiful church than here in the sunshine, where the breeze softly rustled the trees.

By the next Sunday, the foundation stones had been laid

for the church building, and the walls were rising. By the second Sunday in November, only the shingled roof was lacking, and that was finished the next week—just in time, for the wind blew up a gale from the north. Cloud upon cloud rolled into the sky until the whole dome of heaven was filled with darkness, and it looked as though the earth lay in eclipse. Thunder rolled and reverberated. Rain fell in torrents for two days and cascaded from every roof and cliff.

When the rain finally ceased, Rose went outside. The stream below had grown into a thunderous river. The next day word came up that it had flooded the miner's claims. Before long, the sharp drop in temperature brought on pneumonia and rheumatism, causing most of the men to flee to Sutter's Fort or even to San Francisco. Looking down toward The Flats between storms, it occurred to Rose that the river, rushing now where the saloon and gambling tent had stood, cleansed the earth wherever it ran. Only a few miners remained on high ground to build cabins for the winter. *Where was Joshua now?* she wondered.

During their devotions the next morning, a knock sounded at the cabin door. Rose's father answered it. When she heard Joshua's deep voice, Rose's heart beat so loudly that, between it and the pounding rain, his voice was nearly drowned out.

"Come in, Joshua, come in!" her father said.

Joshua asked, "Do you mind if I stay in the spare cabin again? I started a cabin below, but it's flooded out."

Her father replied, "Come in for coffee before you get sick. We have Lars in the spare cabin, but I'm certain he won't mind sharing it. Hang your poncho on a peg."

Rose sat up stiffly at the table.

Joshua entered the room, and she was appalled. His

auburn hair was long and matted, and he had grown a beard. His clothes were so filthy that he looked no different than the other miners. "Good morning, Rose," he said with a trace of embarrassment.

"Good morning, Joshua."

He nodded at Lars.

Her father said, "You must know each other from the ship."

Lars strode across the room to shake hands with Joshua. "Yes. It is good to see you again, Mr. Talbot. I would be pleased to share the cabin with you."

Joshua shook his hand. "That's kind of you, Johnson."

"Lars, if you please."

Joshua nodded, discomfitted.

Still startled at his appearance, Rose finally said, "We hope you will be here for Thanksgiving dinner next week. There will be no turkey, but we are hoping for venison."

"Thank you." His brown eyes moved to her father. "Hopefully I can provide the venison."

Rose thought his polite manner was a far call from his last words to her: "Don't expect me for anything, ever again!"

Her father said to Joshua, "If you do the hunting, we'll have more time to complete the church."

"The church?" Joshua inquired.

"Yes, we are building one just across the way."

"I thought I saw a new building through the rain." He looked at her father curiously. "I heard someone was building a church . . . but you?"

Her father smiled broadly. "Not just me. Rose, Lars, Maddy, Moses, and a number of the miners. It is for the entire community. You are welcome to attend and to help us build it, too, if you like."

Joshua looked at Rose, and she inclined her head as

though to say, yes, she was part of the church-building effort.

Maddy brought in hot coffee and Joshua accepted it gratefully, although whether he was more grateful for the coffee or for the interruption was difficult to say.

Rose asked, "Are you finding much gold?"

"Not enough."

She found herself pressing on. "You were going to search for gold for only a few days, a week or two at the most."

"Matters change," Joshua replied with a defensive tone.

How many men had changed their minds? she wondered. How many men would never in their lives stop seeking gold? One heard of men who traveled from one part of the country to another, even to other lands, in search of it.

The rains continued, and Joshua joined them for meals again, Rose avoiding his gaze when his eyes sought hers. In return for his room and board he insisted upon caring for the livestock and repairing the outbuildings, including the stalls where his horse was now kept again. Rose helped her father, Lars, and Moses chink the log walls of the church building, staying as far from Joshua as possible.

The rain finally stopped the day before Thanksgiving, and the earth flashed with sunlit splendor. Joshua left to hunt, bringing back a young buck in the morning, then disappearing to search the hills above for gold the rain might have washed down.

Rose and Lars hunted in the forest for mushrooms and wild onions. As they knelt on the ground, filling the basket, Lars looked at her, his blue eyes serious. "Rose—"

His ardent expression dumbfounded her. "Yes?"

"I am actually pleased that the sailors jumped ship. Otherwise I would not have had this opportunity to be with you."

"And to help build the church," she hastened to add.

He frowned slightly. "Yes."

She had only imagined his wanting to say something else, she decided with relief. He wanted only her friendship.

On Thanksgiving Adam Townsend and two other miners came to worship with Rose, her father, Lars, Maddy, and Moses. Sitting in the unfinished church, Rose saw Joshua step in tentatively. He had shaved his beard, cut his hair, and dressed in his fawn frock coat and trousers for the occasion.

"May I sit beside you?" he asked, ignoring Lars who sat on her other side.

"Yes, of course."

He settled on the bench beside her, joining in quietly as they sang out, "Come, ye thankful people, come . . . raise the song of harvest home. . . . "

At least he has remembered the words, she thought and prayed for him again.

During the sermon, Adam reminded them, "In his first proclamation of Thanksgiving, George Washington gave thanks to our great Lord, the Ruler of all nations. Ever since that time, we have remembered the first Thanksgiving and how it was celebrated by the Pilgrims, who made their *Mayflower* voyage for the glory of God and the advancement of the Christian faith.

"They came to this land, in part, so they could read the Bible, for it was against the law to even own a Bible in England in that day," Adam explained. "When they bought smuggled Bibles, they were ousted from the Church of England.

"They formed a secret underground church, but their worship was discovered and they were arrested. When they were released, they fled to Holland. They found it a free but worldly country, which they feared would corrupt their children. Finally, they were convinced that they must cross the ocean and build a new community in which godly people had the right to frame their own government and to shape a culture on scriptural principles. May Thanksgiving ever be remembered in that way."

"Amen," Rose pronounced with the rest of them

They had invited the miners for dinner, and Rose and Maddy set out venison, corn bread stuffing with onions and mushrooms, potatoes with gravy, biscuits, and apple pie for dessert. It differed from their Thanksgivings in Georgetown, Rose thought, but this was where God wanted her now. Her spirits plummeted after dinner, however, for while the worshipers visited with each other, Joshua departed to search for gold.

The rains began again, occasionally turning to snow on the forested hill across the river. Whenever the sky cleared, Joshua would disappear, finding his meals elsewhere, if he ate at all. She worried about him. Whenever it rained and he joined them, he had little to say. If the subject of gold was broached, a feverishness filled his brown eyes. Gold had become an obsession, a mania, the ruling passion of his life.

Willard had lusted for women and drink, others for gambling . . . and Joshua for gold. It was a sickness born of temptation. The only cure Rose knew was for him to turn to God. She prayed for him again and again. Some days when she saw him, she scarcely recognized the man he had been, and other days she saw past his gold-crazed demeanor, remembering how he had looked and spoken when he had cared for her more than gold.

The weather cleared two days before Christmas, and Rose and Lars wandered through the wet forest to find a pine tree that wasn't too full for the cabin's small parlor-dining room.

In the cabin, they decorated the tree with pinecones and golden grasses fashioned into circles and stars. They hung the rooms with pine swags and placed a wreath with pinecones on the front door. Decorated, the rustic cabin was transformed into a charming Christmas scene.

Joshua was nowhere to be seen, not even on Christmas Day. After Christmas dinner Rose and Lars wandered along the river, both of them searching the hillsides.

Lars said, "I must return to San Francisco, to the *Californian* tomorrow."

"I shall miss you," she replied with sadness.

Lars reached shyly for her hand. "How much, Rose?"

"Very much," she returned with a warm smile.

"Rose, don't you know? Can't you guess that it is not only building the church that has kept me here . . . that I would give up the sea and stay if you wanted me to?"

She removed her hand from his.

"I care for you so much," he said, his blue eyes looking hopefully into hers. "It began the night Nichola had me escort you to the Wainwright dinner in Boston."

"No, Lars, please don't tell me!"

"I must, Rose. I must." His Adam's apple bobbed and he continued, "I saw right away that you loved him, yet I couldn't help myself—"

"Oh, Lars! I hope I didn't give you false hope."

"No, never. My only hope is that you will realize how little chance for happiness there is for you and him. It is no good when a man and a woman do not share the same faith. We share that faith, Rose. We love the Lord and would work all of our lives to serve Him. Perhaps you would come to love me."

"Lars, please!" she protested, tears of regret welling in her eyes. "I—I would like to keep our friendship."

His eyes closed and, after a moment, he opened them and managed a small smile. "Friends, then, Rose. I knew from the beginning I stood so little chance. Only don't forget me if you change your mind."

A quiet sob shook her. *Oh, Lord,* Rose prayed, *am I making a mistake? What am I supposed to do about Joshua?*

It rained the day after Christmas, as though the sky wept at Lars's departure.

Joshua, however, returned.

At dinner he looked at the Christmas tree with its pine-cones and golden grasses fashioned into circles and stars. "Unfortunate they're not real gold," he said about the grass ornaments.

"Gold is not so terribly important, Joshua," Rose replied at his absurd comment.

"It is for someone who has always had success handed to him on a platter," he said "Finding a great deal of gold is extremely important to me."

"Joshua!" Pushing away from the table, she hurried to her room, her chair clattering on the floor behind her.

The next morning they found his note as well as a gold nugget on the table.

> Dear Rose and Mr. Wilmington,
>
> I am returning to work in San Francisco. I realize that I've become obsessed with gold. Please accept my heartfelt gratitude and this nugget for your hospitality.
>
> Sincerely,
>
> Joshua Talbot

Rose's heart sank. Now she had driven away both Lars and Joshua.

12

March was arriving like a lamb, Rose thought as she stood in the warm sunshine in front of the cabin. Months of rain had blanketed the foothills with green grasses, and melting snow in the mountains kept the river high. On the opposite bank of the river, the forested slope of oak, cedar, and pine shimmered green in the morning light. Soon the miners would return in force to the diggings in The Flats—and, she hoped, to the log church. Despite the unremitting ache for Joshua, her heart filled with joy at the surrounding beauty.

Later that morning a miner returning from San Francisco delivered a letter from Abby, and Rose sat down on the front step to read it.

February 21, 1849
Dearest Rose,
We were so pleased to learn that all is well with you and that your church is nearly complete. Daniel has found window glass for it, and we would be honored to offer it as a donation. We will send it up with the rest of your supplies before Easter. You will surely have it in time for your

church dedication service on the sixth of May. We hope to be there, too! I can't believe that you helped to chink the logs and lay the slate floor!

As you know, Joshua has been in San Francisco since the first of the year, working at the chandlery and trying to sort out the shipping difficulties. He set up a cot in the warehouse and toiled night and day as though to atone for his absence while at the diggings. However, he now informs us that he, too, will "jump ship" to return to the diggings as soon as the rains cease. Uphold him in prayer.

He is coming back! Rose thought, her emotions roiling. She took a long, calming breath before reading on.

We also keep Nichola Wainwright in prayer. She and the baron established a gambling house in the city with money they won in Oak Flats. It was successful beyond belief, but last week it burned down in a terrible fire. It is thought the fire was started by a drunken miner. Nichola and the baron survived, and we pray they will soon see the true light!

The lawless coming into the city now are filling it with violence, despite all of Seth Thompson's and William Palmer's strong sermons. The more heartwarming news is that a growing number of miners are coming or returning to Christ.

Rose prayed that Nichola might learn from the disaster. She read on, hoping for more news about Joshua. Everyone in the family was well. The *Californian* had finally sailed in January. Thanks to the rains, Caleb and Lars had been able to gather a sufficient number of seamen to sail for Boston. Rose reread the letter, thinking perhaps she'd missed something, but there were no other references to Joshua.

Days later, word came up to Oak Hill that miners were arriving at The Flats. Toward the end of March, when the river had receded, the diggings were flooded anew with unwashed, unshaven, undisciplined humanity. The newcomers called themselves the Forty-Niners, and if last year's crowd had seemed roisterous, they had been mild by comparison. Almost immediately there was a stabbing and a shooting; at some of the other diggings, the miners had taken lawlessness in hand by hanging and flogging criminals, which held down crime for a while. Word came up, too, that Nichola, the baron, and Gilda had returned, this time with a far larger gambling tent. And then word came up that Joshua had also returned.

Rose half yearned to see him, to see if he had changed. Perhaps she would ride down alone to the "store" at The Flats. How could anyone fault her for going there for provisions? She would wait until tomorrow morning when her father and Moses rode off into the distant mountains with their Indian friends, who spoke of a new gold area washed out by the rains.

The next day she waited until her father and Moses had left. When Maddy went out to pull weeds in the vegetable garden, Rose hurried out to the corral. She was in the midst of saddling Chessy when Maddy's voice stopped her. "Jest where you think you going, Miz Rose Anne?"

"Why—" She faltered at the knowing look in the old housekeeper's dark eyes.

"I knows why," Maddy said, "and if yo' daddy find out you was riding there alone, you'd have plenty of trouble. But if I be going to the store, too, well, there not be much he can say. I been wanting to see what's happening in The Flats myself."

"You want to go?" Rose asked in surprise.

Maddy lifted her chin, then nodded. "We could use flour and sugar. I got eggs and milk to trade so we doan have to pay too much. I hear they want six dollars for pickles! Half a month's wages for some folks in Georgetown!"

"Don't tell me this idea just occurred to you, Maddy."

"You think you can fool me after all these years, Miz Rose Anne? I knows yo' need for seeing Mistuh Joshua was coming on stronger and stronger. I knows what it be like to be young, and that's why you ain't going alone!"

Rose protested, "But you can't ride, Maddy!"

"We be walking down and that be the end of it," Maddy declared. "Let's hope yo' curiosity doan get the best of us!"

An hour later, they started down the riverside trail carrying a pail of milk and another of well-wrapped eggs. Maddy also toted a stout club for warding off snakes, skunks, bears, and other "varmits."

The grasses and bushes along the trail were greening again, and this morning there were no varmints. The entire scene was pristine until they rounded the bend in the river. Below them, hundreds upon hundreds of miners panned in the cold water and pickaxed along the slopes.

As she and Maddy drew nearer, Rose thought she had never seen such a mixed and motley crowd in her life. It was said that many of the men came with no more than the clothes on their backs and slept in them, using their boots for pillows—and they most assuredly looked it! Her father claimed that most of them existed on salt pork and flapjacks, and that they rarely found more than an ounce of gold a day.

"Doan look at them, Miz Rose Anne. Jest pretend we be walking to the market in Georgetown."

"I doubt that Georgetown, even in its beginnings, ever looked like this!" Rose returned. Aware of the men's eyes on her, she heeded Maddy's advice as they walked along the river. Nearing "town" on the muddy road, Rose glanced quickly about for Joshua, but did not see him.

At last they arrived at the "store"—a tent with a counter consisting of planks laid upon wooden barrels. The bearded storekeeper was as unkempt as the miners, some of whom were already lined up for rum to be ladled into their tin cups. As if there weren't enough other places to buy spirits, Rose fretted. The dirty white canvas gambling tent was next door, and the saloon tent was directly across the road.

One of the ragged miners reached for Rose's arm. "What's a pretty thing like ye doin' here?"

Rose pulled away, and Maddy made a show of her wooden club. "You mind yo' manners, mistuh!"

The miners backed off, and the nearby men guffawed at him. One said, "Let them ladies go first. Don't ye know nothin' about eti-quette?"

While the men ragged each other, Maddy edged toward the storekeeper. "I got milk and two dozen eggs to trade for good flour and sugar . . . and I doan want no weevils in it!"

"Eggs!" a miner exclaimed. "Why I'd pay ye a dollar fer one!" The others agreed and bid up to an ounce of gold dust—sixteen dollars!—for a cup of milk.

While the others discussed prices, Rose scrutinized the nearby gambling tent. A wooden sign over the tent flaps proclaimed "Gilded Palace." If only she could speak earnestly to Nichola! It was still morning; Nichola would likely be in her tent. Rose thought it must be the Lord prompting her to care about the woman's welfare, for she had no other reason to do so.

As Maddy discussed the transactions further with the

miners and examined the storekeeper's flour, Rose slipped away and followed the path around back of the gambling tent to the individual tents. "Nichola?" she called out hesitantly.

A nearby tent flap opened and, to her astonishment, Joshua stepped out. He was bearded and in rough miner's garb. "Rose! What are you doing here?"

She might have asked the same question, but disconcerted, she replied, "I've come to speak with Nichola."

His brows drew together, but before he could speak, Nichola called angrily from inside the tent, "Keep her away from me!"

Rose backed off, still unnerved that he had emerged from Nichola's tent. "I—I only wanted to be her friend."

"You shouldn't be here, Rose. It's a rough place."

"Maddy is with me, and I feel safe."

"I thought the Lord took care of you," he said with a trace of sarcasm.

Determined not to be baited, she replied quietly, "He does take care of me. I planned to come alone, but Maddy found out and wouldn't allow it."

Joshua stared at her without speaking, and she began to back away. Moreover, Maddy was calling for her around the gambling tent.

"Miz Rose Anne, where do you think—" She hesitated at the sight of Joshua. "Morning, Mistuh Joshua."

"Good morning, Maddy." He scowled. "Can't you keep Rose from coming down here?"

Maddy blinked. "She be a grown woman now."

Anger surged to Rose's throat and she was tempted to retort, *Can't you stay away from Nichola?* Despite her ire, she wished he would say she was mistaken in her assumption about him and Nichola. But he said not a word, and she turned away quickly at the threat of tears.

Adam Townsend, from the church, appeared behind Maddy, leading his mule. He halted at the distressing scene before him, then ventured, "I saw you two coming down the trail and thought you must be buying supplies. I brought the mule to give you a hand going back up to Oak Hill."

Maddy darted a confused look at Rose and Joshua, then nodded at Adam Townsend. "We be mighty pleased to see you, Mistuh Adam. You be a real gempmun, and we be thankful for yo' help. I got more supplies in trade than I expected."

And I got more than expected myself, Rose reflected.

Joshua nodded politely at Rose and Maddy. "Good day."

"Good day," Rose responded, clenching her fists. She turned and started down the path. At the last moment she looked back and saw that he was reentering Nichola's tent.

Rose whirled away, biting her quivering lip. If it were not for the miners staring at her, she would have wept like a child all of the way back through the diggings.

When they returned to the cabin, Rose lay down on her bed and tearfully recorded the day's event in her journal. At the end of her account, she added, *How hopeless it is between me and Joshua. How utterly hopeless.*

As though that were not enough, that evening Rose heard a horse whinny outside the cabin. When she opened the door, her breath caught in her throat. "Joshua!"

He had just dismounted, and stood there, shaven, wide-brimmed buckskin hat in hand. "Could we walk out by the river for a few minutes?" he asked, his brown eyes pleading. "I would like to explain about this morning if I may."

Stunned, she nodded.

The twilight imparted a purple tinge to the landscape,

and they started out toward the river in silence. Walking side by side, she noted that he remained carefully distant. Painful memories assailed her: their first meetings in Georgetown when she'd been so drawn to him . . . sailing together on the *Bostonia* . . . seeing him daily in his office in Boston and their romantic interlude on his skiff . . . their trip around the Horn. How could it all have ended in such anguish? And why hadn't God removed her longing for this man?

"Rose," he began, "I could see you thought the worst when I came out of Nichola's tent."

She looked up at him quickly, but his expression was masked by the lavender twilight. "It—it is not really my concern, is it?" she asked, her tone braver than she felt.

He glanced at her, then away at the river. "I felt as though it might have upset you."

"I don't understand. . . ."

He turned to her, his hands stiff at his sides. "I would not want you to think there was anything amiss at my being in Nichola's tent. The fact is she was accidentally wounded during a brawl in the gambling tent. A bullet meant for the baron struck her shoulder, and she's not well. I was attempting to help her."

"I see." Emotions rushed through her: relief that he was not involved as she had feared . . . shame at her suspicions . . . jumbled feelings about Nichola.

She and Joshua gazed at each other in the lingering rays of light, and she said, "How kind of you to ride all the way here to explain."

For an instant she thought he might reach for her, but instead he stood stiffly away.

"I felt that I at least owed you an explanation, and I thank you for listening to it."

She was confused by his sudden coolness.

"I had better return," he finally said, appearing as uncomfortable as she felt.

They turned and walked back in uneasy silence until she asked, "Why was there a shooting?"

"One of the miners felt cheated at cards," Joshua said.

Rose felt cheated herself.

At the cabin, he swung up onto his gray stallion. "Good night, Rose."

She stood watching as he dug his heels into the horse's flanks and rode off. Even his explanation about coming from Nichola's tent—welcome as it was—had not healed the rift between them. Deeply disappointed, she turned away. She had felt so certain he'd had more to say. What had she said to change his mind?

Suddenly it occurred to her that perhaps she'd sounded like a Georgetown belle with her *How kind of you to ride all the way here to explain.* How kind indeed! The inconclusiveness of their meeting had surely been her fault.

Stepping into the cabin, it struck her that the month of March was going out like a lion, in her heart if nowhere else. Earlier, she'd had an excuse to be angry. Now nothing remained except pain.

Two days later, on April 1, thirty miners arrived at the log church at Oak Hill to celebrate Palm Sunday. Adam Townsend conducted the services again. Following the sermon, they sang "His Triumphal Entry," and during the final verse, Rose was only slightly conscious of a wagon creaking to a stop outside. Despite all of her heartache, God loved her and the Lord had died for her, and she sang out the words with God-given joy,

"Hosanna in the highest!

That ancient song we sing,

For Christ is our Redeemer,
The Lord of heaven, our King.
O may we ever praise Him,
with heart and life and voice,
And in His blissful presence,
Eternally rejoice!"

After the benediction she heard a horse whinny, then footsteps running toward the church door. Turning, she found Joshua, unshaven and gaunt—looking for her at the back of the church. He made his way through the departing miners and called to her in a hushed voice, "Rose?"

Her instinct was to flee, to not be hurt again, but seeing the alarm on his face, she found herself moving toward him.

"It's Nichola," he explained. "Her wound has worsened. I brought her with me . . . thinking that you and Maddy might help."

Oh, Lord, must I care for her, too? Rose asked, and an inner voice replied, *You must not only tend to her, but love her.* She was reminded that it was Palm Sunday, the beginning of Holy Week.

She told Joshua, "I shall ask Father and Moses to help you carry her into my room."

"I knew of no one else to whom we can turn. The doctor said she will not . . . live much longer. She's drugged with laudanum. I couldn't let her stay out in that tent, and the baron wants nothing to do with her now."

"I see," Rose replied.

The men carried Nichola on a pallet from the wagon. She moaned, only semiconscious as they brought her into the cabin and to bed. Her face and neck were swollen hideously, and she no longer smelled of French perfume, but of putrefaction.

When the men left, Rose and Maddy tried to make the

groggy woman comfortable. Maddy said, "I never thought it'd come to this . . . and I sho' doan think she did, either! I wish I'd tried to like her more."

"As do I," Rose said. She recalled the haughty Nichola the first time they'd met at Elisha Wainwright's house in Boston . . . the voluptuous entrance Nichola made coming down the staircase . . . her disdainful greeting, "So you are Rose."

Maddy soon left, and Rose sat down in a chair to watch the sleeping woman. Opening the Bible she kept in her room, Rose turned to the Gospel of Luke and read the Lord's words, "Love your enemies, do good to them which hate you, bless them that curse you, and pray for them which despitefully use you." She read on, "Judge not, and ye shall not be judged; condemn not, and ye shall not be condemned; forgive , and ye shall be forgiven. . . ."

Knowing that forgiveness was a decision, not a feeling, Rose prayed, *I do forgive Nichola for the wounds she inflicted upon me . . . real wounds and those imagined, for I do not know what was in her heart. Only Thou knowest what is in our hearts, Father. Help me to love her.*

When Rose opened her eyes, she did feel a faint stirring of love for the woman who lay dying in her bed.

Later Nichola moaned and her eyes flickered open. "What are you doing here?" she rasped. "Where is Albert?"

Rose caught her breath, trying to think what to say. What else but the truth, lovingly told! "It is my room, Nichola. Joshua brought you. Your tent was too cold. And I don't know where Albert—the baron—is."

Nichola's eyes fell shut and she moaned as she drifted into an uneasy sleep.

Joshua arrived later to sit with them, and Rose saw he'd shaved off his beard.

"Thank you for doing this, Rose," he said.

She nodded and they sat in silence, Rose's emotions as vacillating as her thoughts. Had Nichola been so important to him?

He opened a book of Shakespeare to read, reminding her of the afternoons on the *Californian* when he had read aloud to her. She opened the Bible to the Gospel of Luke again, rereading from the Sermon on the Plain.

During the midday meal, they took turns staying with Nichola, and in the afternoon Maddy insisted that she sit with Nichola for a while.

Rose went out for fresh air, strolling off toward the church, and was surprised that Joshua accompanied her. She stopped at the church doorway to admire the flowers sprouting nearby from seeds she had planted, then wandered into the log sanctuary.

"I have been curious to see your church," he said, looking around the rustic space. After some time he added, "In a sense it is more beautiful than a great cathedral, because you used the trees from these hills and the slate from the riverbank . . . and because you have all built it yourselves."

"I love it," she said, "though I never in my life dreamed I would help build a church building with my own hands."

"Your father says you are a tireless layer of slate floors."

"Not as tireless as I was determined to be." She inspected her hands, still rough and cut from the effort. After a moment, she asked, "Does Nichola have friends or relatives whom we should notify?"

"Only Uncle Elisha, I think."

"I see," she replied, no longer quite so sorry for herself. She had a loving family and friends, even though she and Joshua were apparently meant to be no more than companions. He was a good man, if not a godly one. Unless he consecrated his life to the Lord, there could be nothing for them. They had different gods, which in turn affected everything else.

When Nichola awakened, she was in such pain they had to administer more laudanum. In her agony Nichola grumbled, "Don't start preaching to me! I have heard all about hellfire and damnation!"

Rose inquired, "Have you heard of God's love?"

Nichola glared at her.

Rose said, "One cannot force God upon anyone. Each must come of his own will." She bowed her head and began to pray silently . . . for Nichola, for Joshua, for their congregation, for Abby and her family, for every miner in the foothills.

As the shadows of evening began to lengthen, Maddy brought in a candle. When she closed the door behind her, Nichola whimpered deliriously, "Mama! Mama, don't go!"

Rose went to the bedside to hold the woman's hot hand.

Nichola's eyes opened. "It is you, so like Mama."

"Yes, it's me, Rose—"

Tears filled Nichola's eyes. "Too late for me. Too late for God."

Rose's eyes went across the bed to where Joshua sat reading on the other chair. His pained expression made it clear that he had no answers to offer, and she looked into Nichola's tear-clouded eyes. How terrified she appeared! "It is never too late for us to know God."

Nichola's voice sounded faraway. "I can't be forgiven."

Rose insisted, "Christ died on the cross for our sins. We need only reach out to Him . . . by His sacrifice He can bring us to God. He stands at the door of our hearts, but we must invite Him in."

"Yes," Nichola murmured. "Mama said I must invite Him

in." She drifted away, her breathing becoming labored.

In the evening the men brought in a mattress upon which Rose might lie, for she was determined not to leave Nichola alone in such pain. Joshua moved out to the spare cabin.

Nichola lay moaning and breathing irregularly, and Rose wished she had shared more spoken moments with her. In the middle of the night Nichola whispered, "Lord, Jesus Christ—"

Rose sat up, startled. The candle flickered brightly, as though there were a presence in the room. "Nichola?"

The woman made no reply, but her breath was no longer so labored. When Rose awakened in the morning, Nichola's spirit had departed.

After breakfast Joshua asked Rose with a frown, "What did you say to her last night?"

"Nothing more than you heard."

He looked down at the plank floor. "I'm sorry."

She stared at him, understanding his reluctance at last. "You are angry with God, are you not?"

His eyes brimmed with anger. "That is my affair."

"And mine because I care about your soul." She understood that he warred within himself, almost as though he were two different people.

His chin was set. "I suppose you won't bury her in the churchyard."

"That decision rests with our members. I hope we shall."

He stared at her, then abruptly departed.

The next afternoon, the burial service took place in the log church, and the sanctuary was packed with miners. Rose wondered whether they had come out of curiosity. Whatever brought them, she decided, the Lord could use it. She sat on a rough bench in the second row. Looking back briefly, she saw that the baron was not present, and that Joshua sat in the back row, as though ready to bolt.

Standing beside the rustic pine coffin, Adam Townsend began the service with prayer. After the miners' fervent "amens," he said, "Before her spirit passed on, Nichola Wainwright called out to the Lord."

Adam Townsend led them in the twenty-third Psalm, and as the familiar words filled the room, Rose was amazed at how many of the miners knew them. Tears rolled down some of the grizzled faces as they spoke the words, and again as the service concluded with the singing of "Amazing Grace."

At the graveside, she found Joshua beside her. He listened thoughtfully as Adam said, "God regards death very differently than we do. We see it as an ending, but in the life Nichola has entered now, it is a beginning."

He read the Lord's words from the Gospel of John. "In my father's house are many mansions; if it were not so, I would have told you. I go to prepare a place for you."

There were other verses about eternal life, then Adam Townsend said, "In this Holy Week, it is fitting that we conclude this service for Nichola Wainwright with the promise of resurrection that our Lord gave to us. 'I am the resurrection and the life; he that believeth in me, though he were dead, yet shall he live; And whosoever liveth and believeth in me shall never die.'"

The miners appeared touched and, after the service concluded, many asked for the time of Easter worship on Sunday. Rose hoped that Joshua, too, had been touched. She looked up at him.

"I appreciate everything you have done for Nichola," he said. "I know it could not have been easy to show her such . . . love."

Rose shook her head. "Don't think too well of me,

Joshua, for at first I did it out of duty. I had to pray for the love."

He inclined his head, then walked away.

When Good Friday morning arrived, it seemed that spring was about to burst forth. Wildflowers showed their colors across the green foothills. The pungent high sierrra sagebrush gave hints of yellow and purple flowers; scarlet gilia thrust up buds of scarlet, yellow, and pink; purple-blue pentstemon, rose-purple elephant head, and yellow mule ears offered tinges of their hues; even the crooked manzanita bushes obliged with a few pink buds.

To add to spring's wonders, Benjamin Talbot arrived with a shipment of goods, including the glass for the church windows. "I tried to imagine what your church might look like in this setting from your letters, but I didn't think it might be this beautiful," he said as he admired it. "I would move here myself if we weren't so fond of Rancho Verde—and if my horse hadn't been stolen during my gold-seeking visit!"

Rose had to smile at the way he put it. She was unsure whether she preferred Rancho Verde or Oak Hill herself.

"What a pleasure to be here for Easter," Benjamin said, turning serious again. "Tell me how everything goes with your church now."

He was heartened to hear of their progress, especially about Nichola. He said, "We are moving along at a good pace in the city, too."

"Tell us about it," Jonathan Wilmington urged.

"Well, in November a conclave of San Franciscans invited the Presbyterian Timothy Dwight Hunt, who'd been in the Islands, to act as town chaplain on a nondenominational basis," Benjamin said. "Now we have C. O. Hosford, a

Methodist, who was sent down by the superintendent of the Oregon missions. Every month more churches are established. The Baptist, Osgood C. Wheeler of New York, has organized the San Francisco Baptist Association and serves as its first moderator. A Congregationalist minister and Dartmouth College graduate, Samuel H. Willey, arrived at Monterey in February. The Episcopalians are organizing, as are others. Why, a ship came into Monterey recently with four missionaries aboard!"

Rose's spirit soared. For all one heard about the violence all around them, God's people moved onward, preaching His word and building churches to His glory. No matter what happened, God would prevail.

"It's most encouraging," her father said, "but I have always thought it a shame to have so many denominations."

"It sometimes seems so," Benjamin replied, "but the Church is like a river that's divided into countless streams and brooks, flowing in all directions from one source. Instead of being one church, we are now 'the churches'—one in Christ, but each going under a name of its own, and doing the work as seems wisest. We are already bonded by our faith, and we are planning bigger camp meetings this spring and summer."

Benjamin brought out the hams and potatoes that had been sent up, and they decided to invite the congregation for a ham dinner after the Easter worship service.

On Saturday, the miners installed the window glass, and Rose and Maddy washed windows until they sparkled in the sunlight. When they finished and stood back, the log church looked so perfect in its setting that it seemed God had blessed it.

That night Rose dreamed she was entering the golden glow of glory with the Lord. She saw her mother and William and Nichola—and someone so like Joshua! They awaited her across a meandering stream, beaming and arms joyously outheld. She awakened in awe.

Easter Sunday dawned with magnificence, the hillsides ablaze with color as though to proclaim their joy, too. After breakfast the miners began to stream up the hill to the church, nodding politely at each other, smiling with anticipation.

Before long, they had to carry out plank benches from outside the cabin to add to the benches in the church. Rose's father said, "Some of the new miners say they have come because of Nichola's decision and because we allowed her to be buried here! Strange, what sometimes brings man to God."

"Yes, strange," Rose agreed.

In the log sanctuary, the miners brimmed so with expectation that Rose's spirit overflowed with thanksgiving and hope. She looked about for Joshua, but he was not there.

Adam Townsend began the service with prayer, then the congregation sang "Hail the Day That Sees Him Rise" so joyously that the log sanctuary seemed filled with love. The Scripture reading was from the Gospel of Mark, about the women coming to anoint the Lord's body and finding the stone rolled away from the tomb. The wondrous events unfolded as though before the miners' eyes, and such a hush came upon the sanctuary that it was as if the Lord were among them.

At length they sang out with jubilation,
"Jesus Christ is risen today, Al-le-lu-ia!
Our triumphant holy day, Al-le-lu-ia!
Who did once, upon the cross, Al-le-lu-ia!
Suffer to redeem our loss, Al-le-lu-ia!"
The joyous hymn of praise rang through the sanctuary

with such exultation that it seemed to Rose they might rise to glory from where they stood on the slate floor. When they had sung out the triumphant "Amen," and stood awaiting they knew not what, Adam Townsend said, "I feel in my spirit that there are those here this day who wish to step forward to receive the Lord, Jesus Christ, as their Savior, and others who wish to reaffirm their faith. Shall we sing the last verse again while they come forward?"

Rose sang out hopefully with the others,

"Sing we to our God above, Al-le-lu-ia!"

At first only a few miners walked down the middle aisle, then others started up from the sides. Two ran as though they were propelled. Tears rolled down Rose's cheeks as she sang on with the others, "Praise eternal as His love, Al-le-lu-ia!"

There must have been a dozen already making their decisions for the Lord, she realized, and two more still walking up the aisle.

"Praise Him, all ye heavenly host, Al-le-lu-ia!

Father, Son, and Holy Ghost. Al-le-lu-ia!"

It was on the last note that she saw Joshua step determinedly to the altar. Her voice stopped in such wonder that she was unable to pronounce the amen. *Thank Thee, Lord, thank Thee!* she prayed instead.

Adam Townsend said a prayer for those who had stepped forward and then, before he gave the benediction, invited the entire congregation to join in the ham dinner.

At the final "Amen," Rose stood in place, still stunned, watching Joshua walk down the aisle to her, beaming.

She closed her eyes with thanksgiving at the gentleness in his expression. Opening them, she discovered that he was still smiling at her.

He said, "I presume I stood little chance of not going

forward eventually . . . not with you and my father and so many others praying for me."

"Oh, Joshua, I am so happy for you!" How different he looked, how exposed and unguarded and overcome by love. Tears of joy filled her eyes, for her golden dream had come true.

A moment later, Benjamin Talbot embraced his son. "Praise God, Joshua! You will never regret this, I promise!"

Joshua nodded, his eyes closed as he held his father. "I was a long time in coming, for I have always resented . . . resented Mother's death so. At Nichola's funeral I began to understand that God sees death differently—" His voice shook, and he pressed his lips together.

"I know . . . I know," Benjamin Talbot replied. "I was angry at first, too." He faltered. "For me, one of the best aspects of growing old is that I shall see her sooner."

They patted each other's shoulders manfully and blinked hard as they drew apart.

Rose pulled out her handkerchief and gave her nose a most unladylike blow, and she was not alone in doing so.

Several miners stopped by to pump Joshua's hand. "God bless you, brother," they said, then moved on to welcome the other new believers. The log sanctuary buzzed with congratulations, introductions, and heartfelt blessings.

Joshua said with a wry grin, "I never thought to see such a friendly company of miners in my life."

"It's the love of the Lord," a nearby miner responded. "Amazin' as it is, He loves even us!"

Everyone laughed and Benjamin Talbot said, "Guess I'll help carry some of these benches over to the main cabin for our outdoor dinner."

Rose told Joshua, "I have to help get dinner."

The lines between his brows deepened momentarily,

then he smiled. "If you can chink logs and help lay a slate floor, I expect I can slice ham."

They carried a bench to the cabin, then he followed her toward the kitchen. Rose had no idea what to expect. His lack of faith had stood between them, but now . . . What if it had been more that had kept them apart? Perhaps she had deluded herself about his caring. No, she must not imagine.

As Rose stepped into the kitchen, Maddy looked up from the potatoes and smiled. "I never had such a surprise in my life as when that Joshua—." She stopped, her eyes wide, as Joshua followed Rose into the room. "Oh, land!"

He laughed. "You are not the only one who's astonished, Maddy. I was somewhat surprised myself."

"Well," Maddy said, recovering with aplomb, "I congrat'late you, Mistuh Joshua. I sho' do. You found the way to have joy in yo' heart, no matter what."

"Thank you, Maddy," he responded. "I am going to look to you as my example in being a Christian."

"Land, no! Doan look at me and not at any human being! You got to look to the Lord!"

Joshua replied, "That's as fine a sermon as I've ever heard," and they all laughed together.

Rose set the cutting board, a knife, and five large hams before him. "He claims that he wants to help us get dinner."

Maddy blinked. "I do believe that's the first conversion I heard about that makes a man take up kitchen work!" She smiled at them curiously. "I thinks you two can handle the kitchen for a while. I be going out to see about the table and benches. Jest doan let the carrots boil over in the pot." She handed Rose the long stirring spoon.

When the kitchen door closed behind Maddy, Rose found Joshua gazing at her. "Rose?"

Her heart faltered, remembering that look. He wanted

her in his arms. "Yes, Joshua?" She felt rooted to the floor, yet poised to fly to him.

"I love you . . . and I swore at the altar to give up the chase for gold, with God's help. I cannot do it alone."

She flew to him, stirring spoon in hand, and their lips met. Engulfed in his embrace, she wanted never to leave his arms. How blessedly right she felt with him. It was as though God had made Joshua just for her, and her for him.

When they drew apart to catch their breath Joshua said, "I infer with you holding that spoon over my head I had better propose marriage."

"Only if you wish," she murmured happily, for she knew without a doubt that he would. "

"I have had no choice in the matter since the day we first met. Rose, I do want to marry you."

"And I want to marry you, Joshua!"

The carrots boiled over and the hams waited, uncut, but Rose and Joshua were unaware. When Maddy walked in and forcibly removed the stirring spoon from Rose's hand, they returned from the heights of bliss.

"Doan mind me," Maddy remarked dryly, "but somone got to do the cooking."

Rose felt her cheeks turn pinker than ever. "I forgot all about the carrots!"

"That's what comes of having a man in the kitchen!"

Joshua inquired, "Now, Maddy, how would you know?"

Maddy looked up at him slyly from stirring the carrots. "How you expect I got my Moses? The kitchen be a good catching room, except for ruining the food."

At their surprised laughter she announced, "Now shoo! You two go on down by the river for yo' courting."

"Shall we tell her?" Rose inquired of Joshua.

"I judge by that look in her eyes that she already knows,"

he replied. His voice became solemn as he turned to the old housekeeper. "Maddy, I require your opinion. Is Easter dinner an appropriate time for Rose's father to announce a wedding?"

"Oh, it be a fine time!" she assured him, beaming. "In fact, when we celebrating the Lord's resurrection be jest the right time . . . the most joyous day of the year!"

Joshua reached for Rose's hand. "I tend to agree, don't you?"

"I do," Rose replied. "Oh, Joshua, I do!" Then her heart leapt for he was not leading her out the back door toward the river for courting, but toward the front door where her father and his father stood with the guests.

Jonathan Wilmington and Benjamin Talbot smiled as though they knew what was transpiring, and their blessing was evident. Uncle Elisha would be thrilled too, and Abby and Daniel and the rest of the Talbots. Rose sent up a prayer of thanksgiving to her heavenly Father, for with so much love and joy and beauty all around them, His blessing, too, was wondrously manifest.

ABOUT THE AUTHOR

Elaine Schulte is a wife, mother of two sons, and a writer whose short stories, articles, and novels have been widely published. *The Journey West* is Schulte's first book in The California Pioneer Series about the Talbot family and their covered wagon journey to California in 1846.

The second novel is *Golden Dreams*, which describes Rose Wilmington's travels to California by clipper ship, while Benjamin Talbot carries out his call in the new city of San Francisco. Of this novel, Elaine tells us, "It was heartwarming to learn that gamblers and dance hall girls weren't the only early inhabitants of California, as is so often suggested in books, television shows, and movies. From the beginning, the decent people started the churches and schools. Camp meetings were held in rural areas where no suitable buildings for services existed. Families journeyed for miles, jolting in wagons over rough roads, to reach the meetings, which often took place in a grove of trees along a stream. According to accounts from that day, as many as ten to twenty thousand people camped and worshiped God for periods as long as several weeks! By 1855, San Francisco alone had thirty-two churches with denominations that ranged from African Methodist to Welsh Presbyterian."

Eternal Passage is the third novel in the series, which brings Louisa Talbot Setter from Virginia—by gold ship, the jungles of Panama, and coastal steamer—to California in 1849.

Betsy Talbot is the heroine of the fourth novel, *With Wings as Eagles*, which takes place in the gold rush town of Oak Hill in 1854.